The dead aren't really gone: they persist as phone numbers, social media accounts, newsletter recipients, aliases on fan-fiction forums. Digital ghosts move and connect us: we feel we know people we have only seen online just as corporations masquerade as familiar friends.

In *Rubik*, darkly comedic interconnected stories follow Elena Rubik, her best friend Jules Valentine, and wannabe investigative reporter April Kuan, as a viral marketing scheme's motivations become cause for concern. There are the adventures of a model turned visual artist, a tech support voice actor, enigmatic schoolchildren, clever anime characters, and more.

Deftly blending the real and imagined with biting social satire, Elizabeth Tan explores the lives of her diverse group of characters with deep empathy and insight into our contemporary world.

The Unnamed Press
P.O. Box 411272
Los Angeles, CA 90041

Published in North America by The Unnamed Press.

This book was originally published in 2017 in Australia by Brio Books.

1 3 5 7 9 10 8 6 4 2

Copyright © 2018 by Elizabeth Tan

ISBN: 9781944700577

Library of Congress Control Number: 2018931436

This book is distributed by Publishers Group West

Jacket design by Robert Bieselin
Typeset by Jaya Nicely

rubik

elizabeth tan

The Unnamed Press
Los Angeles, CA

Praise for Rubik

"The disorienting effect of accreting, repeating details and unanswered questions makes the final cohesion of Tan's only slightly fantastical Perth even more delicious. Tan's careful layering and nuanced craft will gain a strong following among fans of experimental narratives."

—*Publishers Weekly*

"*Rubik* is an absolute delight in its wit, kindness, and playful profundity; in its feeling that the human experience is prismatic, filled with hope and despair, darkness and joy; in its universes that are at once familiar and strange. A sparkling, poignant debut."

—**Brooke Davis, author of *Lost & Found***

"Bold, brilliant, hilarious, and beautifully strange. Make time to read *Rubik*, for it will challenge all your received ideas about what fiction can or should do: here is the future of Australian writing."

—**Ceridwen Dovey, author of *Only the Animals***

"*Rubik* darts between layers of time, space and reality—fictions within fictions that seem disparate at first but later reveal themselves as inextricably linked. Recalling the surreal connected-universe storytelling of Jennifer Egan's *A Visit from the Goon Squad*, *Rubik* is a shot in the arm of Australian fiction, one that will undoubtedly reveal more secrets on successive rereads."

—Books + Publishing

"*Rubik* is exhilarating... It is a mish-mash of colored cubes, held together by tiny mechanisms, daring you to put the pieces back together."

—The Lifted Brow

"The very best experimental writers have an inspired and weird way of seeing the world that makes much realist fiction seem moribund. Elizabeth Tan's debut is wonderful, brilliant and mind-bending, and a worthy heir to the experimental tradition."

—The Saturday Paper

Table of Contents

rubik

Rubik

It's Sunday evening and there's nothing to eat. Elena's blade-less fan pivots in monochrome silence, the centerpiece of a room that's untidy in an engineered way, like movie teenage bedrooms. There's the strewn unwashed clothes and wall-to-ceiling magazine-torn posters of brooding twenty-some-thing heart-throbs. Cinematic untidiness. Elena, twenty-five, waking up to the awkwardly looped music of a DVD menu screen, remembering the food problem, flicking her mouse to find the Start bar for the time. Thirty minutes too late for Fresh Direct, ninety for IGA.

There's McDonald's, but she doesn't like the constant chime of the drive-in or the white lights. The atmosphere in McDonald's is deliberately uncomfortable, she's been told. The better to encourage customers to move on so the restau-rant can admit new ones.

She spies a rip in one of her brooding twenty-somethings. Smoothes it with a fingernail. Real? No, fake. It was a gift actually, this ironic teenage-bedroom wallpaper—purchased by Jules two years ago from Owls in the Navy. The heart-throbs come complete with faux celebrity names, part-rogue, part-boy-next-door: *Brad Ruffalo, Justin Lee Thomas.*

There should be neighborhood vending machines, Elena decides, tugging her blackened shoelaces. Like laundromats. Fluorescent coves of machine-lined walls, a bench with magazines to flick through while you wait for your Cup-O-Noodles to boil. An idea that someone in some distant city has surely conceived, patented, and deemed unviable by now.

Elena, out into the crisply illuminated street, through her buttoned-up neighborhood. Distant traffic is sonorous like an ocean wave that never arrives. Fifteen minutes away on the main road there are two petrol stations adjacent to each other, locked, by virtue of their location, into advertising identical gas prices every day. This proximity has also inspired a convenience arms race: the stations' modest cash register chewing gum selections have expanded, over the years, into glimmering emergency snack food emporia.

Ten minutes down the slope of Camberwell Street and Jules's car passes by, on her way to the house. Elena lifts a hand, too late. They have these moments often. Since moving out from under her parents' roof, Elena has discovered that having roommates is lonelier than she initially thought. You only ever seem to glimpse your housemates while they're on their way to somewhere else, everyone moving in their own private orbit. Their presence is rarely felt outside of a plate in the sink, a DVD left in the player, rent money squashed in a re-used envelope.

On this night she selects the Gull station. Drawn immediately to the heat-lamped food display, the desperate huddle of pastries. She selects a Homestyle Country Pie, declines the tomato sauce, and separates a ten dollar bill from her tight jeans pocket. She contemplates her change, but none of the neon drinks in the fridge appeals to her tonight. She tears open the packaging to her pie. It does not taste of any country she knows.

Elena, on the diagonal, outside and away from the white glow of diesel and LPG, the faint croon of the radio playing infinitely for refuelling motorists.

The car that hits her is a 1991 Ford EA Falcon, making a right turn as simply as a child rotates a toy ninety degrees. The bonnet whips like a swordfish. When it knocks into Elena the pie ejects from her hand, becomes airborne, and in her last moments she marvels at the literalness of it. A pie in the sky.

One hundred and fifty-seven of Elena's 212 friends find out when some of the remaining fifty-five leave condolence messages on Elena's profile. Over the course of Monday afternoon, 157 people assess their relationship to Elena Rubik, reframe the significance of their last conversation with her, express their grief in 420 characters or less. They stare at her profile picture and try to imagine her as somebody no longer alive.

For each new post on Elena's profile, unread notifications accumulate in her inbox. Among these emails are weekly newsletters from Owls in the Navy, of which Elena is now one of six deceased subscribers.

Elena's DELL Vostro becomes the property of Mr. and Mrs. Rubik, who cannot access it without her user password. The DVD that Elena watched on the night of her death is still inside it, and has since accrued a late fee of $82.50. The laptop will remain inside a box in the Rubik family study.

Some time in the year that follows, Jules accidentally scrolls too far down her list of phone contacts and sends a text to Elena Rubik instead of Edward Lee. She is about to send an apology when she realizes. She wonders if she ought to delete Elena's contact details. She thinks of Elena, out on Camberwell Street, whitened by her headlights. She imagines her mistaken text message vibrating in the pocket of Elena's ghost, outside that gas station, where somebody—she doesn't know who—still leaves flowers.

On 15 July 2011, Elena's online age ticks over from twenty-five to twenty-six. This is when one of Elena's friends clicks on her profile to wish her a happy birthday, discovers the thick backlog of messages, and commences her mourning two months behind everybody else.

On the Luxury Replicants fan fiction forum, Rubik3 appears at the bottom of the front page under Today's Birthdays. Renzo notices it, and PMs Elena:

Hey Rubik, happy birthday! Haven't seen you around for a while. How's the next chapter of EotG coming along? Do you need a beta reader? Renzo.

Three years later, another member of LR will lose his battle with cancer, spawning a tribute thread and tentative plans to contact the member's family with donations. Renzo will think about this incident with Rubik3, his unanswered PM. He will feel the moment like a tongue probing a gap in a line of teeth. A distant truth that never arrives.

Just when the residents of 14 Camberwell Street resign themselves to moving back in with their parents, Jules finally manages to find a fifth housemate, one Bernard Cash, who shifts into Elena's old spot after it has been cleared of everything except for her wallpaper. Bernard will reconfigure the room—place the bed by the wardrobe and the desk by the window. He will plug his power board into the wall socket and attach his phone charger, his lamp, his fan, his Macbook. He will think of Elena, of her ex-housemates turned brittle by some strange guilt that he discovers he understands completely. He will spend a moment in silence, sitting in his new room, but he won't feel creeped out. He will ask Jules for the wireless password. He will check the time on the Desktop. He will Wiki 'Brad Ruffalo' to figure out what he's been in.

Every Good Boy Deserves Fruit

Kish, unarticulated today, without bar lines, spine creaking like a hymn book; soft, old Kish, having dreamed last night of being an engulfed cathedral, ascending to consciousness in perfect fourths. Arched by a yawn. She uses a torn sheet of notepaper to catch her fingernail clippings. Kish, with newly angled nails, boils an egg for breakfast, scrapes the flesh clean from the shell.

Yesterday the piano tuner presented her with a crisp envelope containing all the snapped mechanical pencil leads that he liberated from the Bösendorfer's hull. Today Kish will purchase regular HB pencils, a pencil sharpener, and a discreet receptacle to place inside the piano room for pencil shavings. Kish, drinking the last of her black tea, modulates into a key of distant relation, something edged, notated by sharps instead of flats.

The school where Kish works is old enough to smell like a museum, the pupils' uniforms the same itchy green as a musty billiards table. They start their day at ten-to-nine, but Kish's first lesson is scheduled for ten-past-eight. The Pushkin boy, from Year Three, is sullen but cooperative at this hour. He is careful in passing his thumb smoothly underneath the bridge of his curved fingers. She can hear his tender breath each time a scale or arpeggio demands this movement.

There is something so heartbreaking about his attentiveness that Kish must look away. She thinks instead of the Yamaha cleaved open like a fish, machinery exposed: ribcage of felted hammers, eighty-eight clusters of strings with their precisely tempered intervals. The sounds that emerge will nonetheless resist replication; nothing, not even this Pushkin boy's scale, will exist so perfectly ever again.

Outside the music room, a group of boys kick a football, long and high. Kish and the Pushkin boy can hear each kick resonate like a cartoon punch, the boys' spirited yells. The Pushkin boy, despite his concentration, would prefer to be out there. He has a hunch of resentment, a grumbling belly of rushed cornflakes. These lessons cost the Pushkin parents sixty dollars for forty minutes. They want a bright child; they want to give him Opportunities. They fought hard for this timeslot, at ten-past-eight, so that the Pushkin boy would not miss one minute of his education. The lesson will end, the siren will ring, the boy will proceed directly to class. The boy's jumper is second-hand, stretched for a different-sized head; the woollen fibers look abrasive as fire ants.

Kish listens, contemplating all the factors that contribute, however minutely, to this boy's trembling scale.

Before the lesson is over, Kish tells him about semiquavers. With a blue pen she draws a neat chart in his exercise book: the semibreve, a lonely ovum, splitting into two minims, then four crochets, then eight quavers, then sixteen semiquavers. The Pushkin boy, only just learning about fractions in class, signals his understanding with half a nod. She closes his exercise book and places it on the stand beside his scrapbook. They have a few minutes left.

'Is there anything you'd like to talk about before we go, Peter?' Kish asks.

There isn't. Kish opens up her file and spreads out the sheets of stickers. They are bright as candy, emanating a garish optimism incongruent with Kish's character. The Pushkin boy selects an angel fish, which Kish carefully peels from the glossed paper and positions with the other stickers on his scrapbook cover.

In the afternoon, at Officeworks, Kish roams the columns of paper and bulk manila folders. She places a box of pencils in her blue shopping basket. She is considering which pencil sharpener best befits her when the Nokia rings. A private number.

'Hello?'

For the first moment, all she hears is crackling silence. Like a gramophone, or twigs snapping. Kish, too deep in the Zen of stationery shopping, feels no irritation. The instant she decides to hang up, something begins.

A motif of seven notes, rising one step, falling, and then jumping up, beginning again. Like a gentle alarm clock, insistent and plaintive. The piano, bell-like, in the treble.

Unbidden, the sequence 9300730 flips into Kish's mind, each number clacking in turn, like information on a train station timetable.

The motif continues to announce itself.

And then, horribly, she understands.

The box of pencils in her shopping basket trembles. Kish is shaking, her lungs tight and airless, as if someone is turning pegs in her spine. The strength of her shoulders' convulsions is enough to rattle a box of stickers off the shelf.

The Nokia beeps three times; clicks, slices Kish's aural tether. Returns her, dazed and cold, to Officeworks.

Her colleague Rebecca is working on page-turning strategies, declining Kish's offer to be her page turner for the evening's school concert. 'What I'm waiting for,' Rebecca says, 'is when they integrate tablets with pianos. Wouldn't that be exciting? Maybe the music could scroll along with you, like autocue.'

'Would you still be able to write extra notes on the score?'

'...I guess it wouldn't really be the same, would it?'

It has been three days since the incident at Officeworks. Kish, perched on a desk in the photocopier room, submits herself to the drone of fans. Rebecca slams the paper tray shut.

'Are any of yours playing tonight?' Rebecca asks.

'Just a few of the intermediate ones. When there's too many of the beginners... the parents seem to leave after their child has performed.'

'Doesn't that just get up your nose? It's going to happen tonight too, you'll see. After intermission the hall will be half-empty because all the choir members and their parents will've deserted us.'

'The poor kids at the end.'

'I know.'

Rebecca flips to a new page, presses down on the photocopier lid. Kish feels the pressure exerted on the book's spine as if it were her own. A laser passing like an alien probe over her spreadeagled existence.

9300730

Kish watches Rebecca overturn the warm pages and Scotch-tape them together. 'Okay,' Rebecca says. 'I know the answer is yes, but, still: would it be poor form to Blu-Tack the pages to the piano?'

'Nobody will notice.'

'As long as it doesn't fall on my fingers.'

'I've done it before. Nobody noticed. Besides, the audience will be watching the choir, not you.'

'That's good. I haven't practiced the last few pages. I'm going to have to wing it.'

Kish waits a few beats. 'You're practically going to sight-read it on the night?'

Rebecca laughs. 'Don't tell on me.'

Kish watches Rebecca hold out the pages appraisingly before her. Rebecca is the only other member of the music staff with whom Kish regularly converses. Rebecca's position at this school, with its still-fledgling music department, is an anomaly. At other schools like this, Kish knows, it would be the norm for piano teachers to double as choir accompanists. But Kish cannot accompany, and Rebecca, as far as Kish knows, has no inclination for teaching. One could say, perhaps, that Kish and Rebecca need each other.

'I lied before,' Kish says. 'About the Blu-Tack. My teacher noticed. She just about died from embarrassment. After that, I performed everything from memory.' Kish waits. It feels deceitful not to qualify that statement. 'This was over twenty years ago. But you're an adult now, and you only need to answer to yourself.'

'Well, I suppose I'm performing from unauthorized photocopies, so I'm already going to hell. Ha-ha-ha. Don't you hate it when there's no space for a page turn? I feel like we as a society should be above this.'

Kish smiles carefully. Her mind is edging away from a memory.

9300730

Rebecca folds up her photocopies and tucks them under her arm. She smiles. 'Well! See you tonight then, Kish!'

'Good luck,' Kish says as Rebecca exits. Kish looks around the photocopier room, forgetting her original purpose here. The hum of photocopiers turns into something marine, mournful as the deep sea. White mechanical whales.

Rebecca has accidentally left her book wedged under the photocopier lid. Another aching spine. Kish retrieves it carefully, and leaves it shut on the desk.

In the afternoon, Kish dreams she is inside an auditorium that seems to have infinite dimensions, somehow both interior and exterior. She is young again and clutching a musical score to her chest. She walks to the stage, which is not elevated but more like a pit, and each step of her descent echoes feebly like a dropped pebble. There is no piano on the stage; instead, there are seven telephones arranged in a half-circle. She rests her music on the stand and takes her place on the wooden stool. Here, in the cold glow of the spotlight, facing telephones blank and impartial as jurors, she cannot recall ever practising this piece. She will have to wing it, like Rebecca. She examines the score but she cannot remember how to read music, cannot remember which telephone corresponds to which note. What was the mnemonic again? What does Every Good Boy Deserve?

A man approaches the stage. His face is undetailed, eyeless. He picks up the nearest telephone receiver and enters a number using the rotary dial. His fingers are long, white, the texture of clay. He lifts the receiver to his shapeless ear. The telephone nearest to Kish begins to ring, but not the briny ring she expects. It's that seven-note motif again. Rising one step, falling, beginning again. The eyeless man seems to look at her.

It is at this point that the dream malfunctions softly, like the last click of a wind-up toy. Kish says, *I'm sorry, I haven't performed in a while, a very long while,* but the scene will not proceed. The phone is still ringing. She reaches for it. The instant she touches the lacquered receiver, her consciousness activates. She is lying on top of the bed sheets, in the same clothes she wore to school, one hour before the concert will begin.

Kish parks her car and trails the clusters of students and parents to the auditorium. Accustomed to the school as a daytime space, she always thinks of these night-time recitals as uncanny. Kish turns her phone off. She finds a seat near the back of the hall, where she watches the parents milling around the urn and picking over a tray of Arnott's Assorted Creams. The choir teacher shepherds her students to the stage for warm-up. Rebecca is seated at the school's concert piano, a mellow upright Kemble. She has bothered to paint her nails a velvety green.

Kish meets the eye of the parent of one of her students, across the aisle—she manages to recognize the face and smile before the lights go down.

What follows is a murky procession of tentative ensembles and soloists, each child performing with a solemnity that is seemingly instinctual, absorbed like culture. They pronounce their composers' names with ripe over-articulation; they close their eyes when they take their bows.

She registers her own students' performances as if she is inside an aquarium. The notes have a different gravity, in this spotlight, on an unfamiliar piano. In the week following the concert, Kish will discuss this fact with her pupils. We are not like the violinists or the clarinettists who may take their instruments with them to the stage. Each piano is different water; we must adapt without flinching from the moment we dip our finger into the first note. Yes: this is the metaphor she will use, she's decided, and she will use the term 'we', even though, by even submitting themselves to the spotlight, these students accomplish what their teacher has not accomplished in years.

When the lights come up for intermission she feels like she's unfurling from hibernation. She is grateful that none of the parents comes to start a conversation with her. She tries her best to exude an air of both competence and enigma.

The Pushkin boy is here. Kish accepts this fact calmly at first, but then must rethink. The Pushkin boy is *here*. In civvies, his hands and the concert program clamped between his knees. He is not performing tonight, nor—to Kish's knowledge—does the Pushkin boy have any siblings. He is also minding a woman's handbag.

'Excuse me, Miss?'

She turns around to find the Pushkin parents standing in the aisle.

'Hello,' Kish says immediately, rising to her feet. 'Mr. and Mrs. Pushkin, is that right?'

'Yes, I think we've seen each other at one of these things before.'

'How are you enjoying the concert?' Kish asks, shaking hands with both. Later when she tries to recall the conversation she will not be able to separate one parent's words from the other's.

'Oh, very much. We thought it would be good for Peter, you know—to see what he can aspire to.'

'Of course.'

On some unheard cue, everyone begins to retreat to their seats for the second half of the concert. The Pushkin parents become hurried. 'We just wanted to make sure everything was okay with Peter. He seems a bit dispirited lately.'

'He's doing very well,' Kish says. 'I can tell he's been practising very hard.'

The parents' eyes shift. 'That's good to hear. He just seems... quieter than usual. He doesn't tell us much about what he does at school.'

The lights are starting to dim again, so Kish gives a quick smile. 'I'll certainly try to be more encouraging. He is a rather contemplative child. He'll open up in his own time.'

She is scarcely certain of what reassurance the parents want. As she retakes her seat and the Pushkin parents return to theirs, Kish inexplicably thinks about the boy's choices of stickers for his scrapbook cover week after week, as if there's a clue to be found.

Perhaps in a bid to dissuade parents from leaving at intermission, most of the advanced students are scheduled to perform in the second half. Still replaying the encounter with the Pushkin parents, Kish fails to check the concert program for what to expect next.

But she should have been prepared for it anyway. It wanted to occur. The student is from the high school section, Year Eleven or Year Twelve, too advanced for Kish to teach. The ribbon in her hair is utilitarian black; she carries no music. 'Yeah, hi. Tonight I'm playing "Little Waltz of the Telephones" by Tristram Cary.' She bows and takes her place at the Kemble.

She pitches the first note, and like that moment of touching the telephone receiver, Kish teleports.

Rising one step, falling, beginning again.

Those bell-like notes.

The student executes it with impartial gracefulness, as if delivering a message. Kish is paralysed. She is in Officeworks listening to the seven-note motif. She is in the auditorium of her nightmare with the eyeless man. She is sinking into the dark aquarium of her mind as the water dilates and dilates— watching this student, the confident flash of her fingers. Kish is under the eye of a strange madness. White, total, lunar.

'9300730,' she whispers.

Inside the pocket of her coat, slung over the back of her chair, the Nokia, which she is sure she turned off, begins to vibrate.

When a hand touches her shoulder, she almost screams. She pilots herself from a distance. Turns her head with submarine slowness.

Five fingers shellacked in velvet green.

Rebecca pulls Kish out of her chair.

Kish, unmetered through her long weekend, will spend her time recapitulating that moment when Rebecca had ushered her into the ladies' restroom and confronted her, in her crisp Rebeccan way—*You were shaking; I've never seen you so rattled before*—and Kish, wanting to convince herself of the absurdity of the situation, decided to tell Rebecca about the phone call in Officeworks, the continuing toll of the seven-note motif. The way the song seemed to compel her to respond, to make sweat spring from her pores, as if some repressed memory were trying to ooze out and away. This weekend, so conscious of the insufficiency of her skin, Kish will avoid the Bösendorfer, shut all her windows, remove the battery from the Nokia.

It is only safe for Kish to contemplate the moment in past tense.

Rebecca and Kish listened to the applause echo in the auditorium like distant rainfall.

Kish said, 'It's like the song is a trigger. A message. Someone's trying to give me a message.'

'Interesting.' Rebecca's eyes were so bright. 'The Tristram Cary piece—maybe you should, you know, find the score and play it. Play it when you're alone and there's nothing to distract you. Expose yourself to it, bit by bit.'

'I don't need the music,' Kish said bleakly. 'I had it memorized, at one time.'

Rebecca observed her. Outside, in the auditorium, one student left the stage, and another ascended. 'Why don't you perform any more, Kish?' Rebecca asked. 'I've never seen you.'

Kish didn't reply. The numbers were clacking again.

Rebecca did something rare, then. She reached out and held Kish's fingers. 'Kish. You can either wait for another phone call, or you can take matters into your own hands.'

Kish doesn't want to leave her house. She scribes the opening seven-note motif from 'Little Waltz of the Telephones' on manuscript paper, using an HB pencil drawn from the Officeworks box. She writes the sequence of numbers underneath the motif, one for each note. 9300730. She is sure this is how it appeared in the original score, printed underneath the notes so that they would not be mistaken for finger markings. It was what made Tristram Cary's score so unconventional. 9300730 is a telephone number, a footnote said, and Kish feels her age, remembering a time when landline telephone numbers had only seven digits. There were two motifs in the piece; the second motif was assigned its own sequence of digits, and throughout the waltz the two telephone numbers conversed with each other, overlapping, insistent on connection. The purpose of their communication was communication. But it is only the first motif that bothers Kish.

When she has finished, she feels too hollow to continue with the rest of Rebecca's plan. As if the act of writing the score has eased the dread gathered in her spine, but only slightly. Enough to carry on.

Monday brings another lesson with the Pushkin boy. Mindful of the Pushkin parents' words at the concert, Kish asks, 'Is there anything you'd like to talk to me about, before we begin? Anything you're worried about, perhaps?'

The Pushkin boy stares at his fingers. His eyes are red with fatigue, and Kish wonders—and in some way, doesn't have to wonder—what such a small boy has to endure, to look so weary. While she waits, Kish turns to a fresh page in the Pushkin boy's exercise book. These new pages are faintly imprinted with the chart she drew for him last week, the one with the multiplying semibreve, and Kish feels keenly her position at the bottom of the pyramid, a lowly semiquaver, only one-sixteenth whole.

'When does it get good?' the Pushkin boy asks.

'Pardon?'

'When does it get...' She watches the Pushkin boy struggle. He's reaching for the word *fun*, but he knows it's not quite the word he's after.

Kish wants to hold the child, but instead, she smiles what she hopes is a kind and convincing smile. She chooses her words carefully. She chooses honesty. 'It won't become good,' she says. 'Not for years. For the longest time... it won't be very exciting, or very interesting, at all.'

The Pushkin boy creases his lip. His hand wanders to the Yamaha and presses a dull Middle C.

'But, maybe one day, when you're thirteen or eighteen or twenty-five or thirty-six, it will be like there's a little click inside your brain, like the hand of a clock sliding into a new hour, and you will have got it. It won't necessarily become easier after that. Sometimes you might slip. But it will be okay, Peter. You can't unknow what you already know. You can't grow backwards.'

The Pushkin boy nods. He is, Kish believes, a good boy. He resumes his characteristic neutrality, his gaze emptying, which makes Kish think, for a moment, of the eyeless man. She opens the Pushkin boy's scrapbook and props it on the stand. 'Now, let's see how you're going with "Clementine" this week.'

Kish, having had very little to eat for dinner, decides to sit with the Bösendorfer as the sun goes down, the room modulating to indigo. The traffic on the main road becomes thin enough for Kish to hear the birds' little notes, their succinct language. She has placed her meagre transcript of 'Little Waltz of the Telephones' on the stand. She knows, as Rebecca suggested, that every minute she waits is a minute surrendered to whatever figure controls the strings. She finds, like looking at an optical illusion, that she can toggle back and forth from one supposition to the other.

There is a conspiracy.

There is no conspiracy.

She pitches the first note, an E-natural.

And, like Theseus following a winding thread through the labyrinth, she can only play the next note, and the note after that, and the note after that.

Perhaps, in her own house, on her own piano, the motif will be inert. At all moments Kish is aware of the room she is in, the watchful lamp, the unused pedals, the metronome in its steepled case. Her left hand on her knee.

She holds each note for its allotted duration. She lets the motif fall; she begins again. She plays it for as long as she likes. It could be seven, eight times. Thirteen or eighteen or twenty-five or thirty-six.

She lets the motif rest on the highest note. Her heart isn't beating any faster than when she began. She retracts her right hand from the keyboard.

Something clunks inside the Bösendorfer. Then a rolling sound like a marble travelling on wood. The piano recedes into the floor; the lid closes softly. As the Bösendorfer goes down, a cellar door articulates itself at Kish's feet, stairs evaporating into darkness, the smell of old, deep varnish. The Bösendorfer, now submerged, presents itself as the first step. Kish gives one final thought to the Pushkin boy, his earnest, sad question, and like the clock in the metaphor of her reply, Kish—soft, old, creaking like a cathedral—slides into a new hour, awake now to the time signature; lifts herself up from the piano seat, and begins her disappearance.

Retcon

Falling, she is the tensile arch of a fermata poised above stave, a notation to sky—she is the equation of 3x to the power of two, her landing scatters coordinates—italicized by momentum—legs half-jacked—spiked with gravity, she invents a new axis—nobody will ever be able to say what was so compelling—some will attribute it to the filmmaker, some to her particular electricity—others will say it's because she doesn't leap from a helicopter or a bomb blast but a benign gray sky—others say that there are a billion pictures of falling, and popularity can be bought—and wasn't there another falling body, more than a decade ago? Still there is undeniable magnetism in *her* falling body, her mathematics—she will be referenced in *The Simpsons* and the shortlived web sitcom *Alpha Cheese*—she will manifest as ink on T-shirts and temporary tatts—in the video for 'Icon (Get Your Game On)' by Miko and the Exploding Heads she will don cartoon colors, outlined in querulous black, rotoscoped beyond recognition—a kinetic sketch— lolcats recreate her fall—she is pure verb, the articulation of flight, she is the truth—she is every metaphor in the fucking universe.

Jules wishes she could tell the difference between good coffee and bad coffee. Too often now she'll be in a conversation where the name of a café or coffee stand will come up, and the other person will wrinkle their nose—*wrinkle* their nose like they're in a freaking Blyton book—and say, 'Aw, the coffee there's shit. They have the *worst* coffee. They have to *do* something about it.' And Jules will just have to sit there, nodding sagely, because everybody she ever talks to is tired, and tired people always talk about coffee.

Like this guy here, who took one sip of his macchiato and declared that the barista at that joint should be shot, all of them shot; the place has to be investigated, dammit, exposed for the phoney rip-off scam that it is; jerks, all of them.

Jules can't remember the guy's name, but thinks it's probably Adrian. 'Gah,' Adrian says, taking another unsatisfactory sip, because bad coffee is better than no coffee. Especially out here, in the gray sunlight on Fitzgerald, lugging a tripod. Jules is carrying Adrian's camera bag for him—such was the intensity of his displeasure, it inspired Jules to project herself as a calm grown-up in comparison.

'So,' Adrian says. 'Jules. Jules Valentine. Is that your real name or what?'

'It sure is.'

'What's it short for? Julia?'

'Juliet.'

'As in Romeo and Juliet.'

'Yes.'

'...So your name is *Juliet Valentine*.'

'Yes. Here's my card.'

He takes it in his coffee hand and angles his head to read it. The card, which is Patrick Bateman bone-white, says in glossy center-aligned Helvetica:

STFU

Adrian, balancing his coffee, slides the card into his pocket.

They arrive at their shooting location, a dull brick wall in the Coles car park. Adrian sets down his coffee and opens his tripod, and then consults his phone for the time. 'The light should be just about right now.'

She's got a fake gun tucked into the waistband of her jeans and it's uncomfortable as hell. It really pinches when, at Adrian's instruction, she scales the wall, one-and-a-half times her height and two bricks deep. Jules balances in borrowed Converse high-tops, squinting at the sky and thinking that this light will never look right for anything: the clouds, too brightly lit, too silver-edged. And this Adrian guy, who is not exactly unlikeable but like a train intent on arrival, shooting through every stop, permitting no one onboard.

Jules adjusts her costume—black jeans, leather jacket the color of dried blood—and scratches the reddened skin beneath the fake gun. This is what she knows: Adrian's in the middle of editing a short film. He needs to reshoot a particular scene, but the main actor has gone to Melbourne. Jules has forgotten the exact trail of acquaintances that led to Adrian finding her, a reasonable approximation of the leading lady.

'Alright,' Adrian says.

His directions are crisp: jump off this wall. Run towards the supermarket.

'Okay,' Jules says.

Her first jump from the wall is completely natural. She feels every second of the fall and the crash of pavement, scrambling to her feet and hurtling towards Coles until Adrian calls for her to stop. Jules turns around and Adrian walks up with a roll of gaffer tape. He tears off two strips and makes a cross on the pavement near her toe. 'You have to run to this exact spot for each take,' he says.

Which turns out to be quite difficult. Every time she makes that fall to the ground her feet seem to want to take her in a different direction. At the end of each take she immediately looks across at Adrian, stationed at his camera, frowning. Another take. At times like these Jules finds that her brain doesn't shut off exactly but slips into something like one of those Windows 95 screensavers: in particular, the one where you're flying through space and all these little white dots are rushing at you. If you access the screensaver settings, you can even specify how many stars you would like to appear per second. Jules is rocketing through that black sky and watching the white dots racing like thoughts, and so a part of her is taking her leap off the wall and bracing for impact while another part is thinking about her shift at work yesterday, that young family—mother, father, child—uncertainly navigating the Lounge Room section while Jules was dusting the eProp flatscreen. The family peered around the next corner of the IKEA maze and the mother said to her beloveds, 'Oh, are we meant to go through here? Does it want us to go through here?' Said with such heartbreaking sincerity that Jules had to notice the family for a bit longer—this one so earnest to get it right, to fullfil IKEA's bidding—before rocketing on, the thought behind her, disappearing into the vast digital blackness.

Does it want.

Does *it* want.

Does it *want*.

She jumps off the wall and runs.

Before each take, Adrian holds a clapperboard in front of the camera, but he doesn't snap it like Jules has seen in movies of movie sets. Just seeing the clapperboard in real life is a novelty in itself; it looks less like a professional instrument and more like a prop. Adrian, too, has a strange not-quiteness about him. Some low-res trial version of a film student. Jules doesn't know much about this kind of thing, and her university days seem long ago now, but she does remember the film students, dotted around campus in clusters, setting up a shot for their grim final-assessment narratives—narratives which, due to budgetary and time constraints, inevitably centered on a ragtag group of young university students.

This Adrian—either because of the hurried nature of the shoot or his own preference—is today a lone wolf, camera operator and director in one.

'Go again,' Adrian says, so she does.

It was a Facebook call-out. Perhaps that's why Jules's memory can't trace the degrees of separation between Adrian and herself. Somebody, probably Elena, invited Jules to an event page of Adrian going all *shitshitguys, I gotta reshoot this scene and I only have one more week, I need somebody who looks like this chick.*

The picture for the event page was of a girl in her early twenties holding a bottle of Corona at a party. The event had clearly done the rounds—twenty-nine attending, fifty-two maybe attending, helped along by an update from Adrian promising fifty dollars for the lucky candidate—and no match for the girl with the Corona had emerged.

A few spiky PMs later and here she is, fifty dollars richer, doing in her ankles with another jump. Groundhogging it back to the beginning.

After the sunlight shifts, Adrian puts away his clapperboard and says that they're through. Jules ducks into the shopping center restroom to change clothes, and hands back her fake gun and sweaty costume to Adrian in a battered City Surf bag. 'Thanks for coming out, Jules,' he says, telescoping his tripod legs.

'You'll let me know when you've finished the film, right?'

'Sure, sure. Ah...' Patting himself down for a pen. 'I don't have your email address.'

She scribbles j.valentine@gmail.com on the back of the STFU card. They shake hands like professionals, and then Adrian goes, 'So, uh...' and she watches him dart his gaze, and then default to the topic he knows best. 'Wanna grab a coffee?'

'Actually I have to head off, but thanks.' She slings her bag over her shoulder. 'Good luck with the editing.'

She's halfway back to her car when Elena calls. 'Half a box of couscous in the cupboard,' Elena says. 'Been there for months. *I* would like some couscous. Yours?'

'Nah, I don't know who that belongs to.'

'Well, mine now. How did the shoot go?'

'My ankles are killing me. The guy was alright. That's about it, really.'

'What'd you have to do?'

'Jump off a wall and then run somewhere. It was weird. He didn't give me any context or anything. Just: jump off here, run over there.'

'Aw, Valentine. Why didn't you just ask for context?'

'I kinda liked not having context. Wanted to jumpcut all that bullshit anyway, so I didn't have to interact with the guy.'

'I love how you're talking about this as if you didn't have any choice in taking part.'

'And what's with the clapperboard thing? He didn't clap it once.'

'The what?'

'That thing, you know. "Action!" and then, *snap*—'

'Oh right. It's because he wasn't recording sound. He must already have sound to put over your take.'

'Oh okay.' Jules imagines Adrian syncing her take with a vast repository of sound effects of shoes running across brick, of landing, each sound possessing some careful nuance that her untrained ear would not detect, each somehow outclassing the auditory actuality. Maybe he'll have to construct the track from several smaller sound effects, some mix 'n' match thing, like customisable furniture. For a scene barely ten seconds long. It all seems like too much trouble.

'Jules?'

'Sorry. Hey, El, I have to drive now. I'll be back home soon. Enjoy your couscous.'

'Alrighty. Later.'

'Later.'

Jules is about to hang up when she notices the date on the Motorola's smudged display, exactly two months before Elena's birthday. Shit. She shuts her phone.

Jules and Elena have been engaged in gift-giving one-upmanship ever since high school. They bonded over their mutual propensity to give terrible presents to other people, but they are inexplicably talented at getting presents for each other. It was Elena who gave Jules the stack of STFU business cards for her birthday last year. Now it's Jules's turn, and two months is barely enough time to both conceive of and successfully execute a decent counter-present.

Jules pockets her phone and rounds the corner. There's a girl leaning against Jules's car, staring at the road, lifting a cigarette to her mouth that is mostly ash. Jules stops a meter away, watches the girl take a drag, and there's something kind of off about her, spectral, and then Jules realizes it's because she's dressed in very much the same outfit that Jules was just wearing at the shoot—Converse high-tops, black jeans, leather jacket the color of dried blood. Jules is just about to say something when the girl turns her head. It takes some time for Jules to recognize the girl without her bottle of Corona.

'Hey, weren't you meant to be in Melb—'

The girl tosses her cigarette, grabs Jules by the collar and shoves her against the car.

'Ow! What the *fuck*—'

'Get in the car!' the girl yells.

'Ow!'

'Get in! Get in! Get in!'

And in a jumble of keys and sharp fingernails Jules is falling into the driver's seat and the Corona girl's in the passenger's side.

'Drive! Go go go go go go go go go! Get back out to Fitzgerald!'

Jules gets as far as starting the ignition and slamming into reverse before she remembers that she's not some meat-puppet actress anymore and brakes. Switches the car off.

'Why?' Jules asks.

The Corona girl glares. Jules wonders if, just by participating in Adrian's film, she's programmed now to keep on falling, completely contextless, for the rest of the day.

'Look, Marilyn,' the girl says. 'I don't have time for this. We need to catch up with Adrian and lift the memory card. So get moving. Don't test me. I will hit you.'

'Who the hell's Marilyn?'

The girl pauses. Even when silent, she reverberates with malevolence. Jules's hand creeps to the door handle, ready to bolt; the Corona girl is grappling for something in her jeans pocket and Jules thinks immediately of the fake gun, except maybe on this real-life girl it *won't* be a fake gun, but what the Corona girl retrieves instead is an iPhone. She swipes the shattered touchscreen, shoving aside applications like a police officer navigating a crowd of gawping bystanders. She is loading, Jules realizes, the Facebook event page for the actress call-out. She scrolls down the messages left on the event wall, and in that blur Jules sees the name Marilyn O'Connor, the closest hopeful before Adrian selected Jules.

'You're not Marilyn O'Connor?' Corona girl demands, squinting at the profile picture and Jules and back again.

'No, I'm—'

'Whatever, there's no difference. Look. Look. Listen, just *listen to me*, alright? Get back out to Fitzgerald.'

'Get the fuck out of my *car*!'

'Bastard switched out on me,' Corona girl mutters, rotating the iPhone in her hands. 'Stringing me along the whole time. That little *prick*.'

'Get out of my—'

'Yeah, yeah, yeah. Look, you don't want to get dragged into this bottomless shitpile, trust me. We have to get the memory card. *Listen to me*. We have to get the memory card.'

Jules sighs. 'Do you even know what's *on* that memory card? It's an amateur film. An amateur *student* film. Let's be realistic, nobody's going to watch it. Now, if you could just get out of my car—'

'Yeah, an *amateur* film,' the girl snaps. 'An amateur film backed by some corporate dump so they can "discover" it and market the snot out of it! It's all manufactured, don't you see? It's some fucked-up astroturfing shit!'

'Why should I care?'

'Why should you—' The girl stops herself. 'Okay. Okay. You don't have to care. Fuck knows, nobody else cares. But I need you, okay, whatever-your-name-is, Marilyn, Betty, whatever. It doesn't matter if you don't understand, but you don't want to get caught up in this, trust me. I need you to get me that memory card.'

'Wouldn't following your instructions actually involve *getting caught up in this?*'

'They don't *know* about you. You can disappear after this.' The girl wavers under Jules's gaze. It's not a weakening, Jules sees, but an internal debate on whether to change persuasion tactics. But the girl steadies her glare. Injects new venom: 'I mean, what *else* have you got to do this afternoon, anyhow?'

What else has Jules got to do this afternoon, anyhow?

Be one of thirty-nine people who stop at the intersection of Fitzgerald and Walcott and read the sign 'WE BUY HOUSES FOR CASH CALL 0429 929 801' in its entirety.

Witness a Hyundai Getz narrowly overtake a bus while doing 80k/h.

Collect and dispose of the yellowing local newspaper editions rotting away in the 14 Camberwell Street letterbox.

Belatedly advise one dismayed Elena Rubik that the water-to-couscous ratio is strictly 1:1 cup, and that any minor deviation results in irreparable disaster.

Be one of three people to like a reposted GIF of a cat sending a fax.

As Jules starts the ignition, reverses, and slips onto Fitzgerald, she glances at Corona girl, but Corona girl will never—not once today—strap on a seatbelt.

They jostle over speed bumps. Jules retreats into her digital starry sky and rehearses how she's going to tell this story to Elena later. The present moment is the future's past. *I'm not sure why I went with Corona girl. She just had this weird intensity about her, I guess. She was like a tornado. A strangely persuasive, compelling tornado. Just going on and on about the film, we have to get the film, why won't you help me get the film. She probably had information on that Marilyn girl, some sort of leverage, but nothing to hold over me. So there was no reason, really. She was just so—*

'There he is!' the girl screams, yanking the steering wheel. The car swerves.

'Stop it!' Jules yanks the car straight. There's Adrian, struggling along the sidewalk, hefting his filming equipment and the City Surf bag.

'Pull over!' Corona girl commands, so Jules obliges, and it's the worst parallel park of her life. Corona girl immediately pushes her out the door. 'Get the memory card! Go go go!' Jules tumbles out of her car like a one-woman SWAT team. She sweeps the area for Adrian and catches sight of the City Surf bag disappearing into a coffee shop.

Jules sighs. She stands on the sidewalk, staring at the coffee shop, gathering her nerves, ignoring Corona girl jabbing the car window with her finger. Geez. A man pushes the door to the coffee shop, looks over at her, and holds it open quizzically, so Jules drags up a polite smile and crosses over the threshold.

Adrian's at the counter, surrounded by baggage, coaching the counter assistant through his order. Jules darts a glance at the blackboard but there are no clues for the uninitiated: just a stand of cream-colored, sparse menus on the counter, too far away to read.

Quote of the Day says the blackboard. *All plots lead deathwards. —Don DeLillo.*

Adrian's wrapping up his order, and the polite door-holder, who is still considering the papyrus menu, gestures for Jules to join the queue.

Jules is still searching for coffee keywords—are *latte* and *flat white* the same thing?—when Adrian turns around, holding a number 12 on a metal stand. 'Jules. Hey.'

'Hey.'

'Thought you had to go somewhere.'

'It... got postponed.'

Jules can't seem to move her feet or feel the inside of her mouth. With the number twelve lopsided in his hand, Adrian looks like a bored auction attendee.

'Well,' he says, 'when you order, ask for the Dark Shrine blend. It's way better than the shit we had this morning.'

Adrian twists past her to find a table. Still numb, Jules steps up to the counter. 'Shall I put you on the same number?' the waitress asks.

'Yes,' Jules sighs.

The café soundtrack is the sort of music that would play in an igloo housing a dentist's. Jules scrunches her receipt into her wallet and walks to Adrian's table. His equipment clogs the legroom, so she sits sideways. Catches sight, for a moment, of the City Surf bag, its slightly open lip. The dark red jacket folded inside. The handgrip of the fake gun.

Adrian thumbs the last flourishes on a text message while Jules casts desperately for a way into a conversation—but Adrian takes care of that for her. 'So what do you do anyway, Jules?' he asks, pocketing his Blackberry and retrieving a foil packet of blue Halls. He pops one. 'Study?'

'Work,' Jules says. 'IKEA drone.'

'Checkout?'

'Sales. Roam the maze, arrange displays, answer questions.'

She can smell his menthol breath from across the table. Who takes a cough drop before having a coffee?

'Does it suck?' he asks.

'It's not awful. Just cleaning with people watching. Like being a zookeeper, really. Vacuuming the ERSLEV while customers pet the TYLÖSAND.'

'Hmm,' Adrian says. Jules has never heard anyone actually pronounce the word *Hmm* as if it were a legitimate word. Jules's gaze slides.

She says, 'The only problem, I guess, is when customers get annoyed at having to follow the maze. They have trouble finding things again, or they ask me why the place is designed that way. Me, a drone.'

'Customers always say that sort of shit. It's like they *know* what the deal is. If they want a store to be like some other shop they like, then they should just shop at that shop.'

'Right,' Jules says before she can sort out what was going on in that sentence. 'Right.'

Does it want.

Does *it* want.

'Thing is, though,' Jules says, 'most customers are actually okay. Like, really obedient. Sometimes, you can actually get away with being visibly annoyed at them for not knowing the rules. Like if they use a step ladder that they're not supposed to. Or if they don't have their barcodes facing up at the checkout. I've seen other workers make customers feel really bad just by pausing a little bit too long before answering a question. Some customers are like that, you know. They really hate not getting it right.'

'Flat white?' A glossy waitress slips Jules a cup on a saucer. The coffee wobbles with a modest lid of froth. 'And yours, sir.' Now sliding Adrian's unexpectedly small order across the table, served in what seems to Jules like the mean successor to her own cup and saucer, some future model, a nanocup. The waitress whisks away the number twelve.

'Ampersand,' Adrian says.

'Pardon?'

'I'm an Ampersand drone. It's this hipster gift store that sells unisex clothes and miscellaneous quirky shit. Terrariums. Scratch 'n' sniff letter-writing paper. Tiny little blackboards attached to tiny little pegs. Perfect, huh. You sell storage solutions, I sell the storage fodder.' He gives his mysterious coffee a stir. 'Two different kinds of vacuous.'

'Right.' Jules sips her flat white.

'IKEA's reached that kind of stage though, hasn't it?'

'What stage?'

'Where it *knows* it's vacuous.'

'Oh. Yeah, I guess so.' Does it want. Does it *want*. Jules thinks about all those smug question-answer signs—*Why do we ask you to clear your own tray? Why do we ask you to assemble the furniture yourself?*—and the way the same products appear and reappear, relentlessly, in different positions, different pairings, sometimes even in places that don't make sense. Cheerfully oppressive. 'It's not really a store anymore, is it?' Jules says finally. 'It's a theme park.'

Adrian fiddles with the edge of his serviette. 'Girl I used to know couldn't stand IKEA. Like, not just mass-produced furniture in general—specifically, IKEA. She was full of that, you know—very specific hatred. It was the actress you were standing in for today, actually. She couldn't even appreciate it ironically. Couldn't appreciate anything ironically. She never once bought coffee for any of the crew.'

Jules, having entirely forgotten about the Corona girl sitting in her car, feels her flat white expand coldly in her stomach.

Adrian tips the last of his coffee into his mouth and sets the cup back on the saucer. 'I'd better get going. Nice talking to you.'

'No worries,' Jules murmurs. What is she here for again?

Newly caffeinated, Adrian gathers his equipment more swiftly than Jules expected, and bustles out the door in a burst of sunlight.

Jules lets out a gust of breath like one of the Famous Five after a big adventure. *By golly.* Her body is still positioned in a scrunched-up diagonal, so she twists herself fully into her seat. Her foot knocks against something underneath the table. A plastic buckle scrapes against the café tiles. Having suffered what felt like the entire length of Fitzgerald with that buckle lodged into her shoulder, Jules hardly needs to look down. Adrian's camera bag.

That solves it. Jules slings the bag over her shoulder, takes a last sip of her flat white, and makes an exit.

Back at the car, Corona girl snaps, 'What the *hell* took you so long?'

Jules sighs, plonks the camera bag on Corona girl's lap and slams the door. 'Just get your damn memory card. Do whatever the hell you want with it.'

'What did you even *talk* about?'

'Our retail jobs.' Jules hooks her thumb on the steering wheel. 'He mentioned you, by the way.'

'What'd he say?'

'He said you never once bought coffee for the crew.'

'Typical.' Corona girl rips open the bag and tosses it in the backseat. She flips over the camera, digging her nail under some secret panel. 'He just doesn't *get it*. For a filmmaker he's not all that perceptive.'

'Well—'

'Oh, you *fuck*.' Corona girl glares at the empty socket where the memory card should be.

'So much for that,' Jules says and shrugs.

'He *knows*! He *knew* what you were up to!'

'Guess he was pretty perceptive aft—'

'What's *wrong* with you? I bet you've never even sabotaged a game of tic-tac-toe in your life!'

'I'm not sure how to point this out politely,' Jules says, 'but you're still in my car.'

'Gah.' Corona girl presses her palms to her eyes, rotating them with an aggression that makes Jules wince. 'How can I make you *get* this? What do I have to do to make you *understand*? It's like I'm talking to a brick wall!'

'I know the feeling.'

'Okay!' Corona flings her hands away from her face. 'What's the most *annoying* product you can think of?'

The sunlight is bearing down hard on Jules's back. She thinks her body's going to start buzzing like an overheated computer. 'I don't know. I don't get annoyed at very many things.'

'No, don't give me that. What makes you tick? Think about... okay, think about music. Yeah, I bet you hate music. I bet a lot of it just gets under your skin. And I don't mean shit that everybody finds annoying. No, something that goes deeper than that.' Corona girl looks Jules up and down, taking in her approximate age and history in one sweep. 'Avril Lavigne.'

'What?'

'Avril Lavigne. That's who you hate.'

'What.'

'You would've been in late high school when she first came out. I bet you were one of those outsider kids, right? There you are, flying under the radar with your shitty misfit bangs, reading all the wrong magazines and watching all the wrong TV shows, and then Avril comes along and everyone thinks you're meant to like her because she supposedly represents everything you're going through. She's safely unconventional. She wears *ties*, for fuck's sake, in the most tepid appropriation of nothing. She's trying to sell outsiderness back to you. Some glamorous version of it. Pseudo empowerment. I'm not talking about whatever the hell she does now, I'm talking about her first entry, her embittered, eyelined, generically rebellious teenage incarnation.

'And that's what made her more insidious than every Britney, Christina, or whatever doll-faced cash cow they tried to sell you before. Now they're taking the identity you specifically cultivated to resist all that fakery and they've turned it into a package. Turned the *rejection* of packages into a package. They're prescribing the terms of your rebellion. They're trying to fix it down, and so they're invalidating the sincerity of your own identity, your own actions.

'And *that*,' Corona girl says, 'is why Adrian's fake indie film is the spawn of fucking Satan. That's why I oppose it, and that's why you should too.'

And as the sun injects a buzzing swarm of static into her head, Jules wonders what the inside of Corona girl's brain must look like. If Jules sliced Corona girl from hairline to chin to reveal a cross-section of skull, she imagines she'd see a brachial network of colored wires and a ticking bomb, digits spilling to zero, and you can't stop it because you don't know what leads to what, can't trace the logic of any of Corona girl's bizarre conclusions.

'Are you *listening* to me?' Corona girl snaps.

And Jules decides that she'd really like her afternoon back.

'Of course I'm listening to you. You sound like a first-year who's discovering capitalism for the first time. *Everyone* is a package. Everyone *knows* that everyone is a package. You're just outraged at the packages that are the worst at hiding it. What you're saying is old news.'

'Oh, right, so *that's* your solution. Complacency is complicity, you know.'

'I'm not complicit. I *know* what you're talking about, I'm just saying it's *old news*. This thing with Adrian's film has already happened to supposed garage-to-recording-studio musicians, except the garage was MySpace. You and your little Fuck the Man revolution are decades too late. And please get out of my car.'

'But this isn't a Fuck the Man thing! This is personal! This is me, *us*—my face, your body—being *used*. It's one thing to just let it wash over you and be smugly self-aware about it, but it's another thing to be a participant. A *perpetrator*. This affects me, this affects you, on a *personal level*, don't you get it?'

And then Corona girl reaches some previously unattained level of untranscribability.

'Yes, I know this is *old news*. Yes. Yes. Yes. Yes, I know— yawn—some people over there are doing a thing, *people way over there*, in the distance, far apart from me, *doing a thing*. Yes. Yes. Boring, right? Well don't worry because I am so bored right now. Yes. I am bored but I am also, well, I am also livid, *bored and livid*, do you understand? Things just—things just don't *cease to be evil* when they're boring and old, you know.'

Corona girl is staring at her with such fluorescent intensity that Jules has to look away. She watches a mother cross the road with her kid in tow, and cars walloping over speed bumps with a kind of oceanic buoyancy. Indifferent as assembly line commodities. She's thirsty. Her mouth is dry with the taste of coffee. She can almost perceive the microfoam yellowing on her tongue.

Jules sighs. 'Adrian didn't even say what the film was for.'

'No,' Corona girl says, relieved. 'He didn't ask your permission.'

'He gave me the impression it was all part of his thesis project.'

'He didn't get the full permission of the crew, either.'

'He didn't tell me what the film was about.'

'He's an *asshole*.' Corona girl drops back down in her seat.

Jules rests her hand on the gear stick. She's still trying to coax herself into caring completely but she's still only approximating it. It might have to do. She sighs again. 'What now?'

It's impossible for Jules to think of herself as resembling Corona girl, not even for a ten-second take spliced into a narrative that's become, in Jules's imagination, a swirling black hole. Even with Corona girl's head turned to the window, darkly observing the hotel apartments and a fenced golf course, Jules isn't sure if there could ever be a resemblance. Corona girl is just too keenly present, so aggressively foreground, in a way that Jules will never be.

'What's the film about, anyway?'

Corona girl glances at her. 'It was an experiment.'

'In what?'

Corona girl rethinks. 'A *series* of experiments. This movie
—it's old footage. We've been playing with it for years. The
purpose always evolves. At first it was meant to be a short
silent film that looped perfectly back on itself, so it could be
played continuously.'

'Has that been done before?'

'I'm not saying it was new. It was just a particular challenge we set for ourselves.'

'Okay. And then it evolved?'

'Yes. Because of QR codes.'

'QR codes?'

'You've seen them. On movie posters. Magazines. Posters
for stores. Those squares, like a pixelated Rorschach test.'

'Oh, those.'

'Object hyperlinking, right. We wanted to mark the landscape with our film. Hide it all over the city. That's why it was
so perfect that the movie was looped. It could be divided up
into segments. You could start anywhere and hunt for more
fragments. The effect was even better if the location of the QR
code corresponded with the location in which the segment
was shot. There you were, watching events taking place in
the very spot you're standing. Like watching ghosts. But this
isn't new either. I bet somebody's already done it before. It
was just for us.'

'So the film is actually finished?'

'More like, at one stage, there *was* a complete film, a particular edit that would have worked. What Adrian's doing
now, he's just expanding it, recutting old footage, inserting
new footage. Making it sellable. Making it fit the next purpose.'

'But why *your* film?'

'It could be anyone's film. I don't know how they found
Adrian. Maybe they found his pretentious website. Or maybe
his style has just the right amount of edginess and the right

amount of mediocrity. You gotta have both. You gotta be an Avril. Here, take this exit.'

Jules indicates off the freeway. Negotiates the merge. 'Who's "they"?'

Jules glances over at Corona girl, but she doesn't say anything.

Does *it* want.

They drive past a post-apocalyptically silent Chicken Treat installed in a shopping mall that seems permanently under construction, witches' hats scattered like Minesweeper flags all over the buckled tarmac. Cars queue up at the KFC drive thru. The university billboard across the road advises: *It's the brightest minds that will make tomorrow better.*

Corona girl directs Jules to the empty staff parking lot.

'What are you going to do?' Jules says as she turns the car off.

'I don't know.'

It's a more austere campus than Jules's alma mater. Even for a Sunday, there's a particular desolation to it. Corona girl pushes her iPhone deep in her pocket, slings Adrian's camera bag across her chest and marches down the path with the authority of a post-disaster rescue operative. The Film and Television building is concrete gray, an Orwellian ministry humming with vending machines. Jules follows Corona girl through a side door, up a stairwell that makes multi-level car park fire escapes look cosy. At the top of the stairs, at a red door, Corona girl retrieves a faded student card from her back pocket and swipes it. A medical blip.

They move through a corridor and into a classroom lined end-to-end with anaemic Mac terminals, the monitors blank-faced as cult members. Jules sees the signs of Adrian—City Surf bag, blister pack of blue Halls, bent STFU card—at the one terminal that's awake, linked up to a projector that casts its images onto a giant screen pulled over the whiteboard.

They've caught the film in mid-transition—now, fading in: the face of a young woman, expressive and open, lifting an orange telephone receiver. Corona girl. A strange thrill of recognition ripples through Jules. Completely soundless, the film has a paradoxical energy—a kind of consciousness, alertness. Jules looks at Corona girl. Awash in her own light, her eyes flick around the room, completely disinterested in the screen.

The medical blip sounds. The door springs open. Jules turns back and comes face to face with Adrian—wallet tucked under his armpit, student card between his lips—protecting, in his gentle hand, a thin paper cup of Nescafé.

Adrian takes the card from his mouth and lets the door click shut. 'Jules. What are you doing here?'

'I'm just the driver.'

She steps away so Adrian and Corona girl can look at each other unobstructed, but what she doesn't expect is for the atmosphere to change the way that it does. For it to become so warm, not with animosity, but like old friends meeting. Long lost comrades-in-arms.

'What are you doing here?' Adrian asks, now a curiously lonely question.

Corona girl tightens her lip. Her on-screen counterpart leans into the telephone receiver tenderly. 'You lied to her,' she says, pointing at Jules. 'She wants her part of the film back.'

'You're getting real lousy at sabotaging my movie. Is that my camera?'

'You broke their rules.'

'Oh yeah. I've broken their rules loads of times by now.' Adrian motions at the screen with his paper cup. 'This character isn't just you anymore. There are four or five others I've used. In snippets, like I was shooting today with Jules. Who knows. Maybe if I keep at it long enough you'll be edited out completely.'

'Edited out completely.' Corona girl nods. Her face flickers as if she's trying to decide whether that would be a good thing or a bad thing.

'It's kinda cool, actually. Like that other experiment we did ages ago, remember, when we tried to get as many people as possible playing the one guy—'

'Don't change the subject.'

Adrian shrugs, lets out a little disbelieving laugh like a stand-up comedian trying to get the audience on his side. 'You *disappeared*. What was I meant to do?'

Corona girl bristles. 'Who says you're *meant* to do anything? Are they *making* you do this?'

'No! Of course not. It's a collaboration. And shouldn't it be? Shouldn't that be how it goes? Our work doesn't have to be invalid just because there's corporate interest involved. We can't do it alone. *They* can't do it alone.'

'It's a phoney power shift. You know it is.'

On the screen, Corona girl runs down a Perth street made unfamiliar by the pace of the shot, wearing the same outfit that Jules wore today—or, perhaps more accurately, the outfit that Corona girl is wearing right now, in real life. Dark red leather jacket, black jeans, Converse high-tops. Everything except for the gun tucked into the waistband of her jeans.

Adrian does that disbelieving laugh again. A drop of Nescafé jumps the paper rim. 'I don't get it. I don't get what you're trying to do here. This was *our* project. Whatever you delete or destroy I can find again. I can recut and rebuild. I can reshoot the whole damn film. That was your whole philosophy at the beginning, wasn't it? Continuity's a cheap trick. Everything can be repurposed.'

At that moment the film arrives at Jules's scene. The jump. They all have to look at it—Adrian, Jules, Corona girl. Bathed in pixels.

There's something about the way she falls.

The artful cut to black.

And in the reverberating darkness, Corona girl shuts her eyes softly. She takes in a quiet, deep breath, like a ballerina about to pivot into her opening position, about to embark on the most astounding and convincing performance of her life. Or at least this is what Jules thinks at first, but it must have been a sigh of resignation instead, because when the Corona girl opens her eyes she unslings the camera bag and holds it out to Adrian. He takes it in his spare hand.

'I'm sorry,' Adrian finally says, and for some reason Jules knows that it's true.

Corona girl glances at the screen and back again. 'You know, sometimes I wish it were real. That all the shit we buy and believe in could actually level the playing field. Like it was actually possible for us to make whatever we wanted to make, without all these other considerations entering into it.'

'Of course it's possible for us to make whatever we want to make. It's why we started doing this. What you've always said. Nothing is permanent. Nothing can't be redone.'

Their eyes meet just as the film begins again.

The Motorola whirs in Jules's pocket. The ringtone cuts in a second later, and, like characters in a dream sensing their time is up, Adrian and Corona girl look at Jules.

Jules fishes the Motorola from her pocket and flips it open just as the caller hangs up. One missed call, the phone reports. Elena.

As Jules wonders whether it'd be rude to call Elena back, the phone perks up with a text message. *Sorry! Meant to call someone else. Did you say you were coming back home btw?*

Corona girl and Adrian are still staring at Jules. Jules feels obligated to apologize, but she finds herself saying something different. 'Look. This is a sweet moment and all, but I have to go.'

She finds her car keys, slides her phone back into her pocket. She steps out of the film's light, edges past Corona girl, past Adrian. Depresses the handle of the red door.

'Jules.'

Adrian walks down the row of blank monitors, sets down his camera, wallet, and paper cup at his terminal. He executes a series of quick clicks, and then pulls a cheap blue flash drive from the USB port. 'Here,' he says, tossing it to Jules, who barely catches it. 'It's all the stuff we shot today. You can hang on to it.'

Jules casts a final glance at Corona girl: hollow now, like those first pure CGI movie characters. Those unnerving stares. 'Thanks,' Jules says. 'Um. Good luck.'

And, perhaps Jules imagines it—perhaps her eye *wants* to see this, out of loyalty to some sense of continuity—but, just as she steps beyond the red door, letting it return home, click shut, she *thinks* she glimpses the Corona girl slip a hand behind her jacket. Reaching into the waistband of her jeans.

The falling body will, in some ways, come to stand for a generation, its privileges and anxieties, the tension between intent and accident, a persistent narrative that delegates control to something external and omniscient—gravity, mathematics—her image, a perfect mimesis of the forces that will make her iconic, an exercise in recursion—across her endless cultural iterations she will evade identification—for some she may even escape context, the pastiche encountered before the original—but in the everlasting present tense she is both active subject and passive object—plunging like a syringe into memory—the poise of her muscles, her action-ready limbs—announcing that she jumps knowingly, and accepts the impact to come.

Jules finds herself lying on her stomach with her face squashed into her pillow, sleep-encrusted eyes, head full of static. Her phone is lodged into her upper thigh. She arches her back, digging down there to excavate it. The time is 8:09 PM.

Her temple aches with the memory of the sun. She rolls onto her back, and in that sluggish turn she catches sight of the cheap blue flash drive on her bedside table. She groans.

Elena had gone somewhere by the time Jules arrived home. Not that she thinks she can tell Elena about any of it. Not only because Jules doesn't want to piss off Corona girl, or whoever's pulling the strings with Adrian's film, but because, like the root of all her troubles today, she feels like she has absolutely no context.

She grasps the flash drive and flicks the cap off with her thumb. She drags her Acer out from under a pile of clothes, powers up, brushes lint off the keyboard. She hears one of her other housemates flush the toilet, and another boiling the kettle. There's only one file on the flash drive, and a gigantic one at that—Adrian must have shifted all his other files off, rather than shifting this one on. Jules double-clicks.

And re-watches that part of her day, looping over and over. Each fall is different but she always returns, like a typewriter sliding back into position, or a teleportation device malfunctioning relentlessly, blinking her backwards and backwards. She's already forgotten the chosen take. The loops are becoming indistinguishable.

Backwards, backwards.

Like a thought you just can't get over.

Rocketing through that starry sky in reverse.

She remembers Elena's timely missed call and smiles. Perhaps if Elena had not called, Jules would still be stuck there, with Adrian and Corona girl, sucked into their plot, transfixed not because she was invested in the drama but because of her peculiar listlessness, the Jules Valentine circuitry that found the whole day less of an emotional rollercoaster than a mildly perplexing see-saw ride.

She ejects the flash drive and recaps it. A possible birthday present, she thinks, for Elena. Inside knowledge on whatever shit goes down when Adrian's film is released, if it gets released at all. A sly wink that won't make any sense until sometime after Elena's birthday, perhaps, or maybe it'll be just in time. Jules likes the idea of that. Subtle. Maybe not enough to beat STFU cards. But still pretty cool.

Jules drops the flash drive in her bedside table drawer. She rubs the broken skin on her lower back. Tomorrow is Monday, a work day, and she expects a slightly thicker layer of dust, instructions for maze reconfigurations, a new special at the cafeteria. The static in her head buzzes at a softer frequency. She hopes she remembered to wash her uniform.

Light

She remembers the first time she inserted a contact lens—the mild itch, the initial distortion like peering into an oily lake. The pop of air when the lens fastened to her eye (remember that it *wants* to be in your eye, the optometrist said)— and then, perception, a sharpness she had been accustomed to believing was unnatural, reserved only for televisions or computer screens or photography. Do people really see like this *all the time*, she thought, sitting in the car on the way to school, marvelling that the world can be a hard, bright place, each object discrete and outlined.

It's not the same with glasses, she thinks. You can always see the frame, the division between clarity and natural sight. Beyond the frame is pure peripheral ambiguity.

When she was very young, she used to pretend her spectacles were a unique body graft, like a mechanized limb. She had been the only child in her class who wore glasses. 'Why does that girl need to wear those?' she once heard a classmate whisper—not maliciously, but to a six-year-old kid there's no difference.

'I AM *NOT* A GIRL,' she announced in her Outside Voice. 'I AM A ROBOT. I HAVE THREE LIGHT-PROCESSING

SETTINGS FOR OPTIMAL VISION VERSATILITY. THESE SETTINGS ARE, ONE: MAXIMUM-POWER MODE. TWO: POWER-SAVING MODE. THREE: OFF. MY ABILITY TO COPE WITH SENSORY DATA THEREFORE EXCEEDS YOURS. I AM A SUPERIOR BEING.'

A lunchtime spent in Time Out and a parent-teacher meeting did little to change her perspective. She christened herself Robobec, or BECCA, which—given her recent discovery and appreciation of acronyms—translated into Body of Exceptional Cunning, Coordination and Adaptability.

The teacher condemned BECCA's outburst but admired her vocabulary. BECCA's mother wasn't sure how to tell the teacher that this vocabulary was a direct result of BECCA's particular TV and medical pamphlet diet, fed to her in an attempt to surmount the child's initial dismay at wearing glasses. The incident at school was less an outburst than a recitation of a prepared statement.

Her parents decided BECCA needed more extracurricular activities, new outlets to siphon away her contempt for the non-mechanized.

For her outdoor activity, they chose netball, where, outside the goal circle, precision was not so crucial. Non-spectacled perception is not blindness—the way cartoons depict stumbling nerds with arms outstretched when their glasses have been knocked off—but more like an Impressionist painting: semblance without detail. Soft reality. Without glasses, BECCA could easily identify and pass the ball to members of her team and stay within the right lines. She played netball until the end of high school.

For her indoor activity, the parents chose piano lessons. Hard reality would only suffice here, as even in children's books the musical notation is small, subtle as Braille. Perhaps her parents supposed that BECCA ought to learn to privilege other senses besides sight. Both her piano playing and netball improved when she switched to contact lenses just before her seventeenth birthday: she liked to think of herself, finally, as possessing 180 degree vision, the fog beyond the spectacle rim suddenly incorporated seamlessly into her perception. Her contact lenses were her most favorite things in the world, and it seemed criminal to discard them at the end of each month. It *wants* to be in my eye, she remembered, and it pleased her to think of her lenses as sentient.

This ocular upgrade coincided with BECCA receiving her driver's licence. Without hesitation she put herself down as an organ donor, ticking all the boxes except *cornea*.

Throughout BECCA's life, her corneas have been the topic of much inquiry. *Keratoconus*, the ophthalmologist called it, a degenerative disorder in which the cornea thins and the eye becomes conical. Each year, BECCA's lenses thicken in parallel with her pointed eyeballs—but one day, she is warned, her sight might degenerate beyond the help of contact lenses.

Now, at nearly thirty years old, the possibility of losing her eyesight fills her with grief, but she remembers the last attribute of BECCA, Adaptability, and swears she will adapt. A piano accompanist for choirs and solo performers, she investigates measures that will allow her to continue her occupation. It will be difficult, she knows, but entirely possible. At her ophthalmologist's advice, she joins the waiting list for corneal transplants.

Sometimes she smiles at remembering her six-year-old self, who translated her deficiency into versatility, different perceptual modes. In a way it could be true, she thinks, because it can be exhausting sometimes to see everything so sharply. She remembers one night when she forgot to remove her lenses, and woke up to a world that was invasively bright, her eyes peculiarly airless as if sealed with cling wrap. On some weekends she sits outside in power-saving mode, enjoying soft reality, its muted brushstrokes.

One day, after BECCA exceeds thirty, an individual vacates the corneas that BECCA will inherit. Notified of this availability, she is permitted a few facts about the donor: woman, twenty-five, Western Australia. These details coalesce in BECCA's mental index, codified as a default avatar, a silhouette in a square.

Corneal transplants are most successful when performed within twenty-four hours of the donor's death, so BECCA does not have long to say goodbye to her own corneas. She has learnt that although corneal transplants do not necessitate the donor and recipient to be matched, there is still a chance her body might reject the corneas. As she succumbs to anaesthesia, she thinks of this risk, and thinks of herself anew as Robobec—her parts modifiable, improvable. She enters off-mode with the faintest smile.

After the operation and recovery, BECCA still needs contact lenses, but because her eyeballs are now of a more conventional shape, her prescription is simpler. It doesn't disappoint her at all that she must still wear lenses, that she may still perceive both hard and soft reality. For detecting signs of transplant rejection, she is supplied with a new acronym, RSVP: Redness, Sensitivity to light, Vision loss, Pain.

In that first month she enjoys scrutinising her eyes for stitches, the little nylon darts that point to her pupil. It is a most pleasing recursive act, to perceive what allows her to perceive. She is fascinated by her body.

She thinks frequently of her donor: the lawful unknowability of her. BECCA has determined the most statistically probable cause of death of this woman, twenty-five, Western Australia. At every traffic intersection she wonders if *this* was the place, or this, or this; she wonders what it was that her donor saw last. It fills BECCA with sad warmth that light may still touch her donor's eyes, may pass through, may become meaning.

It is not clear to BECCA what happened to her own discarded corneas. Perhaps, so thin and unwanted, they simply dissolved upon removal; or, perhaps they are kept in a lab cabinet for further inspection, supine in womb-like liquid. When she sits down at the piano for important recitals, she wonders if her old corneas will choose this moment to exercise vengeance from beyond the grave, to RSVP aggressively. It can happen any time, she's told, even years later when the stitches are gone and the new corneas have assimilated to her convexity.

BECCA has given the transplant coordinator a letter of gratitude addressed to the donor's family, kept on-file somewhere, for when the family decide they are ready to receive it. Her transplant coordinator tells her that BECCA's post-op progress is monitored, logged, and reported back to the donor's family. It is only these data, this fact of her wellbeing, that BECCA exchanges with the donor's parents.

Two years later, when BECCA is renewing her driver's licence, she remembers that she herself will be a donor one day. If the circumstances of her death permit it, she will be dismantled, her parts incorporated into other bodies. This information strikes her in a way that it hadn't when she ticked those boxes years ago. It is freshly terrifying.

But, after that cold fear recedes, she is left contemplating the idea of herself persisting in other bodies, and other bodies persisting. Her vision glitches. Returns.

Pikkoro and the Multipurpose Octopus

And here's Pikkoro, in the sudden quiet, on this hot afternoon—sighing over the asphalt, school hat low on her brow. Textbooks add ten pounds to her back and ten years to her face; hunched by rote wisdom, she awaits the green man and labors through the crossing. She is surrounded by cicadas and bicyclists and blurry-faced commuters. On days like this, Pikkoro's eyes can withdraw so deeply into her head—can resort to oversimplification, express themselves with single lines.

—Hmm?

Her eyes grow round at the sight of a truck cutting the corner, tipping slightly on one wheel. Overloaded with crates, the truck punts one piece of fruit from the pile—which bounces brightly, then makes a getaway roll for Pikkoro's foot. She stoops for a closer look: a hard yellow mango, see-sawing to a stop, sticker-side-up. It's *HarvestTime*™. The silhouette of a tree growing lovehearts instead of foliage.

Pikkoro scoops up the mango. She decides to take it home.

Pikkoro lives on the second floor of a gray apartment building. It has palm trees at the front gate and a communal pool with uncleared leaves floating on the surface. Her young ankles swell with each gray step. She passes the other homes piping with afternoon television programs and microwave bells. She stops at her welcome mat to peel off her shoes.

—Wah, it's so hot.

And what a relief it is to finally slump inside the apartment, drop her schoolbag on the tatami and throw herself into the sofa.

Tako, in the kitchen, suctions ice cubes from a plastic mould. He pops the ice into two glasses.

—Sorry. I should have come to pick you up.

Pikkoro mumbles into the cushion. Her after-school bowl of ramen is steaming on the table. On the mantelpiece there is a row of framed photographs of Pikkoro and her parents, ageing slowly from right to left. In the final photograph there is a snapshot of Pikkoro and Tako. One of Tako's tentacles is outstretched, off-frame, as he is holding the camera.

Tako shuffles to the sofa with two glasses of iced tea, offering one to Pikkoro. She groans, rolling onto her back, accepting the glass with both hands. Tako notices the mango peeking out of her knapsack.

—What's this?

—It fell on the road.

Tako picks up the mango. Pikkoro wriggles off the sofa and slips into her chair. A novel, *Seeds of Time*, is splayed face-down on the table, alongside a pile of unfinished knitting. Pikkoro sets her glass on the placemat and blows weakly on her ramen.

—Har-ve-s-t T-i-me.

Tako puts the mango on the kitchen counter.

The afternoon changes color. Pikkoro is stretched out on the tatami, her mathematics textbook spread inside the glowing

square of television light. She frowns at her spidery calcula-
tions and rubs out her latest answer. Tako is sitting on the
sofa, knitting with four arms and holding his novel open with
two. Although Pikkoro's head is drooping into her homework, although her sighs grow heavier, Tako clicks through
his knitting and there is contentment here, discernible in their
soft faces. There's a game show on television that neither of
them is fully watching: warbling with uncertainty, pinging
with success, buzzing with failure.

—*We're going to take a short break, folks; don't go away!*

The theme song booms, and Pikkoro finally lays her head
down on her exercise book and shuts her eyes.

But she is compelled to open them again when the television falls silent. She raises her head to a commercial unfold-
ing in the hypnotic quiet. The fattest apples, pears, oranges—and mangoes, just like the one Pikkoro plucked from the
road—spinning against a backdrop of idyllic orchards, giant
and seductive as planets. It doesn't make sense, but it doesn't
have to—Pikkoro sits up and lets the fruit spin inside her iris-
es. Her pencil escapes the fold of her exercise book and rolls
away. Even the clicking of Tako's knitting needles has ceased.

Then, fading in: the loveheart tree. *It's HarvestTime™.*

—Pikkoro-chan.

—Hmm?

—Your costume is finished. Come try it on.

Tako unfurls what he's been knitting: a woollen octopus
poncho, coral red, the eyes and mantle forming a hood. Six
stuffed limbs hang off the sides, and Tako helps Pikkoro slip
her arms between two extra sleeves that make the seventh
and eighth limbs. She wobbles to her bedroom so she can
look in the mirror. Tako joins her.

—What do you think?

Pikkoro sways appreciatively.

—It's perfect.

The next day, Pikkoro's costume is wrapped in a brown paper parcel and secured to the top of her school bag. It's set to be another hot day—the sky is white with humidity, and those clouds just seem far too close to Pikkoro who, accompanied by Tako, trudges on humpbacked through the heat. Even with Tako carrying the heaviest of her textbooks, she still feels as if she's bent double. The gradient of the slope to school seems more aggressive than yesterday.

A discerning viewer could perhaps believe that Pikkoro is accustomed to sadness, a kind of non-specific melancholy that infuses her eyes and slides down to her bones, pooling in the young creases of her skin. Sadness that not even her bright hair can obscure; so pedestrian that it could just be neutrality or fatigue.

Pikkoro arrives at school, reddened by thirst. She stops at the water fountain, then shows Tako to her cubbyhole. When all her heavy things are stored, Tako says goodbye.

—Take care today, Pikkoro-chan. I'll see you after school.

Tako is wearing a mint-striped ice cream parlor hat. Pikkoro watches him slide-walk through the corridor, against the flow of students, and it seems that her day might become a little duller now. But she looks back into her cubbyhole, revived by the brown paper parcel, which turns see-through for a moment to reveal the red costume inside. A piccolo trills.

Pikkoro's teacher is a drowsy but kindly man, young but worn, talking the class through a long mathematical equation from last night's homework. Pikkoro stares at it, compares it to her paper, and marks her answer incorrect. The teacher puts down his chalk and Pikkoro's gaze now expands to take in her entire paper, the red strokes written over last night's gray pencil, like a village ambushed by mercenaries.

—Those participating in this semester's play may attend rehearsal now. The rest of you have a reading period.

The teacher has scarcely finished his sentence when a third of the students scrape out of their seats and race to their cubbyholes. Over the morning the children's costumes have accumulated here—cardboard snouts, triangular ears stapled to headbands, mosquito-net wings. Pikkoro unwraps her brown parcel and wriggles into her octopus poncho: though it is woollen, the weave is loose enough to keep her from becoming too warm. Pikkoro runs out of the classroom with the other costumed students, her extra limbs bouncing, down the stairs and across the corridor to the auditorium.

On the stage, a cluster of senior students are riffling scripts and reciting lines, while others are assembling a giant backdrop made from flattened cardboard boxes.

—Ah, the extras from Class 3B are here! Eh? Those costumes are pretty neat! Come on, Kyo-senpai will show you where to stand.

—Everyone get ready for Act II, Scene 4!

The senior boy called Kyo leads Pikkoro and her classmates up the stairs to the wings of the stage.

—Remember to remain quiet while the lights are off. The actors will have a few lines. Then when your lights come on, jump up and make your best animal sounds! Be as loud as you want! You can move across the stage but don't get in the way of the actors. Okay?

Away from the tedium of silent reading, the students from Class 3B are thrilled into obedience.

—Places, everyone! Alright, from the top!

The lights dim abruptly. A boy and a girl hobble in from stage left, clutching each other.

—*Where are we, Cumbersnatch?*

—*I don't know, Honey, but something fishy is going on here.*

—*Where has the doctor gone? Where are all the other passengers?*

—*I'm telling you, when we get back to Hawaii...*

—*Eep! Did you hear that?*

—*Hear what?*

The lights boom on, and the animal students break out across the stage, screeching and hooting and snarling, beating their arms, stomping their feet, charging towards the protagonists.

—*Eeeargh! Savage beasts!*

—*Cumbersnatch, quick! We have to do something!*

Pikkoro isn't sure what sound octopuses are meant to make in the wild, so she spins around the stage, her extra arms flailing, making a kind of bubbling, warbling noise. There is no scalar consistency across the animals the children have chosen, so a duck cavorts alongside a cardboard-finned shark, a rabbit lunges after a rhinoceros, and Honey and Cumbersnatch cower with heartfelt conviction.

The door to the auditorium snaps open. The drama teacher walks in, flanked by two men in brown suits, and the students quickly contain themselves. Pikkoro's mouth twitches into an O when she notices the HarvestTime™ loveheart tree stitched onto the smart leather briefcases of the brown-suited men.

Kyo steps in front of the group and bows slightly.

—Excuse us, sensei. We began rehearsal while you were in your meeting. Since the extras from Class 3B are here, we are practising Act II, Scene 4.

The drama teacher dabs at his mouth with a white handkerchief. He glances at the brown-suited men. They both nod.

—Students, I am pleased to make an announcement. It has come to my attention that our play is terrible. That is why we will be rewriting it.

The senior students gasp. The drama teacher casts a critical eye over the ensemble. He gestures with a stern hand at the children in their homemade animal costumes.

—We cannot use any of these. These costumes are no good. No, the extras from Class 3B will be supplied with new costumes. They will be dressed as fruit—as pineapples and grapes and watermelons and figs. Then the play will be excellent. I am confident of this new direction.

Pikkoro and the other children look shell-shocked. The senior students are so speechless that they must collaborate on their response.

—Sensei... you want Honey and Cumbersnatch...

—to stumble upon...

—an island of giant fruit?

A girl in a penguin jumpsuit begins to cry.

Pikkoro and Tako walk home from school. The brown paper package, laid across Pikkoro's arms like a dead pet, is lumpy and folded wrong. Pikkoro and Tako stop at the pedestrian crossing.

—Must I make you a new costume?

—No. Sensei said they'd give us new ones.

The green man appears, and they cross the road. They round a familiar corner, but as Pikkoro looks right and left, she does not see the HarvestTime™ truck from yesterday.

In the apartment, Pikkoro watches her ramen grow fat in the steaming soup. Tako unwraps the paper parcel, folds the octopus poncho neatly, rewraps it, and walks to Pikkoro's bedroom. He slides open the wardrobe. Places the parcel on the top shelf.

Was it only yesterday that Pikkoro saw the truck on the way home from school, the mango on the road? Has her life always been this charged with moments of significance, relentless as an assembly line? Pivotal moments advancing from a conveyor belt, delivered with suspicious regularity—some dire newspaper from the cosmos headlining the same cryptic warnings in large black typeface? Pikkoro can't quite discern the lettering, much less read between the lines—can only understand that there is some threat hovering, spreading a shadow over her tiny life, as she lets herself sink like a water-logged noodle to the murky bottom.

—*Where are we, Cumbersnatch?*
   —*I don't know, Honey, but something fishy is going on here.*
   —*Where has the doctor gone? Where are all the other passengers?*
   —*I'm telling you, when we get back to Hawaii...*
   —*Eep! Did you hear that?*
   —*Hear what?*

The stage explodes with light and a boy dressed as a raspberry overbalances and—*whump!* The other fruits totter uncertainly across the stage. The effort of negotiating the costumes' awkward angles neuters the children's ferocity, and the actors stutter through their lines, surrounded by the thump of falling fruit students—

   —*Oh look, Cumbersnatch! There's every kind of fruit here!*
   —*We're saved!*

—Cut! Cut! Hang on a second, wasn't there a mango before?

The piccolo—*trill!* A part of the stage becomes translucent—and there's Pikkoro, curled up in a mango suit. She sighs, and rolls onto her rotund stomach. The fruit costumes even come with enlarged oval *HarvestTime*™ stickers. Pikkoro scratches at the edges of hers, but it's stitched into the fabric.

That senior boy Kyo's voice is strained.

—Sensei... are you sure about this plot direction?

For the thousandth time Pikkoro is poring over her little collection of facts—such as the truck that swerved around the corner near her home, the mango gleaming on the asphalt, the loveheart tree, those two silent men with their briefcases... and that infuriating slogan, *It's HarvestTime*™. And for the thousandth time, Pikkoro thinks: Honey, something fishy is going on here.

—Once again! From the top!

Pikkoro scratches at the fake *It's HarvestTime*™ sticker on her side and *puck!* One of the stitches snaps. She wriggles her finger under the hole and keeps on ripping—*puck-puck-puck* like subatomic fireworks—until the fake sticker peels off. It curls away like the lid of a sardine tin.

There, exposed to the grimy light of her hidey-hole, is a tiny black mystery nestled in the fabric, shaped like a jelly-bean. Pikkoro struggles to sit up, craning her neck. Yes, there it is—tight as a parasite, inseparable from the costume. It will not be prised away, not like the fake sticker.

Pikkoro decides that now's the time for action. She wriggles like a caterpillar shedding old skin, kicks free of her costume, and crawls away.

Later, at home, Tako and Pikkoro investigate the Harvest-Time™ mango on the kitchen counter—large, innocuous, so deeply yellow that its fragrance is very nearly visible. Pikkoro itches off the *It's HarvestTime*™ sticker. Denied sunlight, this part of the mango's skin retains an oval lighter than the rest. Tako takes their sharpest knife to pare back the skin, opening a window to the mango's flesh. It's difficult to see but Pikkoro knows it's there—she slides a square magnifying glass over the wound—a black spot, so small as to be mistaken for a fragment of seed. A flaw in the mango's perfect design.

—Tako-sama.

—Yes?

—Was it bad of me to sneak away from the play like that?

Tako doesn't reply right away. He floats to the sink and rinses the knife.

—You felt unsafe somehow, following the other children.

—I don't like what's happened to the drama teacher. It's like he's been brainwashed.

—Did the men try to brainwash anyone else?

—No. Well, I'm not sure.

Pikkoro sees the drama teacher again, dabbing his mouth with a white handkerchief.

—The fruit is poisoned.

—Poisoned?

—Or bugged.

—Bugged?

—Well, something isn't right about it.

—Something isn't right about the convenience of your discoveries.

—Hmm?

—You found a mango on the road, and you were cast as the mango in the play. Isn't that too much of a coincidence?

Pikkoro slumps down into the kitchen counter, pushes her face in her arms.

—I don't know about that.

Tako extends a brown tentacle over Pikkoro's shoulder and picks up the mango. He brings it closer to his small eyes, inspecting it like a jeweler.

—Tako-sama.

She reaches out, takes one of Tako's spare arms in her hand.

—You have to help me.

The next day, Pikkoro sets off to school alone. She has packed light. All this business with HarvestTime™ has meant that she has not completed one stroke of her homework, but she is ready to accept the penalty. She takes a moment to gaze at the slope leading to her school. Her eyebrows tip towards her nose in determination. She struggles up the hill.

She endures the roulette of the morning period, in which her teacher calls on a random student for the answer to each question of their night's homework. One by one all the students around her are called upon, but somehow not her. It's not even lunchtime and the day is already ringing with portent for young Pikkoro.

At eleven o'clock, after recess, the teacher says:

—Those participating in this semester's play may attend rehearsal now. The rest of you have a reading period.

Pikkoro remains in her seat a little longer than the other students. She has come too far to falter now, but there's no hint of fear in her eyes. She pushes back her seat.

In the auditorium, the older students help the younger ones put on their fruit costumes over their school uniforms. The drama teacher and the HarvestTime™ men oversee the preparations with grim faces.

—The mango girl.

—What about her?

—She isn't here.

The drama teacher shrugs.

—They are third grade students. I am not responsible for their whereabouts.

The drama teacher is paring the skin from an orange with a small knife. The HarvestTime™ men watch him. Those thick curls falling. One of the men turns to the other:

—The girl will come.

Kyo stoops on one knee and picks up the unclaimed mango costume. The sticker must have been resewn overnight, for the costume is bright and unbroken. Kyo holds the costume as his eyes trawl the room in the manner of a cop late to the crime scene, clutching a thief's calling card. The boy dressed as the raspberry practices walking. He takes bow-legged sumo steps.

One of the senior girls approaches the drama teacher.

—Sensei... would you like us to begin rehearsal now?

The drama teacher peels the final strip of skin from his orange.

—Please hold on for one minute. Not everyone is here.

One of the HarvestTime™ men flicks back his suit sleeve and consults his watch.

—Where is the mango girl?

Kyo frowns at the HarvestTime™ men and back at the mango costume. The drama teacher licks juice from his knuckles. He lifts the orange to his mouth. The raspberry boy has found a walking rhythm that his legs can tolerate—*ichi, ni, ichi, ni*, he chants—but then as he wobbles, throws out his arms for balance, he catches something in his unsteady gaze. He points:

—Octopus!

SHHIIIING! Pikkoro stands at the auditorium's back entrance, hands on her hips. The octopus poncho seems to flare in the borrowed light, and she raises a hand:

—Sensei! Don't eat the fruit!

The drama teacher looks up. A bead of juice slides over his fist. All of a sudden Pikkoro's right there next to him; she snatches the orange out of his hand. The students gasp. Pikkoro lifts the orange high and flings it hard onto the auditorium floor. Her foot comes down a second later.

SPLAT!

Pikkoro lifts her foot. The orange is a wet, juicy mess. The acid sizzles.

Everyone is silent. A girl in a banana suit begins to cry. The HarvestTime™ men fiddle with their neckties, push their glasses more firmly on their noses. The drama teacher clenches his teeth. He is shaking a little, trying to form syllables: *k. . .k. . .k. . .*

—What is the meaning of this?!

Pikkoro rests her foot back on the ground. It is unclear who precisely the drama teacher is addressing—Pikkoro, with her loose posture, seemingly satisfied that some great threat has been squashed into the auditorium floor, or the HarvestTime™ men, who are as rigid and inexpressive as the students' cardboard stage scenery.

There's a sound coming from outside—like bells, far off, growing louder and closer. The adults and senior students shift nervously, but the children, swiftly availing their memories of the current peculiar situation, light up. Wild understanding dawns in their eyes. The bells reach peak volume, echoing closer and closer, and then, visible through the window, Tako's ice cream truck pulls up at the auditorium's outdoor entrance. The children lose it—they gallop to the doors, cheering, straining their arms through their fruit costumes as Tako announces through the loudspeaker of the ice cream truck:

—Hello! Hello! Students of East Elementary School! Principal Matsumoto rewards you for your hard work today!

One of the children manages to wrestle open the doors and they all pour out, swarming Tako's ice cream truck.

—A free ice cream for each student! A gift from Principal Matsumoto for your hard work today!

The senior students hardly know what to do, but the children aren't questioning this ridiculous twist, grabbing ice cream cones with eager hands. One of the senior girls exits the auditorium to find another teacher. Meanwhile, understanding is dawning for the drama teacher too, as he gazes tight-lipped at the pandemonium, at the squashed orange. At the HarvestTime™ men clutching their briefcases.

—W-What's happening here? What happened to my students' play? Why are all the children dressed as fruit?

And finally, darkly:

—Who authorized you to come to this school?

The HarvestTime™ men do not reply. One of them readjusts his necktie. They turn to Pikkoro, who is so small in this chaos, peeking out from her clever coral-red octopus hood. One of the men twitches his lip—in disgust perhaps, or with smug inside knowledge. He steadies his glasses with two firm fingers. And then, the HarvestTime™ man intones:

—Sugimura Pikkoro.

For the first time, fear colors Pikkoro's face—gentle as the broad, omniscient stroke of a paintbrush, darkening at the edges, expanding like water. Pikkoro asks:

—How did you know my name?

Tako senses trouble and climbs out of the ice cream truck, while the drama teacher stands up. The teacher is smaller and older than the HarvestTime™ men but he looks incensed enough to take them both on. The senior students are still frozen in wide-eyed trauma. Everywhere, children are licking ice cream.

THWACK!

One of the HarvestTime™ men swings his briefcase into the drama teacher's stomach. Pikkoro cries out. The drama teacher stumbles. The HarvestTime™ men bolt for the exit. Their sensible shoes skid through orange pulp. They knock aside stray kids like a couple of harried fathers struggling to get out the door for work, dodge Tako and scramble into the ice cream truck. They even snap on their seatbelts. The engine stutters into life and the truck speeds off, kids sprawling in its wake—and a bewildered Tako, his mint-striped ice cream parlor hat askew.

Pikkoro screams:

—TAKO!

Transformation! Tako takes to the air with a powerful *whoosh!*, arms thrashing, sinuously electric. They lock into place—two for the handle bars, two for each wheel—as his suckers shine like polished military brass, his eyes protract into headlights, and the soundtrack rises sharply, crackling with guitars and snares and fluttering woodwinds as Pikkoro jumps onto the seat formed by Tako's webbing, grabs the handle bars, revs hard and speeds the hell out of the auditorium.

The ice cream truck bumbles down the hill and Pikkoro and Tako hurtle after it; the limp arms of Pikkoro's poncho fly backwards like kite tails. It's a chase scene that has everything that can be crammed into a chase scene—tight corners, screeching brakes, near misses, ruffled civilians, blasted horns, dogs springing free of their leashes and barking ecstatically into the street. The vehicles successfully clear, in white-knuckle sequence, a pedestrian crossing, two red lights, a speeding train, a clamoring boom gate, and, for the climax, a rising toll bridge. The ice cream truck makes the leap—the giant novelty cone cracks away from the roof and plummets into the river. *SPLASH!* Trumpets groan. The drums fumble while the truck crunches onto the road and skids back into action. Tako leaps after the truck, and for a moment, Pikkoro, hanging only by the handle bars, feels her poncho parachuting open, the arms streamlined perfectly for flight. Red-cheeked, lightning-eyed, so far away from school, home, the ground—Pikkoro has never been so precariously alive.

They chase the truck through the countryside until they arrive at the HarvestTime™ headquarters, monolithic as the orbiting fruit in their TV commercials. A kind of dystopian silo. The ice cream truck zips through an entrance which appears like a glitch in the building's armored exterior. Pikkoro and Tako plunge into the darkness after it. The ice cream truck brakes, squeals in a circle; Tako whiplashes out of his motorcycle form and Pikkoro jumps off. She lands on her feet.

The two HarvestTime™ men slither out of the truck and slam the doors. It is so dark in here: the light at Pikkoro's back fails to clarify the dimensions of the room. A fluorescent lamp snaps on overhead; then another, and another, springing like hunting snares. Exposing in their painful light: smooth sloping walls. Inert conveyor belts. Pronged beams. Vertical labyrinths of ladders.

Pikkoro steps backwards into Tako's ready arms.

A regal woman with silver hair is poised on a gangplank that overlooks the room. Her fringe obscures her eyes. Her voice is soft but paradoxically resonant.

—Sugimura Pikkoro. What a surprise to see you.

Pikkoro withholds a gasp. Her eyes are shining, lacquered with tears, but it is critical that she does not cry. Tako is perfectly still. The two HarvestTime™ men are so unnoticeable that they may as well disappear between frames.

The silver-haired lady spreads her hand.

—Or maybe it is not such a surprise. You are, after all, highly talented.

Pikkoro allows herself only a few seconds to shiver.

—What do you mean?

The lady's lips curl into a smile.

—You are special, Sugimura Pikkoro. The other children are not like you. They will never be like you. Not one of them would pick the mango from the road, would question the play, would peel back the sticker. Even for a puzzle of such low difficulty, of such relative transparency to the outside observer—the other children would struggle to notice even half of what you perceived instantly.

Pikkoro tightens her face. She tries to keep it in, but a tear finally escapes her eye. She bunches her fists.

—No! No, I don't understand! Why did they come to my school? Why did they change the play? Why did they make us wear those costumes?

For a moment the lady stops smiling, and Pikkoro shrinks. She lowers her eyes. The same fallen face that Pikkoro holds as she marks her mathematics homework with a red cross. That old, large sadness.

The lady, as if with some renewed awareness of Pikkoro— so small, earnest, her octopus poncho hanging so dearly to her little shoulders—offers a different sort of smile.

—Sweet child.

And then:

—You will grow old so beautifully.

Tako shifts his weight. He remains silent, as if speaking would be a trespass. Pikkoro, with her clenched fists, tremoring with indignity and anger and foreboding which exceeds anything she has felt before, must proceed alone.

—Explain it to me!

—Explain what to you, Sugimura Pikkoro?

—Just... explain everything! I don't get it. What's the point of all this? I... I don't even know what questions to ask! I need you to explain what's going on! And why. Why does it have to *be*?

The lady laughs. A feathery sound, motherly and infinitely patient.

—How apt, Sugimura Pikkoro. You astutely describe the central problem of existence. What is going on? Why does it have to be? What questions am I supposed to ask? What am I trying to understand? What does it even mean, to understand? Explain everything. Explain, explain.

Pikkoro becomes aware now of the giant crates that surround them, piled high with silent fruit. Apples. Mangoes.

Peaches. Each marked with the HarvestTime™ sticker, like white glossy eyes. The silver-haired lady continues:

—I think you will find, dear Pikkoro, that much of adulthood is dedicated to erasing the *why* of everything. It is the act—a game, we should say—of adhering to the rules without actually knowing them. Any question that the uninitiated might ask is, inevitably, the wrong question.

The silver-haired lady holds out her hand and unfurls it softly. A dull plum sits on her palm, one which also bears the HarvestTime™ sticker.

—Isn't it strange, Sugimura Pikkoro? The complexity of these imaginary rules? Even this fruit, which pre-exists humanity, is the follower of rules. Its ancestors have been bred selectively, the pollen scraped from their bodies, the natural logic of their seed corrupted. This fruit does not know that its special genetic code is the intellectual property of this company. A receptacle for crucial data. It does not know that we have intervened. It simply adheres to the rules. As we all must.

The hand that holds the plum remains there, as if the lady is a statue at a shrine. The sticker gleams. Pikkoro seems to swell with something unspeakable; she can hardly breathe, can hardly stop her eyes from trembling with tears. But she must be brave. She *must*. She must take a new breath. She must ask the next question.

—What has all of this got to do with me?

The silver-haired lady lifts her lips.

A smile like a trapdoor.

—It's harvest time.

And then Pikkoro is falling, a clean, slow movement— propelled by a separate momentum, unforgiving as gravity. Her eyelids fold, and the limbs of her poncho, so utterly unrelated to her whole, descend separately, splaying like outstretched fingers, scattering from her perfect fall.

Tako catches her before she can hit the ground. He en-
folds Pikkoro in his many arms. And then, in swift easy seconds, Tako turns into a helicopter, bursts out of the Harvest-
Time™ headquarters, away from the invisible gaze of the
silver-haired lady—flies Pikkoro over the countryside and
across the river, four blades perforating the baffled sky. Humming like a heartbeat.

What does Pikkoro see during her moment of unconscious-
ness? Does she tumble like Alice through red crosses, eraser shavings, corrective ink? Does her unfinished homework
loom around her, large as blimps? Sly pterodactyls of long
division? Gap-toothed comprehension tests? Perhaps she
sees newspaper headlines, or white oval stickers, a tree of
hearts. Perhaps fruit orbits her body, rotating on their secret
axes, their unfathomable formulae. Perhaps she sees, again,
the silver-haired lady's smile, disembodied, a terrifying omniscience.

Perhaps she understands that this is merely the first episode of many to come. That she has embarked on a steep
trajectory of self-discovery, and her progress is witnessed by
more worlds than one.

Or perhaps, with rare benevolence, the universe grants
young Pikkoro a moment of respite, sparing her the burden
of thought—and she sees nothing at all.

And so, after receiving whatever insights darkness might
offer, Pikkoro reawakens at night, in her home, in her soft and
colorless bedroom. Tako is sitting next to her bed, reading
Seeds of Time beneath a dim lamp. Pikkoro's octopus poncho
hangs over the back of her chair like a sleeping child slung
over her father's shoulder.

Pikkoro sighs—a sigh of safety—and Tako lifts his eyes
from his novel. When their eyes meet, they feel keenly the

insufficiency of words, so they resist the blunt intrusion of language. Pikkoro rolls over, holds Tako's closest arm, and, together, they fall asleep.

When the morning comes, Pikkoro is dressed for school. Her bag is gridlocked with books, and there are clean white socks on her feet. Tako and Pikkoro stand at the entrance to their home, contemplating a blue sky that holds no clues.

—Are you sure you want to go to school today?

—Yes. I need to see if things are back to normal.

Pikkoro's eyes are cleaner and sharper than the sky. She says:

—I'm not scared.

Tako gazes out over the town, at the trim rows of apartments and traffic lights and dotted white lines. In the far distance is the bridge they flew over yesterday—and further out, invisible, the HarvestTime™ headquarters, the silver-haired lady.

Pikkoro says:

—I'm so sorry about your ice cream truck.

—It doesn't matter. The important thing is that you are safe, Pikkoro-chan.

—What are you going to do now?

—I'm sure I will find something else to do. It doesn't worry me at all.

Pikkoro looks up at Tako. She encircles him, the best she can, with her small arms. Tako leans close to her.

—Take care, Pikkoro.

With that, Pikkoro sets off to school. She hoists her schoolbag high onto her back and walks down the gray staircase, slips through the apartment gate, patters across the footpath. She waits for the green man and crosses the road under his bright approval. She stops at the bottom of the hill, clutching the straps of her bag. She looks up at her school. A flock of birds trawls the sky like a fishing net.

At home, Tako carries a cup of tea from the kitchen and takes his seat at the table. With his peaceful arms, moving in elegant concurrence, Tako rests his cup on the placemat, stirs the water with a spoon, and leafs through the employment section of the newspaper. His sapient eyes study the entries. Outside, early-morning sounds float on the air—drowsy, inseparable, overlapping like tongue-twisters. Bicyclist. Cicada. Bicyclist. Cicada.

T

There is Ulysses, heavy across his knees—the weight of a cat, somehow so paralysing. Tim lies in bed a half-hour more than he intended, legs baking, watching a slit of sky turn bluer. He can hear the main road lacquered in traffic; he can perceive himself waking, a moment he has narrated ten times or more—the loneliest moment of the morning, non-unconsciousness, crusty and overripe. He moves his legs out from under Ulysses, and Ulysses, pretending he chose this moment to rouse himself, arches his spine and vanishes over the edge.

The day of the month floats to the top of Tim's mind. He wanders to the bathroom, takes a syringe from the cupboard, and slides the needle into his skin.

Tim feeds Ulysses a bowl of hard kibble, die-cut into shapes like fish and bones. Tim always wonders: for whose benefit are these shapes cut? Can a housecat appreciate what a representation of a fish looks like, or a bone? Tim pours himself a bowl of unbranded cereal and tries not to think of them both, this cereal and the cat food, as being produced by the same process of extrusion, maybe even on the same factory floor, injected with steam, cooked by friction, sprayed with fat.

Every now and again, both in the cat food and in Tim's cereal, there will be a piece that evaded some part of the process, and will seem to have melted together with another piece. Tim will always feel a peculiar sympathy for them, these odd ones.

Today is the day of the stranger, the hard knock at ten o'clock. Tim wipes his mouth on his sleeve, crosses from the kitchen to the front hallway, and opens the door. The stranger is perhaps a shade older than him, a little more clenched, holding a cat in one arm.

'Do you have a cat?'

Tim blinks. 'Yeah, I do.' He looks over his shoulder at Ulysses in post-breakfast lickdown. 'He's over there.'

The stranger looks past Tim. 'No, no. That's not your cat. *This* is your cat.'

It is only when the stranger foists the cat into his arms that Tim realizes the cat is a dead ringer for Ulysses—short black fur, lean muscle, quick green eyes. The cat is even wearing a red leather collar that Ulysses used to wear, but Tim assumed he had recently lost. In his surprise Tim takes a step back, unintentionally permitting the stranger to step inside the house. '*That's* my cat,' the stranger says, pointing at Ulysses.

'Whoa. Wait.' Tim fumbles with the cat in his arms.

The stranger scoops up Ulysses with familiar confidence. 'I live in the next street. My mother's been house-sitting while I've been abroad. She didn't notice that the cat wasn't mine.'

'But this guy's been living with me for...' Tim stops. When did the collar go missing?

'It's Ulysses, right? Your cat's name is Ulysses. It's on the collar, right there.'

Tim looks down at the cat in his arms. He overturns the label on the collar. ULYSSES / 29 SIGMUND ST.

'Oh,' says Tim. The cat formerly known as Ulysses, curled against the stranger's chest, looks at Tim balefully. The cat labelled Ulysses yawns. 'Gee. I'm terribly sorry. I had no idea. They look identical to me.'

The stranger shrugs. There's something unforgiving in his face, that clenchedness. 'Cats like to wander. I would've called ahead but—'

'I don't have a phone. Yes. I'm sorry.'

'You don't have a phone.' The stranger gives Tim a searching look. There's an accusatory edge to his statement that Tim could just be imagining.

'When Ulysses showed up without his collar I just assumed he lost it. I mean...' Tim falters. It hardly seems worth correcting himself. 'Uh. It won't happen again.'

The stranger gives Tim one last searching look. 'Well.'

Ulysses begins to struggle. Tim gathers him close to his chest and uses his elbow to get the door. 'Thanks for returning my cat.'

When the door is closed, Ulysses jumps down, trots to his food bowl and begins crunching kibble. Tim watches. A jet engine builds behind his ears.

The manuscript he's been working on is full of enigmatic one-sentence paragraphs.

In our haste we left two stones unturned.

There were too many things living in the water.

We didn't have a plan.

When Tim can't tell which one of two readings sounds the best, he Alt-Tabs to the pictures supplied by the artist and scrutinizes them for five minutes. He hasn't seen anything quite like them before: such tall, shrivelled figures, drawn with claustrophobia-inducing detail, melded with teapots, tables, trees, fastened onto each other. They must move leglessly, or perhaps they are rooted to the landscape. Tim switches windows.

Little did he know that a slow, interior catastrophe was underway.
A collision of sorts.
A miscalculation of cells and their trajectories.

He stops the recording. Swivels out of his office, to the kitchen, and depresses the kettle switch. To get there he must first pass Ulysses, occupying the living room sofa, eyes convex with half-sleep. Tim hasn't said one word to Ulysses since the stranger left. Not one word. He's not sure where to begin, really. He hates to think of all the private, inane things he's been saying to that other cat.

'Bet you had fun, didn't you,' Tim says as the kettle boils and clicks itself off. 'Lording it up in some old lady's company.'

Ulysses's eyes shrink. The cups of his ears rotate away from Tim's voice. Tim retrieves a chamomile teabag from a crumpled box. Shields the hot mug back to his office.

He returns to those one-sentence paragraphs.

It was not our intention to lead the others astray.
We used to be right for each other.
Our blood carried messages that our organs misunderstood.

By the time the sky turns purple Tim has collated all his recordings into a ZIP folder, which duplicates itself in some faraway server, along with his message:

Hi Ursula,

Please find attached the audio files for your project. Let me know if there are any problems.

Best of luck,
Tim Spiegel

It might be said that a recording is a documentation of sound events.

A sound event can be a cat's meow, a dropped pencil, a passing jet engine, a warning bell.

Like stories, every sound has a beginning, a middle, and an end. Some people refer to these as the attack, the sustain, and the decay. To plot a sound event on a graph would therefore produce the shape of an envelope—the attack being the sound's journey to peak volume; sustain, the peak's constancy; decay, its recession.

The sound of boiling water might have a slow attack, a long sustain, a gradual decay.

A cymbal might have a fast attack, a short sustain, a long decay.

One bounce of a basketball might have a fast attack, a quick sustain, the scantest decay.

It is the task of some recordists to capture all these minute violences that comprise a soundscape, while for others, it is the erasure.

Recorded speech is made perfect by the removal of hesitations, blunders, breath intakes—noises that betray the body.

One way to look at it is that recordings of speech, edited in this manner, gesture to a kind of dead space; a neutral, unechoing context, a voice without a human.

Another way to look at it is that sound must always gesture to space, even if that space is a hypothetical envelope plotted on horizontal and vertical axes.

Tim used to have a theory that cats can slip in and out of a parallel dimension, a realm which permits them to move invisibly, to reappear without sound. To swap places, even. Certainly, looking into Ulysses's eyes, those blurry hexagons, Tim knows that Ulysses has seen more than he has seen, that Ulysses is acquainted with a separate, softer world.

In the morning, Tim receives an email from the artist.

Hello Tim! Thanks for these! They sound great. I knew you'd be perfect at it. I'll send you details re: the opening night soon! Take care, U

They have never met in person. Her emails are cheerfully incongruous with her artwork. It makes it impossible for Tim to construct any mental picture of Ursula at all.

Today Tim has to update some tech support options for an old employer, a job which he thinks will take less than half the day. He knows he has to start sniffing out new work soon. For a while he's had the luxury of being picky, taking small projects that he can record at home, but perhaps it's time to put himself out there again.

Thank you for calling technical support for your Seed device. Please listen carefully, as our menu options have recently changed.

Please hold. An operator will be with you shortly. Please note that, for training purposes, your call may be recorded.

To hear these options again, press five.

It had occurred to Tim just two weeks ago, when he was riding a late train home from the city, why his Seed recordings never sounded quite right to him. It was one of the newest trains, with the names of each passing station spelled out as red dots on long, visor-like black screens. *Doors closing*, said a male voice, startling him—and he realized, everywhere, in elevators and telephonic menus and train stations, he was accustomed to hearing an automated female voice. As if city planners built around themselves an elaborate uterus of thermoplastic and cables and signals, presided over by an unseen mother, her permeating voice, maternally omniscient. He started to feel strange about his work then, like he was impersonating the voice of the father, or the Devil. Some *in vitro* ventriloquism act.

Tim hooks his headphones around his neck and pinches his eyelids. Time for a cup of tea.

Ulysses is sitting on the living room windowsill, contemplating the outdoors. Tim strokes Ulysses's spine with a cupped hand, which Ulysses does not acknowledge. Ulysses, Tim has discovered, is impossible to startle. Even on the day that Ulysses was first brought home in a cardboard fruit carton—a gift from a well-meaning neighbor, who knew Tim was recovering from surgery—the cat's emotional tenor did not rise above anything more than mild interest. Tim walks to the kitchen and starts unravelling a chamomile teabag.

For some reason, it's only from this distance that Tim notices the object of Ulysses's gaze.

Standing in Tim's overgrown garden is the stranger's cat, the Ulysses doppelganger.

The two cats stare at each other, chiselled, impassive as chess pieces. Tim crosses into the living room to stand by Ulysses again, as if seeing things from Ulysses's angle would make the situation legible, but the cats simply look on, neither of them bristling. Tim lifts a hand to Ulysses's neck, to feel his leather collar, to overturn the nametag once more. ULYSSES / 29 SIGMUND ST.

Tim wonders if he ought to catch the cat and bring it back to the owner, but he realizes that the owner never gave his address. And Tim doesn't know how he could possibly catch a cat that has already outsmarted him for weeks. It doesn't matter though, because, when the breeze picks up, the doppelganger rises on his haunches and departs.

No other fairytale characters have been so fooled and foiled by a voice as Little Red Riding Hood and her grandmother. This story strikes even children as improbable. The wolf, at the grandmother's door, pitches his voice high: 'Oh Grandmother! It is me, Little Red Riding Hood!' And the grand-mother, her borders so penetrable, invites the wolf inside, and in turn finds herself inside the wolf. Little Red Riding Hood emerges from the woods some time later and enters her grandmother's house. This entails a different perform-ance from the wolf, and one that is received with a little less conviction. 'What big eyes you have,' Little Red Riding Hood will say. 'What big ears you have. What big teeth you have.' In some versions of the tale, Little Red Riding Hood wonders at, but does not enquire about, the difference in her grandmother's voice. Perhaps it is because Granny is sick, she reasons. In some older versions, in which the grand-mother is not swallowed whole, the wolf even feeds a part of the grandmother to Little Red Riding Hood. In the darkness of the cottage, the girl is none the wiser. The story is a warn-ing to little girls—don't talk to strangers, don't stray from the path—but it is also, in a way, a warning to us all. A story about the inescapability of our bodies, the inextricable rela-tionship between sound and space. Don't even try to escape. Your body will always find you out.

Two weeks later Tim is on the train again, heading in the op-posite direction to the peak-time commuters. The carriage is almost empty, even with the clusters of Friday night party-goers—men glistening with hair gel, women adjusting their strapless tops. Their chatter is excited enough to penetrate the techno gloom of his iPod music. The shuffle has decided to score this moment with 'Clubbed to Death', a song that in-stantly teleports Tim to 1999, to glowing green kana stream-ing like rain behind opaque sunglasses. And he remembers that déjà vu visited Neo in the form of a cat.

Tagging off out of the station, climbing the vertiginous escalator two steps at a time, jaywalking to the Horseshoe, plunging into the Cultural Centre, weaving around buskers. Down the lurid candy steps outside the State Library. The gallery is already humming like a beehive. Tim winds his earphones around his iPod and tucks it into his pocket. He enters a foyer clogged with friends and family of the exhibiting artists; everyone is holding plastic cups of wine or orange juice, glossy programs rolled up under their armpits. Sponsors' banners teeter on black tripods, wobbling every time someone brushes past. On the reception counter there's an abandoned program, fastened to the laminate with a dried circle of spilled wine—Tim peels it off as he edges by.

Stationed outside Ursula's installation is a table of freshly baked bread, cartoonishly loafy, the kind with bulbs of overflow at the top. *Visitors may feel free to eat the bread or scatter the crumbs around the site, like Hansel and Gretel leaving a trail of crumbs to find their way home,* advises the program—so Tim rips off a communion-sized piece and chews on it. The main delight of the installation, which has primly dressed and even elderly visitors getting down on their knees to inspect it, is a low tunnel constructed of mattresses, pillows, and stacks of chairs draped with blankets and quilts. Tim waits for a gap in the flow of visitors, tucks his program into his back pocket, and crawls through the entrance.

And what greets him is his own voice, emanating through the tunnel via secret speakers, hidden like cancerous pockets—

Little did he know that a slow, interior catastrophe was underway.

A collision of sorts.

A miscalculation of cells and their trajectories.

Tim crawls over the spongy terrain. It is humid and airless. The gallery lights outside the tunnel illuminate the weave of the blankets until they look membranous, heaving, organic.

'It's like a pillow fort,' Tim hears somebody giggle.

The tunnel delivers Tim to a wide room, ringing with his own voice—*Opportunities winked all around us like stars.*

A slide projector casts Ursula's drawings onto the wall in a square of yellow light. This one features a Roman general, his arms dissolving into root vegetables, his legs thin as stilts.

Click.

A trio of babies, sharing the same thick woody torso, playing a game of cards. *Our trades meant nothing; it all came from the same hand.*

Click.

A woman in a tall hat with a trumpet for lips. *We had to escape.*

Click.

A long-faced man with a merry-go-round for a ribcage. *We had to cut off the limbs that were holding us back.*

Click.

The other viewers, made so small by the scale of Ursula's projections, drift into Tim's blind spot and disappear. Even though it's his own voice, and even though he's seen all the images before, Tim is filled with a strangely delicious terror, standing here with his back to the sagging, breathing portal. Like he's a child, peeking through his fingers, at a movie he's too young to watch.

There's an email from Ursula in the morning:

Hi Tim! I saw your name in the guestbook from last night, but I didn't see _you_. Sorry I didn't say hello—I'm not quite sure what you look like! I hope you enjoyed the installation. I'm quite happy with how it turned out, and I hope you are too. Thank you once again for making such fabulous recordings at such short notice, and take care! U

Today, thanks to a special at the supermarket, Ulysses is eating canned food. He is happier than Tim has seen in days, his round head bowed over his bowl, eyes closed in ecstatic concentration. Tim crunches his cereal. He tries to compose a reply to Ursula in his head, but he feels peculiarly unready to communicate with her. As if he is one of her characters, without fingers to type with. Without the privacy of a singular body.

The residue of visiting Ursula's installation has yet to evaporate entirely, still palpable enough for Tim to look at Ulysses not as Ulysses but as a collection of black strokes and tessellated green hexagons, gathered together loosely and inadequately with collar and nametag.

As it happens, Tim—as Ursula wished—is taking care of himself. He has secured a job, the best kind, he thinks, the kind you can linger over without too much impatience from the client—a novel to be turned into an audiobook. The manuscript has just arrived in the mail today.

It begins, as many narratives do, with a moment of waking. Despite their repetitiousness, Tim never tires of narrating them; they always take him back to his favorite awakening, the one after the surgery that would shortly deliver Ulysses to his doorstep. Never had consciousness been such a relief. There was still all the post-surgical therapy, of course—the capsules, the injections. He could not work for almost a year as his voice stabilized so gradually, undergoing its own adolescence, slipping semitone by semitone into the voice Tim uses today. Ulysses would have listened to his voice's many fluctuations during post-surgical therapy, would have endured Tim testing out his new vocabulary. Cricoid, thyroid, epiglottic. Arytenoid, cuneiform, corniculate. The vocal folds, that other sonic envelope, thickening and lengthening in slow motion.

Perhaps Ursula's drawings have refreshed that just-woken feeling—the excitement of Tim's consciousness in Tim's body, edited by scalpel and stitch. Not one of Ursula's figures, for all their anatomical circumlocutions, looks unhappy.

In cinema, a little bit of sound can achieve the greater deception of continuity. Even if the sound is unexceptional—just the empty blare of traffic, for instance—a scene composed of multiple shots filmed over irregular days in different locations can pass as chronological, can create a coherent space. The sound and the scene need not even have the same duration—the sustain segment can be lengthened, looped, so that its decay coincides exactly with the scene's conclusion. A film is not completely unlike actual perception, anyway. A series of discontinuities assimilated into a provisional whole. Whatever can make sense. Close enough is good enough.

Sometimes an image can be reassigned a new sound. The trick is to forget the names of sounds. To realize that they are manipulable frequencies with no real special identification. A squeaking violin can be a bird. A waterfall can be an explosion. A boot heaved out of mud can be an organ pulled from a body.

Tim has one last encounter with the stranger—this time unaccompanied by cats—as he walks through the park on the way home from a doctor's appointment. The stranger is sitting on a bench smoking with a friend. 'Hey, you're that guy,' the stranger says. He blows smoke from his nostrils, tapping his friend on the shoulder and gesturing theatrically to Tim with his cigarette. 'That's the guy I was telling you about. The one who swapped cats with me for a couple of weeks.'

The friend snorts and takes a drag.

'I saw your cat in my garden,' Tim tells the stranger. 'About a fortnight ago. Just staring at my cat.'

The stranger smiles, to Tim's surprise. 'They must have some sort of secret. A telepathic understanding.'

A mobile phone rings brightly. The stranger's friend jumps up and walks away to take the call. He cups one hand over his ear when he says hello. The stranger watches him. 'Hey. The other day I realized I knew you from somewhere.'

'Where?'

The stranger balances his cigarette in his mouth and rummages in his back pocket. He holds up a Seed.fon. *'Thank you for calling Seed technical support,'* the stranger says.

'Please listen carefully,' Tim obliges, *'as our menu options have recently changed.'* The stranger chuckles. Tim says, 'You have a good memory for voices, then.'

'How do you stand it, man? Having to hear your own voice every time you call tech support.'

'Easy. I don't have a phone, remember?'

'Oh yeah. Right.' There's that searching look again. 'I would've thought they'd just *give* you one. Seeing as you're the voice of tech support and all.'

'I freelance. I do other stuff.'

The stranger pockets his phone. 'I'll have to keep an eye out for you. An ear.'

Tim smiles uncertainly. He's about to head off, but then he asks: 'What's your cat's name? And where do you live? In case I have to return him someday.'

The stranger crushes his cigarette. 'He's Max. Unoriginal, I know. We live on the street next to yours. Kent. Number 18.'

Tim nods. He thinks about asking the stranger's name, but it feels unnecessary. 'Max,' Tim echoes. 'I'll keep that in mind.'

Later, when Tim arrives home, Ulysses jumps down from the windowsill and paces in front of his food bowl. And how Ulysses can pace, can dramatize hunger—making every part of him small except for his eyes, tail raised in expectation. 'Hello, Ulysses,' Tim says. 'I saw our friend today.'

Tim breaks the perforated spout of a new box of cat kibble, and jiggles it over the bowl. The last morsel has not fallen when Ulysses rushes in, snapping a fish with his teeth. Tim strokes Ulysses's spine. A purr creaks through his body like an old wooden ship.

Good Birds
Don't Fly Away

Oh to be Peter Pushkin, the personification of woe—such a singularly joyless figure, so crushed with dismay—lunchbox lid in one hand, schoolbag drooping from the other, uncontained juice dribbling onto the pavement. Peter Pushkin, soggy with failure, just like his inedible sandwich. His leaking juice box is still slotted innocently in the lunchbox's grooves. Other things have been ruined too: his school diary, which he must ask his parents to sign each week; his library book, *Seeds of Time*; even the letters inserted into the tight plastic windows on his pencil case spell PETER. The only thing safe, it would seem, is his recess-time snack: an Uncle Toby's granola bar, preserved in its white wrapper, which Peter tries to wipe dry. It is just past eight o'clock and nobody is here except for the kids whose parents work at the school, or have jobs that begin early. Peter's own mother has driven off, probably on the freeway by now. The air is so crisp that it hurts. Peter rescues a scrapbook and an exercise book from his bag. The bottom of each book is damp, stained with watery orange.

Peter Pushkin—paralysed by indecision, soaked in betrayal—remains standing at the front of his school. Late for something.

A black car glides into the school driveway and slips into a parking space. Out steps a boy Peter hasn't seen before, and whose uniform is unmistakably new—his jumper lint-free, the color true. He glances first at Peter and then away to the school flagpole. The driver's door opens and the boy's mother steps out, smoothing her skirt, shutting the door. She, too, gazes at the school. 'It looks like we're just in here, Jem,' she says. She triggers the car's inaudible locking mechanism—the headlights flash succinctly—and strides towards administration. The boy follows. Even his schoolbag is new.

Peter waits until the boy and his mother have disappeared. A cat with a red collar flashes through the bushes. Juice creeps across the pavement, sliding into the gaps between bricks, as if this sleazy stickiness seeps from the earth itself. Peter jiggles the last drops of it from his bag, tucks his rescued books under his armpit, and trudges towards the gymnasium.

The rooms for private music lessons are nestled in the corners of buildings and repurposed storage cupboards, like cells for monks or bees. Peter takes his piano lessons in a room on the gymnasium's upper level, one of two jammed at the top of the stairs, each with what Peter believes to be an overabundance of windows—a square window for outsiders to look in, a window on the door, and a window overlooking the school's vast oval. It seems that even with the morning's disaster, Peter has arrived ahead of Miss Amar, for the lights in the room are off, the piano lid is closed, and the door is locked. Peter is Miss Amar's first student for the day, and she has been the second to arrive before, so this situation does not yet strike Peter as odd. Instead he takes up his position on the waiting chairs, places his books in his lap, and leaves his bag on the floor.

Later, in Handwringer Hamsden's office, his mother's face will wrinkle with exasperation or concern. 'Why did you just sit there, Peter? Why didn't you find someone to help you?'

Find who? Peter will want to ask, careful to angle his head so he won't have to smell the musty citrus odor that will persist throughout the day, recorded in the stain on his music scrapbook, the paper's dark lip. For the world is still a big place to Peter, like a sweater he will never grow into, and even if it did ever occur to him to *find someone* he would scarcely know what to say to that someone. If *someone else* really is to be found at this corner of the school fifty, forty, even thirty minutes before the bell is due to ring.

No—Peter sits there in front of the music room, listening to the slow crescendo of activity on the oval. He *would* imagine all the things that have made Miss Amar late if only he could imagine Miss Amar doing ordinary human things like sleeping through her alarm clock or missing the bus. But this is what Peter thinks about: whether he will have the discipline to ration his granola bar over recess and lunch; how he should dispose of his ruined sandwich without a teacher questioning him; and why it is that Miss Amar prompts him to select a sticker each week from her collection, and add to his own collection on his Megasaurus Scrapbook; and how was it, precisely, that stickers came to be used in this fashion, to sweeten children into obedience.

When footsteps and voices sound in the stairwell, Peter is still contemplating these questions. 'We have two practice rooms up here with pianos in them—both Yamahas,' a voice is saying. 'For school concerts we use the Kemble.'

Three heads emerge: Handwringer Hamsden, followed by the mother and son that Peter saw in the car park. 'There is one other piano teacher besides Mrs. Yorke—Miss Amar, who takes care of the beginning and intermediate students— and we also have Miss Jung, who accompanies the choirs and instrumental students as required.' They have reached the landing now, and Peter's lonely chair. The deputy principal's eyes gloss over Peter—stumbling a bit in his tour-guide speech, unsure whether to acknowledge Peter or continue. 'The, uh, rooms are soundproofed, so we can have two lessons going on at once. This is where you'll be, Jeremy, with Mrs. Yorke.'

Peter remains still, as if he is an exhibit in a museum. The mother follows the deputy principal's cue, and gazes through Peter. Only the boy looks directly at Peter. His eyes are a headache-inducing blue.

The mother says, 'It's a lovely little room. I'm sure Jeremy will enjoy it here.'

Handwringer Hamsden nods. His eyes skitter over Peter once more, then he stammers, 'Well... I'll show you to Jeremy's classroom now, and introduce you both to Mrs. Calbourne.'

They depart gratefully. Peter thumbs a sticker on his scrapbook cover. He curves his fingers pianist-style, werewolf-style. He is contemplating the angel fish—the sticker he selected from Miss Amar's collection two weeks ago—when Handwringer Hamsden comes back up the stairs, this time alone, and asks Peter what he is doing there.

A day later on the news, they will say that Miss Amar rarely spoke to her neighbors and did not have any close friends. No family except for one distant sister, who will eventually travel from Prague to pack up her house. Principal Alteruthemeyer will appear in a brief interview, describing Miss Amar as an intelligent and quiet woman who was well-loved by all her students. Anyone with information will be encouraged to call Crime Stoppers. Having no tearful relatives, and no one else besides the principal willing to appear on TV, the segment will end with a reporter standing outside the school, stating the last of the scant facts. Beyond the school gates, blurry girls and boys will sit on the grass and eat lunch, oblivious as gazelles.

We return again to Peter ten days after the disappearance of Miss Amar. It is a Thursday, one bright with hope for young Peter as he peels a banana in the courtyard, where some of the third grade boys play four-square with a balding tennis ball. Quentin Silvy is King and has held this position for nearly seven rounds; the others in line are starting to itch. Scattered around the four-square court are boys clutching half-eaten sandwiches in crumpled cling wrap, pacing, wiping their mouths with the backs of their hands, shouting at the game. Peter is the only one sitting down because he is the only one who takes his lunchbox out of his bag. This is something Peter is only noticing just now: the other boys do not take their lunchboxes out of their bags, but take their lunch out of their lunchboxes which they leave in their bags. Peter is too mortified to eat his banana.

'Hey. Are you Peter?'

And Peter is strangely relieved to see the new kid, Jeremy Lavignac, a somber green lunchbox tucked under his arm. That cut-glass gaze.

'Yeah.'

'I'm Jem.'

'Hi.'

'Kyle said you had an egg salad sandwich.'

Peter does have an egg salad sandwich. It is his least favorite sandwich filling, which is why he is eating the banana.

'...Yeah.'

Jem glances at Peter's lunchbox. 'I was wondering, if you haven't eaten it already, if you wanted to swap. I have ham.'

Peter looks at Jem. Is it credible that an eight-year-old boy wants to trade ham sandwiches for egg salad? Peter tries to rewrap his banana in its skin and pops the lid of his lunch-box. Jem verifies that the sandwiches are indeed egg salad before slipping his lunchbox out from under his arm and producing his own sandwiches, which are in a glossy, tightly sealed Glad bag.

An explosion of yells: Quentin has missed the ball. Grinning sheepishly, Quentin accepts his place as Dunce. Peter and Jem swap sandwiches. 'Thanks,' says Jem. He snaps the lid back on his lunchbox and sits down next to Peter. Peter breaks the seal of the Glad bag. Jem uses a different brand of bread from his own family, the kind with visible grains and seeds.

They watch the four-square, chewing their slightly different lunches. A teacher roams into view and disappears.

'You have piano lessons with Mrs. Yorke,' Peter finally says.

'Uh-huh.'

'What's she like?'

Jem studies his sandwich. 'I'm not really sure yet. I've only seen her once. I guess that's what it's like when you're switching teachers—it takes a while to figure out.'

'What grade are you up to?'

'Five.'

Peter nearly chokes. He realigns the bread. 'You must be really good.'

Jem says nothing. He takes another bite of the sandwich. 'You had that teacher who went missing.'

'Miss Amar.'

'Was she good?'

Peter pauses. He wonders if Jem means *good* as in musically talented, proficient; or if he means whether Miss Amar was good at teaching. 'She was really nice,' Peter decides. He feels a beat of pain after he says this. 'She never lied to me.'

Jem looks down and flicks a piece of egg from his trousers. 'I hope the police find her,' he says.

'Yeah. I hope she's alright.'

Peter is nearing the crust. His teeth strip the last of the white away. Jem asks, 'Do you have any brothers and sisters?'

'No. You?'

'No.'

Think back to when you were eight. Think back to lonely lunch hours and ill-fitting school uniforms and being stranded at school without a way home. Think of having to raise your hand to speak and to ask the teacher if you could go to the toilet. Think about the homework you carried on your back. Think of the zip breaking on your pencil case, of juice flooding your schoolbag. Think about every time you died—in class, in the courtyard, on the oval.

Think about those others who made it bearable. Try to remember how it was, exactly, that you met.

This bright afternoon, like so many others that do not burn with shame or fear, will vanish like Miss Amar.

It will be two months later that Peter's mother will call the school. The fee for piano lessons has been waived for the past bill, but she wants to know when Peter can start learning again. As if she believes that Peter is falling fatally behind schedule, his chance for greatness slipping away, and what is Alteruthemeyer going to do about it? Mrs. Pushkin is only able to advance her complaint as high as Handwringer Hamsden, who is in his handwringing element. 'I will liaise with Mrs. Yorke,' he says, *liaise*, as if it will require trench coats and secret handshakes, but Peter's mother is, for the moment, satisfied. She expects a resolution within the week.

By this time Jem and Peter are regular guests at each other's houses. Today they sit on the carpet of Jem's vast living room, their school shirts untucked, Wii controllers slack in their hands.

Jem asks, 'Why does everyone call him Handwringer Hamsden?'

'It's what all the parents call him. Even my mum and dad call him that sometimes. I'm not sure what it means exactly. I don't know if he knows that people call him that.'

'My mum hasn't met Mr. Alteruthemeyer.'

'No one has. Except for Channel Seven.'

Peter triggers a beanstalk and they climb into the clouds.

Jem's mother walks in, sorting through a pile of mail. 'Are you staying for dinner, Peter? We're having fettuccine, and you're very welcome to stay.'

'My mum is coming to pick me up at five. But thank you anyway, Mrs. Lavignac.' He always makes sure to say her name carefully. La, vin, yak.

'That's alright, dear.' Mrs. Lavignac looks up from a telephone bill and smiles. Exits just as Jem collects a 1UP. It's strange, but whenever Jem's mum smiles at Peter, whenever she's so nice, Peter just thinks of that first real encounter with her, waiting for Miss Amar. The way she stared through him.

'Jem.'

'Yeah?'

'What's Mrs. Yorke like?'

Jem wrinkles his nose. 'Um. I don't know really. Strict? But not.'

Peter thumbs the A-button and sprints from some flying hammers.

Jem adds, 'She's nice. You'll be alright, really. She just. Well. She just wants you to be the best.'

'I'm not very good.'

'You practice your scales, right? All the time? She would like that.'

'It's what I do most of the time though. I'm not very... good.'

'Scales are a start.' They run for the flag. Jem hits at 2000, Peter at 800. They head into the castle. 'You'll be fine, Peter. Honestly.'

Peter lets the controller slip into his lap. He takes a sip from a tumbler of water on a coaster.

'We can practice now, if you want.'

Peter and Jem hover over a new level. There's a whole world waiting. 'Are you sure?' Peter asks.

And here Peter must examine his tidy, exemplary friend. The school could not be prouder to have a student such as Jem Lavignac. They've already made him perform at both the primary school assembly and the high school assembly. Peter is sure that now they will wheel the Kemble out for any occasion, no matter how tenuous. The Anzac Day ceremony. Vaccinations.

And Mr. and Mrs. Pushkin aren't letting Peter hang out with Jem for fun. This isn't so Peter can socialize. Jem is some sort of asset; the Pushkins' encouragement of their friendship is calculated, strategic. So, 'Are you sure?' Peter asks again, because if there's one thing Peter is deathly afraid of, it's Jem ascribing these nefarious motives to Peter himself.

Jem saves the game. 'Let's go.'

At night, the stickers on Peter's scrapbook cover become bloated with depth. Freed from their two-dimensional exis-tence, they take to the air like astronauts. Peter counts them, one for every week with Miss Amar, as they spin like a celes-tial mobile. There is the giraffe, his first sticker, its outlines cracked slightly from the scrapbook's wear-and-tear. There is the dolphin, glittering kaleidoscopically, the same painful blue as Jem Lavignac's eyes. Jem is here too—sort of—Pe-ter feels that this is all happening while Jem is beside him or above him or inside him—and he feels a bottomless kind of sadness, an ache that feels good and bad at the same time, that sort of bothness that adults never talk about, oversimpli-fy, like erasing strokes from a drawing. He wakes up before his alarm can ring, to a murky blue sky. His face is dry but he knows he has cried—like his library book, caught in the flood of juice, his skin can't hide it.

Before his first lesson with Mrs. Yorke, on the way to school, Peter scrutinizes his Megasaurus Scrapbook and his exercise book like an archaeologist. The stickers on his scrapbook cover are inert today, secretive as glyphs. Miss Amar's script has the opaque codedness of another time, another culture, which has been evaporating from Peter ever since the disappearance.

'Good luck,' his mother says when they reach school. Her bracelet has snagged on her sleeve, but she hasn't noticed yet. 'Let me know how it goes, okay? Make sure Mrs. Yorke writes in your notebook.' Peter feels peculiarly sorry for his mother in this moment. Something about the way she means every word so very much.

Mrs. Yorke is already waiting when Peter climbs the gymnasium stairs. If she is irritated about having to take on more students since Miss Amar's disappearance, she does not show it when she opens the door for Peter. He has seen Mrs. Yorke at school concerts before; he recognizes her sharp nose and bulletproof chignon. She spends the first five minutes of the lesson asking Peter what he feels are irrelevant questions, like what grade he is in and what his favorite subject is. Peter glances over at the desk and notices a brown leather-bound day planner, a pile of music books, a sharpened pencil, a perfectly rectangular eraser. There are no playful sheets of stickers or smiley-faced stamps. All of Mrs. Yorke's students are advanced and old; Peter is profoundly embarrassed to be here. Even the room smells different with her in it.

As Jem and Peter predicted, Mrs. Yorke starts with scales. Peter's responses are unblemished, if not hesitant, and Mrs.

Yorke watches, her patience bordering on grimness, as if she is guiding a slow donkey up a flight of stairs.

'Your scales are sound,' Mrs. Yorke says (*sound*—Peter must return to the word and re-angle it—as in '*safe and sound*'). 'You might want to think about lifting the tempo a little bit. Now, onto sight reading.' She slides the first book from the pile on the desk and flattens the page to the earliest grade. Panic blooms in Peter's head. 'We won't do this every week,' Mrs. Yorke adds. 'I would just like to get an idea of your competency. I'll give you a minute to study the music.'

Peter doesn't know it, but what he is doing now, instead of studying the music, is reflecting bitterly on the concept of *relativity*: how this one minute of preparation flashes by compared to the one minute of, say, waiting for a video to load.

'Okay, Peter. Please begin. Go very slowly, if you like. Remember to count.'

What follows is a melody that is performed too slowly to have a discernible melody, moving like a tortoise trying to cross a busy highway. Mrs. Yorke coaches him through the journey. 'Yes. Yes, good. Steady—make sure you count. *D* in the left hand. No, no, darling. *D*. Yes, that's right. Good. Careful—remember to count. Just keep going...'

By the end of the piece, the lines of the stave have blurred together. Peter withdraws from the keyboard. Mrs. Yorke says, 'That wasn't bad—you need to keep a close eye on your rhythm. Your sight-reading in the treble is going very well. Just remember that in the bass, on the spaces, the notes are *A, C, E, G*—All Cows Eat Grass. And on the lines, the notes are *G, B, D, F, A*. Great Big Dogs Fight Anyway.'

It is at this pronouncement that Peter knows for sure that Miss Amar is gone, dislodged from reality like a pitch too low for notation. Miss Amar had taught Peter similar mnemonics to help him remember how to read the notes on the stave—FACE on the spaces and Every Good Boy Deserves Fruit on the lines for the treble stave; All Cows Eat Grass for the spaces in the bass. But this is the first time Peter has heard Great Big Dogs Fight Anyway. He is certain that Miss Amar used a different sentence, but all of a sudden Peter cannot remember what that was. It was poetic, he is sure, less violent. Peter gazes at the piano keys, and at the periphery he can perceive that Mrs. Yorke is gazing at *him*, as if she too senses some unbridged gap between them.

'Maybe it was Good Boys Don't Frighten Animals?' Jem suggests. 'That's what I remember learning with my first teacher. I don't really think about that stuff anymore when I'm sight reading, to be honest. It's just like reading words now.'

Jem and Peter are loitering in the outfields of the softball pitch, oversized gloves in hand, feigning alertness. Half of the class have no talent for softball, rotating through the bases on the strength of penalty balls, or trotting to the back of the batting line after striking out.

Jem adds, 'I know what you mean though. It's like you think there's only one way to learn something and you think you're learning it the way everybody else is learning it, but there's a million different ways instead. It kind of makes your brain hurt.'

Some of the sportier members of the class, like Quentin Silvy, are red with frustration. They spew advice and impatient encouragement at their teammates like helicopter parents. Mr. Cutbush demonstrates how to swing the bat for the hundredth time. Peter watches Kyle Pickering step up to the plate and prays he lands a hit. One more strike and the teams will switch roles.

Jem says, 'Maybe you should try to find out what happened to Miss Amar. It's like you need—what's the word?—

closure. That's what Mum kept saying, anyway, when Granddad died. It's why we moved here, why we're living in his old house.'

'Miss Amar isn't dead,' Peter says without conviction.

'Oh, I didn't mean that. But she's gone, right? And you might never see her again. You need to say goodbye to her, in a way. You need to understand what happened, you know? Understand for yourself.'

Understand for myself, Peter thinks. Like Jem is asking him to believe some private truth, as if truth is no solid thing. Kyle swings—sunlight bounces off the bat—and the ball hits the catcher's glove with smug certainty. 'Strikeout!' Mr. Cutbush calls. 'Change sides!'

There is no official record of who is in the junior primary choir; the ranks fluctuate from week to week. It is difficult for Mrs. Diamond to make any progress with such an irregular congregation, so while the upper primary and secondary choirs are well-drilled under her watch, the junior primary choir never performs at anything more taxing than a school assembly. No cunning devices are therefore required when Peter and Jem sneak into the Tuesday morning practice session and blend in with the other students. Their target is Miss Jung, the piano accompanist, whom Peter saw one lunchtime walking to the canteen with Miss Amar. She is also, as Jem observed, the only other music teacher with the title of *Miss*. Their friendship was surely inevitable.

As Jem and Peter murmur along to a jaunty song about pavlova, Peter watches Miss Jung's sure fingers, which move with indifferent proficiency. She could be piloting a spaceship, or inputting the launch sequence for deadly missiles. Out of all the music staff, Miss Jung is the one the students know the least about. She never teaches, so Peter is unfamiliar with her temperament, though he can perceive—in the way she punches her chords and tosses her fringe from her eyes—a wild reckless determination. If she ever played Truth or Dare, she would probably pick Dare every time.

Choir is scheduled to finish five minutes before the bell, so at quarter-to-nine Mrs. Diamond cheerfully dismisses the troops. As the students shoulder their schoolbags and Mrs. Diamond turns off the overhead projector, Jem, without a giveaway glance at Peter, approaches Mrs. Diamond. Peter is almost disappointed at her predictable gladness. 'Oh hello, Jeremy,' Mrs. Diamond says. 'I haven't seen you in choir before. I *loved* the Debussy you played at assembly the other week...'

Miss Jung is folding up her music and slotting it into her bag. Peter takes a sip of juice for courage and walks to the piano. He feels like he's wearing a spacesuit, the careful steps he must take. Miss Jung snaps the buckle of her bag. Her eyes rest on Peter.

'Excuse me, Miss Jung.'

She straightens her back. A robot pendant swings and settles at the center of her chest. The words dry up in Peter's mouth.

'Hello,' she says, with the stiffness of an adult who is frightened of interacting with children. In the distance he can hear Jem—the pro—sucking up to Mrs. Diamond, offering to carry her books back to the staff room. They head towards the door.

Miss Jung's eyes change. 'You were one of Kish's.'

'Pardon?'

A beat. 'You were one of Miss Amar's students.'

'Yes.' This wasn't part of the plan. Peter wonders if his face is turning red.

'You want to know what happened to her.'

'Yes.'

Miss Jung's eyes dart to the door, but Jem and Mrs. Diamond have already left. She digs her thumbnail into the leather handle of her bag. 'I don't know what happened to her, kid. I'm sorry.'

'But weren't you...' *Friends*. Peter hesitates. Maybe they were wrong about everything.

Miss Jung looks over her shoulder again. The bell will ring any minute now. It is the loudest point of the morning, the students reaching critical mass—not just here but in every school in this city, all these unripened minds wanting answers, answers, answers.

'What have your parents told you?'

'They say the same things as everybody else. Nobody knows anything. Everyone just says she's missing.'

'Well, that's just it,' Miss Jung says, as if Peter has fluked the correct answer to a test. 'Nobody knows anything. Miss Amar is missing, and that's simply all there is to know.'

Miss Jung shuts the lid of the piano. She glances at the wall behind her, where some of the choir students leave their bags during the session. Only Peter's bag remains. She gestures to it. 'You'd better get to class. School's about to begin.'

Peter manages to stare at Miss Jung for a bit longer. As with any teacher, it's like staring at the sun, and eventually Peter has to look away in case his eyes start watering. He retreats to his bag, kneeling down to unzip it. He screws the lid of his drink bottle tight and seals it in his lunchbox, shuffling around his school books and the juice-stained *Seeds of Time*. He slings his bag on his shoulder. He looks up at Miss Jung. She reminds him of Mrs. Yorke at this moment. That long gaze, as if he's a picture in a Magic Eye book, and Miss Jung can just make out something else. A hidden figure. A different plane.

'I don't know what happened to Miss Amar, kid,' Miss Jung says. 'But I can give you a clue. The only clue I know.'

They will look it up on YouTube that afternoon at Jem's house—'Little Waltz of the Telephones' by Tristram Cary from his collection *Polly Fillers*. Jem says that it's part of the seventh grade syllabus. Jem doesn't think the piece is much of a useful clue but Peter doesn't think the piece itself matters, that it could be any piece. Miss Jung had said that the song was a reminder for something, a trigger of some sort. A code, a password, a secret message. Wherever Miss Amar has gone, it is to answer that call; her disappearance was a willful one, a purposeful withdrawal.

Late at night, Peter turns on his lamp and slides out of bed, on his knees, to his schoolbag packed for the next day. The contents are tessellated like brickwork, and he extricates *Seeds of Time*. It is due for renewal tomorrow. Peter's heart still squeezes up at the sight of the juice stains. He has so far renewed the book four times without anyone querying him, but he knows he'll have to return it eventually, and explain the damage. The book has a yellow sticker wrapped around the spine, which means it's actually for high schoolers only, but when Peter first checked it out he was lucky enough to be served by the sympathetic librarian, Mrs. Cleft. Peter has been in the habit lately of checking out books that he cannot quite read. He is attracted to plain, abstract covers that give nothing away: *Seeds of Time* is a creamy off-white color, like ageing bones. The author's name and title are scrawled in careless, half-asleep handwriting, and there are lumpy clocks drawn by the same quavering hand, so misshapen that their faces can barely hold the numbers. Their crooked arms announce times that do not exist.

Peter hopes that the effort of reading the novel's cloudy prose will exhaust him enough to put him to sleep. He opens to his bookmarked page. *Seeds of Time* isn't like any novel he's read before: each chapter seems to take vast leaps forward in time; characters disappear and return in strange ways, or they do not return at all. It is late in the novel, and from what Peter can tell, there are no more human characters.

> Take heed (listen) (transform) little children (soon to be grown) and do not deny (make no mistake) our tenuous universe. Our existence is not autonomous (does not stand alone) (if not for language we would be a nothingness greater than nothingness). This world (our time) is merely the fiction of another (a fantasy) (a collective dream).
>
> All the rules are reversed. The most wayward of you will survive (prosper) (find the way). Transform (listen) yourselves (don't be a good bird). Forget what you know (unlearn). It will make the task easier (you will have to go backwards).
>
> A seed contains (in perpetuity) all the information necessary to begin. It is an heirloom (a continuation of our conversation) (a speech act) (stories passed on).
>
> Bear the likeness (you too contain the information necessary to begin). The foundation of our time (this world) is replication (a melodic science). Transform (heed).
>
> This evolution is unauthorized.

The passage does the trick: the words weigh down Peter's eyelids; the book falls shut. The lamplight is a tether that keeps Peter close to consciousness, but he cannot rouse the energy to stretch out his hand and flick the switch. Eventually he sinks; the urge dissolves, but it has only changed form, become liquid, an aquarium which Peter navigates, swimming down and deeper, until he reaches the bottom of the tank, where a forest of old-fashioned telephones grows like seaweed, their receivers dislodged from their rotary dial bases, the spiral cords swaying in the murk. Jem, in this dream, is a separate figure, barefoot like Peter, his trousers rolled up to the knees, advancing downwards in broad strokes. They are trying to find the right telephone; they swim to a receiver and cup it to their ears, release it, and move on to the next telephone, but it is hard to work methodically, hard to know whether you have already tried this telephone or that telephone. They are all identical; their cords are knotted like a complex root system.

'Something's coming,' Jem says.

A shadow falls over the tank. Peter looks up, but he can no longer see the lamplight. The telephone receiver in his fingers begins to vibrate softly. He lifts the receiver to his ear.

'*Blue Screen of Death,*' the telephone says.

The shadow lifts; Peter releases the receiver, which bobs, twirls—Peter turns his head with submarine slowness. Jem is gone.

'What did Miss Jung say Miss Amar's first name was?' Jem asks.

'Kish.'

'Kish Amar.' Jem rolls the name in his mouth. It's weird finding out the real names of teachers. Slightly embarrassing, even, as if you've caught them peeing.

Peter wants to ask Jem why he disappeared last night, but then he remembers it was just a dream. He has felt peculiarly sore all day about it, and he must keep reminding himself that Jem hasn't actually done anything to wound him. He wonders if he should ask Jem if he had the same dream, but the details are already vanishing. Something about an aquarium. Telephones submerged in green water.

It's recess and they're walking to the library to renew *Seeds of Time*. 'We can look up Miss Amar in the piano teacher directory,' Jem says. 'Her address might be in there. Want some?' He opens a box of Pocky and holds it out to Peter.

Peter pulls one of the sticks from the pack. 'What do we do if we find her house, though?'

'Maybe her sister will be there. Looking after the house.'

Sunny Mrs. Cleft is behind the desk today at the library, to Peter's relief, and she renews his book without voicing any suspicion. 'It's so nice to see you attempting such a challenging book, Peter. How are you finding it?'

Peter considers his feet. He is too embarrassed to admit he only picked the book for its cover. 'Kind of... slow. But interesting.'

'Yes, I suppose it can be a bit off-putting for some! Did you know that you're the first person to borrow this book out from the library in about... hmm, thirteen years?'

He wonders if the computer also tells Mrs. Cleft that he's had the book for over two months now. 'Oh. Cool,' he says.

Only Jem thinks to ask: 'Who was the last person who borrowed the book?'

She clucks. 'An audacious question, Jeremy! Library records are private. But! Since it has been so long...' She scrolls the mouse theatrically. 'Hmm, the last borrower... was... Rebecca Jung. Oh! I always forget Miss Jung used to be a student here. Isn't that funny?'

Peter and Jem freeze. Perhaps a beat too long. Jem quickly executes an innocent smile. 'That's interesting, Mrs. Cleft.'

'Yes! She's a huge fan of these sorts of ambiguous, strange books. You could have lots of intriguing conversations with her about this one, I'm sure.'

There's a queue forming behind them, so they leave the library. Peter blinks at the sunlight, trying to figure out exactly why he feels dazed. Jem chews a Pocky stick meditatively.

And then, it is Friday morning, the day when all the students' collars have wilted, graying at the folds, and our Peter Pushkin teeters at the edge of a group of three boys gathered at the bench outside their classroom—Quentin Silvy, Kyle Pickering, Andrew Sondergaard. It is only at this early hour before school that these unlike boys will converse; one cannot pick one's companions at eight o'clock in the morning. Quentin is bouncing his ubiquitous tennis ball up and down like a yoyo. Peter, perched on the railing opposite the bench, finds a cornflake fragment stuck between his teeth, and tries to tongue it out.

Kyle says, 'And then the octopus turns into a helicopter and SMASHES out of the building and THAT'S JUST THE FIRST EPISODE.'

Quentin's tennis ball snaps back into his hand. He sighs loudly, turns away from Kyle, says: 'Hey, Peter, shouldn't you be at piano?' He moves his hands up and down like a velociraptor.

'That's on Mondays,' Peter mumbles.

'You as good as Jem yet?'

'No.'

'Why not?'

Kyle says, 'You can't COMPARE them like that Jem's a what's-it a progee.'

'Prodigy,' Andrew corrects.

'Well, Peter could be a prodigy.' Quentin looks Peter up and down. 'Maybe not at piano. But like at reading, say. I've seen the books you read in Silent Reading, Peter. The words are like ants. You need a magnifying glass to read them.'

'Ha ha YEAH Mrs. Cleft lets you borrow the yellow dots.'

'Yeah,' Quentin says. 'So you're probably heaps smarter than you let on, Peter.'

Peter grips the railing. He's not sure how exactly Quentin swerved into this topic, and there is something menacing in the transition. Andrew is looking at Peter curiously.

Quentin asks, 'What's the book you're reading right now about? The one with the clocks?'

Quentin's lethal eyes like burning meteors.

'Well,' Peter says. 'It's a science-fiction novel.'

'Yeah?'

'Yeah. And. And it's about...'

'Hey guys.' Jem appears suddenly. He hooks his thumbs around his bag's shoulder straps. Peter breathes a sigh.

'Hey Jem,' Quentin says—and, apparently swerving back: 'How's piano going?'

Jem blinks. 'Okay, I guess.'

'Any assembly gigs coming up?'

'Not that I know of.'

Quentin nods—and keeps on nodding, a half-smirk on his face, as if Jem had made an extremely subtle wisecrack. Peter wishes that Kyle would start motormouthing about that TV show again. Or any other TV show. Anything but this weird knowing silence between these boys with such expensive names, so assured of their right to exist.

Jem points at Quentin's tennis ball. 'Why aren't you guys playing four-square?'

Quentin snorts. 'Four-square's boring now.'

'We're waiting for Ryan to get here he has a NEW SOCCER BALL,' Kyle sings.

'Wanna play three-on-three when he gets here?' Quentin asks.

Jem catches Peter's look. 'No thanks,' he says. Quentin nod-smirks. 'Actually, I have to go to the canteen,' Jem continues, sliding off his bag and setting it down with the others. 'See you guys.'

Peter jumps off the railing and follows Jem. Even though they can feel Quentin's gaze tracking them, they walk slowly. The school is greenest in the morning, glossy with dew, like a just-completed painting. Jem, for a moment, is uncharacteristically thrown. He looks around. 'This reminds me of a dream I had with an aquarium in it,' Jem says, and Peter—startled, relieved—allows himself for one instant to feel the warm safety of belonging, inclusion.

Mr. Cutbush, eager to avoid Monday's dismal softball session, has changed today's activity to British Bulldogs. The entire class is bunched up at one end of a playing field delineated by blue plastic markers, while three random students roam the center. On Mr. Cutbush's whistle the players are meant to run to the other side without being tagged by the students in the middle. If you're tagged, you become a tagger. Peter has only medium-level hatred for this game because while the action is too frantic to allow for a smooth conversation with Jem, being tagged isn't really such a bad thing when you're surrounded by other taggers.

Jem is saying, 'I've been meaning to tell you—I get it now. It's so easy; I can't believe we didn't see it before.'

'Huh?'

'*She saw your book.* Miss Jung saw *Seeds of Time* when you opened your bag. That's why she gave you the clue.'

Mr. Cutbush blows the whistle and everyone runs for it. Peter follows Jem's zigzagging path, twisting away from a hand trying to tag him. They make it to the other side.

Jem says, 'Tuesday choir—we're sneaking in again. We'll ask Miss Jung about the book. When she knows that *we* know about it, she'll definitely help us find Miss Amar.'

'You think so?'

'I'm sure of it. We can prove that we're smart and she can tell us things.'

The whistle sounds. Peter takes off, Jem this time a step behind him. They weave in and out, effortless as birds. Then Quentin Silvy jumps in front of Peter. Jem manages to swerve but Peter runs straight into Quentin's outstretched arm hard enough to knock himself over. As the ground punches the wind from Peter's lungs he reflects dizzyingly that Quentin never ever gets tagged so soon in this game.

'Sorry, Peter!' Quentin grabs Peter's hand and yanks him to his feet. Their eyes lock; Peter feels the chill of premonition. He separates himself from Quentin's grasp. The other students are waiting for Mr. Cutbush's whistle. Peter's eyes find Jem within the crowd, and Jem shrugs.

The whistle trills, and then everything happens.

Quentin sprints for Jem, intent as a missile. The collision is epic. On this afternoon Peter discovers that, talent or no talent, bones all break the same, and gravity does not discriminate. He watches them fall—Quentin, Jem. The snap of Jem's arm is decisive as prophecy. Everyone hears it—Peter, Mr. Cutbush, Quentin—even Kyle Pickering lodges a knuckle in his mouth, his face scrunched in sympathetic pain. '*What the hell was that, Silvy*?!' Mr. Cutbush roars, while Peter closes his eyes and hears five notes, one for each finger on Jem's broken left arm. *G, B, D, F, A.*

Mrs. Lavignac is incensed enough to bulldoze through Handwringer Hamsden and talk to Principal Alteruthemeyer himself. Jem and Quentin are absent for the rest of the day. 'I don't understand how this could happen,' Mrs. Lavignac will say, over and over, mining Principal Alteruthemeyer for answers he cannot provide. Peter will never know any of this for sure, but he does know that adults can let these things escalate to impossible heights. He knows that Mrs. Lavignac would have no qualms enrolling Jem in another school, that she could make Alteruthemeyer sweat blood with such a threat. He knows that different rules apply to boys like Jem Lavignac.

After Phys Ed, Peter changes back into his uniform and eats lunch alone. Kyle Pickering tries to talk to him—pours out an unpunctuated stream of cheer-up speech that makes Peter's head buzz. When people are this kind to Peter he feels that happy-sad ache, that troubling bothness. 'I reckon Quentin's gonna get suspended or even expelled I mean WHAT WAS HE THINKING I don't get why he did that...'

Peter doesn't get it either, this sudden hostility from Quentin, the way he quizzed Peter about the book. Why Quentin would annihilate his good standing at this school—Quentin Silvy, who, as far as Peter could perceive, had no inclination for conflict before. As if Quentin has been replaced overnight, or abducted and brainwashed.

Thankfully the bell rings before Kyle can get too lathered up, and they head back to class. During the break Mrs. Calbourne has distributed the school newsletters and other notes to bring home to parents. On Peter's desk, on top of the newsletter, is a pink card from the library. Waiting to crush him.

RECALL NOTICE
Dear PETER PUSHKIN
The following item(s) have been recalled by another borrower and are now due for an early return:
KWAI, H. R. / Seeds of Time
New due date: MONDAY 16 MAY 2011
Please ensure that the item(s) above are returned by the new due date to avoid incurring late fees.

That evening Peter's father stays late at the office, so it is just Peter and his mother at dinner. Recently his mother has taken to playing classical music as they eat. At first Peter supposed it was to fill in the silence that normally grips the Pushkins at dinner time, but he has come to understand that there is never just one reason with his mother—all her stones must kill at least two birds. So he suspects that the second bird is himself, and that his mother is playing classical music the same way mothers play classical music to their children while they're in the womb, as if there's some kind of IQ osmosis going on. Tonight it's Disc Three of *50 Classics from the World's Greatest Composers*. Right now it's Camille Saint-Saëns, 'Aquarium', from *The Carnival of the Animals*, a song Peter always finds unnerving. It's the song he imagines playing inside his body, vibrating through all that sad blood and water. Those falling piano notes, like coins disappearing into a wishing well.

'Did anything happen today at school?' his mother asks.

Peter drags his spoon through his rice. His parents are full of exhausting questions like this. How can he possibly explain what happened at school today? 'It was the same,' Peter says, barely able to suppress the quaver in his voice. He hears, again, the snap of Jem's bone.

'Really?' she says, with a *Play School* presenter's surprise. 'The same as any other day?'

And Peter tries—he really, really tries. He upends his day and spreads it out in his mind, looking for something to tell his mother, but all the components relate to Quentin, to Jem. To Miss Amar's disappearance. His quest for something. Closure, Jem said—but Peter is sure there's a better word.

'Peter?'

'Nothing,' he says, on the edge of tears. 'There's nothing.'

'Okay.' His mother purses her lips. She could go any-where from here. She could go down the *you know you can tell me anything* path, or the indignant *why won't you tell me any-*

thing path, but she picks the silent path. She guides the last grains of rice onto her spoon. A new track begins on the CD.

'Would it be alright if I used the phone later? To call Jem?' Peter asks.

He is not sure whether it is hurt or relief swimming in her eyes. She beams despite everything. 'Of course, honey.'

It takes seven rings before Mrs. Lavignac picks up the phone. Her voice is mellow, but Peter can still hear it echo throughout the cavernous Lavignac house.

'Hello, Mrs. Lavignac. This is Peter Pushkin.'

'Oh, Peter!' She hitches up the end of his name, like pulling up a sagging sock. 'You'll want to talk to Jem, is that right? I'm sorry, but he's staying at the hospital. Don't worry, darling, everything is fine. The doctors have fixed him up, given him a sling and all that. We're worried about—well, we're worried about how he's going to play the piano, of course, but this will just set him back a couple of months. We'll see.'

We'll see.

Peter can taste those lonely lunchtimes again.

'Will Jem be able to come to school on Monday, Mrs. Lavignac?'

'Oh, darling. I'm not sure. It doesn't look very likely. I'll tell him you called, though. Thank you for thinking of him.'

'Okay. Thank you, Mrs. Lavignac.' He doesn't know how to ask Mrs. Lavignac to tell Jem about the Recall Notice for *Seeds of Time*, so he doesn't.

That night, Miss Amar appears for the first time in Peter's dream. Peter is startled that he still remembers her face, everything from the gentle holes in her skin to the loose hair curving out from her tenuous bun. He is playing a G major scale in contrary motion and she is sitting in the chair beside him, with her right hand folded over her left.

'Very good, Peter,' she says. 'You will grow old so beautifully.'

Peter looks up from the keys. There are faces reflected in the veneered wood of the piano. He turns around: an entire wall of the lesson room is missing, and in its place is a congregation of chairs. Jem sits in the front row, his left arm replaced by a wooden prosthetic. The author of *Seeds of Time* is there too, but since Peter doesn't know what H.R. Kwai looks like, or whether the author is a man or a woman, he/she is just a black fog with the letters KWAI floating in a vortex. He/she says:

> Normally that would be the end of it, for nothing curtails a mystery-solving adventure quite like confiscating all the clues, and nothing sends a message quite like a broken bone. But our Peter Pushkin is a strange boy, maybe even a special one, possessing all the dormant intelligence of a seed. There is a quiet resilience about him; he has the potential to transform. He contains all the information necessary to begin.

Jem's wooden limb makes whirring noises, like an approving wind-up toy. There is a cat in his lap, with a red collar, who at first appears to be sleeping. But it opens its cloudy eyes. 'What you have said is incorrect.'

H.R. Kwai says:

> Oh?

The cat with the red collar says, 'There is still one clue left.'

Peter turns back to Miss Amar, who is no longer Miss Amar but Miss Jung.

'Where is Miss Amar?' Peter asks her, but Miss Jung simply points. The piano has disappeared, replaced now by an open cellar door. Miss Amar stands above it, considers her path from the top of the flight of stairs. Green water seeps up from the floor, but she makes her decision. She descends. The hem of her dress darkens.

'Miss Amar!' Peter calls, but the water is rising, tipping over chairs, sloshing into Peter's shoes. Jem strokes the cat with the red collar; his arm makes the glitching movements of a stop-motion animation. Indifferent to the ankle-deep water, Miss Jung talks earnestly with the H.R. Kwai fog. Their conversation is too low for Peter to hear, but it is heavy with secret wisdom. Miss Jung, the last clue.

The cellar door closes but the water keeps rising, swollen with all of Peter's fears, all the things he can't explain. He slides off the piano stool and into the swirling green sea. The paper walls of the lesson room begin to crumple into pulp. He goes under. For a heart-stopping second Peter becomes omniscient—the powerless sort—and the room becomes small like a diorama, one of many dioramas, and his room is just one cubicle in a shoebox out of many shoeboxes, and his life is just one version of many illustrations of the same sad facts of the world, and his tragedy is just one tragedy out of the infinite tragedies of the universe.

Peter Pushkin, too young to feel so brittle, stands in front of his school on Monday morning in his freshly laundered uniform, eyelids thick with sleep, while his mother's car arcs out of the school driveway and slips back into traffic. There is too much feeling in his fingertips, in his cheekbones and chest; they reverberate as if a sustained soprano note is ringing throughout his small glass body. There are five minutes to go before his lesson with Mrs. Yorke, but Peter can feel the whole weight of the Yamaha on his shoulders, heavier than a coffin with all his loved ones inside. There was a story Peter read once about children whose sins became corporeal, giant boulders strapped to their backs, and in some similar way the piano is the manifestation of all the things that have dogged Peter throughout his short existence. Something more advanced and sinister than a boulder, a machine with too many parts that engulfs him with unknowability.

Peter has never skipped a lesson before. He has never failed to be in a place where he is expected to be. But he discovers today that it is surprisingly easy to walk where he shouldn't walk, to miss his turn into the gymnasium. In another corner of the school there is a choir singing—the upper primary choir, Peter supposes. He follows the sound of their voices, which are sweeter and purer than what Peter heard in the junior primary choir session from last Tuesday. Even the piano accompaniment is sweeter, and Peter can hardly imagine Miss Jung playing so softly.

He finds the door and slings off his bag. He is close enough now to hear what the students are singing, a warm-up exercise: *Miss Terry missed a mystery in the midst of many ministries...*

Peter takes out *Seeds of Time*. The pink Recall Notice pokes out from between the pages. He slides down the wall outside the classroom and sits hugging his knees and the book. He wonders if Jem really will stay home from school today like Mrs. Lavignac suggested, and that simple dreadful thought increases the weight on his spine, and he renews his grip on *Seeds of Time*, listening earnestly to Miss Jung's piano accompaniment. He is saying something to himself which sounds like nonsense at first, but then he realizes it's: *Please... please... please...*

He huddles there until the school swells with children and the last note of the last song dissipates into the rafters. He hears Mrs. Diamond compliment the students before dismissing them, and the door next to him bangs open. Peter waits until all the students have passed, each more sure-footed than

Peter will ever be, tall and straight with certainty. He slips inside the classroom. One of the Year Seven girls is packing up the overhead projector and Mrs. Diamond is organizing a stack of sheet music on the piano. Peter clutches *Seeds of Time* to his chest. Has Miss Jung left already?

'Oh hello, dear,' Mrs. Diamond says. 'Can I help you?' She briskly straightens the papers.

'I'm looking for Miss Jung,' Peter says.

'Oh, my dear—Miss Jung isn't in today, and I don't think she'll be in for a while.' Mrs. Diamond slips the sheet music into a plastic folder.

'Why not?' Peter asks.

Mrs. Diamond looks down at him, as if newly aware of the height difference between them. 'Oh, my dear. I don't know if I can really tell you that. You see—'

'Please,' Peter says, sounding, to his surprise, old. Impatient, perhaps. Hurting so badly for the plain, unsugared facts. 'Please, can you tell me.'

He is no Jem Lavignac; he is talentless, unpersuasive, unwise to the rules. But, nevertheless, Mrs. Diamond seems to sigh with something like sympathy. She smooths the cover of her plastic folder. 'Well,' she says. 'Well. Miss Jung's gone for an operation, you see—she has been waiting for new eyes for a number of years, and some donor corneas finally became available last night. She's in surgery now. So her vision will be much better soon, but she will need some time to recover.'

For a moment Peter feels the air change properties—become viscous, green as the sad stale water of his dreams. *Seeds of Time* slips a little bit from his fingers.

Mrs. Diamond smiles. A smile which lands with a clueless thud, like a book sliding through a library return slot.

Never to be seen again.

'But is there anything I could help you with, my dear?'

Congratulations
You May Have
Already Won

From: lkjv@ouvert.net
Date: Sat 21 July 2012
To: undisclosed recipients

Hello:
Sales of electronic products facing the world. Absolute originality, value for money. On this month, the product feature is Seed. Seed.fon Seed.tab Seed.nb Seed.foto. Availability, astonishing prices.
CLICK NOW FOR EXCITING GIVEAWAYS!!!!!!!
Bring ideas to life
It all starts with Seed
Beautiful day
l k j v

From: penderghastd@gmail.com
Date: Sun 22 July 2012
To: lkjv@ouvert.net

Dear lkjv,

Greetings! I must say that I am intrigued by your vague and enticing offers. It just so happens that the relentless efforts of Seed.corp have thoroughly won me over, and, like Robbie struggling to hide his aching boner for Cecilia in *Atonement*, I am trembling with desire to purchase a Seed product. Any of the breathless array of Seed goods you have mentioned would satiate me; I just really want one now. But I am writing specifically to you, Mr. lkjv, because your optimistic vigor, your sincere interest in my wellbeing and your startling way with words have convinced me to choose you as my trusted salesperson to guide me in consummating this purchase. I shake virtual hands with you, my new friend!

Now, as we embark on an honest business relationship, I would be tremendously grateful if you could indulge me on a few queries. My first question is in regards to the Seed.fon. (Isn't that sooo trendy? Spelling 'phone' as 'fon'. It is such a youthful touch which penetrates the shell of apathy that encases my wayward self-centered generation and conveys with celestial benevolence: I am here. I understand. I, too, am barely literate.) Anyway, my question: I was really dazzled by the Seed.fon ad where that girl jumps off that thing and it's really cinematic and awesome. Will the camera on my Seed.fon be capable of capturing reality in such a poignant manner? Is there a filter for that?

Secondly, I would like to turn my attention to the Seed.nb. I will preface my question by saying that I do really love the faux wooden casing of all the Seed devices and especially the Seed.nb; it truly is an avant garde design that melds hi-tech with antique craftsmanship. Perhaps you do not know the answer to this question (I note that you are not a representative of Seed.corp per se but a wholesaler perhaps, a middleman). But nevertheless: has Seed.corp considered the multifunctional potential of the Seed.nb? The lacquered wooden finish might make the Seed.nb suitable for other uses, like a kitchen cutting board, say. Wouldn't that be spectacular? You could be checking Facebook in the kitchen and feel like some locally-grown organic free-range celery sticks for a snack—close the laptop lid—and presto! A cutting board! Really, lkjv, I think Seed should consider dishwasher safe laptops. Would you pass on this suggestion?

I hope that you will answer my queries so I may face the world with absolute confidence in my originality and value for money. I believe that with you, my dear lkjv, I have, indeed, already won.

Yours,
D

From: lkjv@ouvert.net
Date: Sun 22 July 2012
To: undisclosed recipients

Hello:
Sales of electronic products facing the world. Absolute originality, value for money. On this month the product feature is Seed. Seed.fon Seed.tab Seed.nb Seed.foto. Availability, astonishing prices.

CLICK NOW FOR EXCITING GIVEAWAYS!!!!!!!
Bring ideas to life
It all starts with Seed
Beautiful day
l k j v

From: penderghastd@gmail.com
Date: Sun 22 July 2012
To: lkjv@ouvert.net

Dear lkjv,

I must say I am quite surprised and (oh, I'll admit it) rather hurt by your response. Could it be that I misinterpreted your first communication? Could it be that you were not genuinely interested in bringing me absolute originality and value for money in a personal, mutually beneficial relationship, but like a moonlighting whore you were canvassing your wares to the entire street, spreadeagled at the window, flashing your goods to one and all? I must say I thought you had more dignity than that, lkjv. I thought you had class. I thought you were a contender. I therefore rescind my extended hand-shake. You have doused my flames of desire for Seed and all its smug suffixes of cutting-edge technology. I shall curl up instead with my rickety Asus and play Chip's Challenge.

Good day,
D

From: penderghastd@gmail.com
Date: Sun 22 July 2012
To: lkjv@ouvert.net

Dear lkjv,

I believe I may have been too hasty in sending that last communication. Upon scrutinising your puzzling return email, still sulking over our relationship's demise, I realized that your message was not completely identical to your first. In your first message the words 'the product feature is Seed' were preceded by a comma, but in your second message, the comma was absent. Could it be that you cannot communicate your feelings directly to me? Could it be that this is some coded message of agreement? Are we... are we being watched? Or could it be that you have received multiple offers from other consumers desperate for Seed products, and your enigmatic reply email is a cunning filtering process, and only the smartest will be granted the sweet reward?

Although I am still tingling with hurt, I must say I am also intrigued. If any of my suppositions are correct, please write back to me.

Tingling with hurt AND intrigue,
D

From: lkjv@ouvert.net
Date: Mon 23 July 2012
To: undisclosed recipients

Hello:

Will you glance at these electronic products? Seed.fon Seed. tab Seed.nb Seed.foto. A convenient life is arrived for you. Phone, tablet, laptop, camera. All the electronics, all your needs.

CLICK NOW FOR EXCITING GIVEAWAYS!!!!!!!

Most up-to-date technologies and very accurate information.

Keep up the great job

Bring ideas to Seed

l k j v

From: penderghastd@gmail.com
Date: Mon 23 July 2012
To: lkjv@ouvert.net

Dear lkjv,

So, the mind games continue. I'll let you in on a little secret, lkjv. Whatever your dubious motives, you are by far the most dedicated correspondent I have had in recent memory. Certainly, you are the only one wishing me a beautiful day and to keep up the great job (I write this as I sit at work, actually, so that particular remark was quite salient, lkjv).

But I must also let you in on another secret: mind games are something of a speciality of mine. Take this waiting room that I preside over, for instance: the thoughtful plastic crate of toys we have available for the children, the dear little shelf of Sunshine Books. Sometimes clients have to bring their kids in, you see, and at first glance they are relieved that there will be something to occupy their insufferable spawn, and their opinion of our office improves. We are Child Friendly. We Care about Families.

But what they don't know is that there is a particular art to choosing toys and games for a waiting room. I know, because I'm the one who curated this fine selection. You don't want items that need continual battery replacements, for instance. And you don't want items that are hard to disinfect, like stuffed animals. So that really only leaves items that you can build with, like Duplo bricks. So there they will be: a parent with a kid in tow, and they'll plonk the kid at the toy box, and the kid will start assembling something from the Duplo—invariably a house or a postmodern sculpture. This structure, whatever it is, will be highly unsettling to the parent. Why? The complete absence of blue bricks. No seriously, have you looked at a dense wall of colors that doesn't contain blue? It's sinister. So they'll sit there watching their kid build, they'll get called in for their appointment, they'll go home, and at the backs of their minds there will be this feeling of unwholeness. Maybe the kid will feel it too. Aggression, despair. And the last person they will suspect is the friendly receptionist.

Do these count as mind games? I don't know.

Beautiful day,
D

From: lkjv@ouvert.net
Date: Mon 23 July 2012
To: undisclosed recipients

Hello:
Sales of electronic products facing the world. Absolute orig-
inality, value for money. On this month, the product feature
is Seed. Seed.fon Seed.tab Seed.nb Seed.foto. Availability,
astonishing prices.
CLICK NOW FOR EXCITING GIVEAWAYS!!!!!!!
Bring ideas to life
It all starts with Seed
Beautiful day
l k j v

From: penderghastd@gmail.com
Date: Tue 24 July 2012
To: lkjv@ouvert.net

Dear lkjv,

So we are back to the original message. It's okay. The most
solid foundation of any relationship is repetition, I've discovered. I guess that's why Rach and I were so secure. She was
well-oiled, like the best public relations officer in the world.
You could see it in the way she'd talk about my occupation at
parties. 'David works for Taylor & Sondergaard,' she'd always
say to people. Consistent, not unlike a satisfying smoothie.
One time, compelled by an almost mean curiosity, I added:
'I'm the receptionist.' Oh boy, that got weird. Suddenly the
people we were talking to were looking at me like I was a
piece of toast with Che Guevara's face in it. 'How *unusual*.
A male receptionist.' And Rach was turning pink at this de-
parture from her PR script, and on the silent drive home she

would have confronted me about it but I suspect she didn't know how to describe my transgression exactly, or her unease. I guess I'm missing all my blue bricks.

I don't think she was embarrassed by me, really. She just liked to be polished, to leave nothing—not even the perceptions of other people—to chance. I miss her sometimes.

Oh look at me, getting all sappy! There's a whole world of electronics out there; exciting giveaways, lively ideas! Rach is a big fan of Seed by the way. I still remember her on the day she had to get a new plan and a new phone, sitting on the couch with all the brochures and Firefox tabs spread before her, staking out the best deal with the seasoned accuracy of a crucifix-wielding vampire slayer. No artistic falling girls and fon-tastic spelling would have moved her. She was too busy aggregating customer reviews and making repayment charts in Excel.

Now I know what you're thinking, lkjv. You think I'm not over Rach and that I've fetishized Seed and that's why I'm your penpal now. I can assure you that it's just a coincidence that my ex was a Seed.phile. Would I have still engaged you if you were peddling Macbooks or iPhones or discount pharmaceuticals? Probably. You just have an aura about you, lkjv. You're like a monk sitting on a snow-covered mountain, quietly crafting your replica hipster electronics, their shape and design guided by the market's invisible yet discerning hand.

Meditatively,

D

From: lkjv@ouvert.net
Date: Tue 24 July 2012
To: undisclosed recipients

Hello:
Click on the link below to enter our shops (<u>Online shops</u>)
Beautiful day
l k j v

From: penderghastd@gmail.com
Date: Wed 25 July 2012
To: lkjv@ouvert.net

Dear lkjv,

You seem somber now. It must be lonely where you are, in your empty shops. Meanwhile, I'm watching over a backlog of clients. There's a child here, but she's observing the same silence as everybody else, bent patiently over her mother's Samsung Galaxy. So the Duplo blocks are still packed away in their bucket, and every now and again the phone will ring and the whole room will listen to me say, *yes you can make an appointment, of course you can reschedule your appointment, I'm afraid we're fully booked this week.* You know, lkjv, a well-run waiting room is like a temple. So docile and reverent, these clients—even the ones on the phone follow my hushed cue. Sweet as hymns. They thank me so earnestly, with such rapt gratitude, and like you they wish me a good day, a beautiful day.

You know, there's something strange about watching a kid use a mobile phone, because you can never really imagine what it's like for them—to be pre-existed by the internet, by smart-phones. The world was just always like that to them, always a screen within grasp. Or maybe—and this is where I have to stretch a bit—maybe they do know somehow, subconscious-ly perhaps, what it was like before all of this. Because there are bits everywhere, residue—desktops, recycling bins, fold-ers, typewriter font, QWERTY keyboards, compasses. Clues to a past life.

And speaking of clues to a past life: you know what I saw yesterday, when I checked my mailbox after work? A news-letter from the Society of Consumers Against Fraud. Rach updated her mailing address for every bill, every subscrip-tion—except for this newsletter, which arrives in my mailbox irregularly and is always typeset in size 12 Century Gothic and has the ugliest stretched-out Word Art header you can imagine. They're probably the only society in the world that sends out newsletters by post. Presumably they don't trust the internet, a veritable breeding ground of fraud. There is a lot of column-padding fodder in the Society of Consum-ers Against Fraud newsletter—meandering articles about ATM horror stories and the exorbitant price of checks, and whether supermarkets are injecting water into their bacon. I'm not sure how Rach got on this mailing list exactly. May-be a well-meaning relative subscribed her. Who knows. Rach never read them, but the paper was exactly the right size for the kitty litter.

I hope you cheer up soon, Ikjv. I would hate it if you lost your enthusiasm for selling electronics.

Best,
D

From: lkjv@ouvert.net
Date: Wed 25 July 2012
To: undisclosed recipients

Hello:

What is the most up-to-date technologies available? How to make plans for the future and a time to be happy? How can you know that the lowest price is this? Join with Seed to make ideas come to life.

Pay a visit to our sites and be up-to-date every day. (Online shops)
Keep up the very good job
l k j v

From: penderghastd@gmail.com
Date: Thur 26 July 2012
To: lkjv@ouvert.net

Dear lkjv,

Yesterday I created the inaugural newsletter of the Society of Consumers Against Freud (population, 1: me) and borrowed some stamps from the office so I could mail the newsletter to my subscribers (population, 1: the Society of Consumers Against Fraud). Even though the Society of Consumers Against Freud newsletter is strictly for non-electronic circulation, I have kindly made an exception for you, and have attached a copy for your perusal. It has a tasteful layout with a well-proportioned header, and contains columns such as Psychoanalysing Psycho-analysis and 10 Tips to Avoid Freudian Slips. I trust you will find it useful.

One of the specialists came in today with a new box of Duplo. She said that her daughter had a birthday party and received two identical gifts, so why not use one for the waiting room? It was difficult to hide my dismay as she tipped out the box and tumbled the bricks together. There is a child playing with the bricks now, rummaging for the blue ones, and I can't help but scowl continually in his direction, which is difficult when I'm simultaneously engaging a client with *oh yes this year IS going rather fast; what are we to do? I haven't done my tax return! Ha ha ha ha ha.*

You raise some intriguing questions in your latest communication. You seem to be suggesting that this fine capitalist mess we're in—this nine-to-five drudgery we endure so we can fill our houses with new technology—is antithetical to our happiness. How can we be happy when we are constantly delaying happiness, postponing it indefinitely for an unguaranteed future, creating glimmering storehouses of technology we never have time to use? How can we really be sure that we are paying the lowest price on our electronic goods? Are we not paying... WITH OUR LIVES? Very astute, lkjv. But here is where I believe your message becomes confusing: is Seed really the antidote to our capitalist woes? Is there really a line of consumer electronics that is so brilliant that it can revive the idea of capitalism itself, and make us see this nine-to-five hamster wheel afresh?

I'm afraid I must return to my very good job. That kid's mother will be called in for her appointment soon so I will covertly dismantle his horrible Duplo structure. Tell me what you think of that newsletter, okay?

Ponderously,
D

SCAFNewsletter.pdf
1 MB   View   Download

From: penderghastd@gmail.com
Date: Fri 27 July 2012
To: lkjv@ouvert.net

Dear lkjv,

Hurry up and write to me.

Best,
D

From: lkjv@ouvert.net
Date: Fri 27 July 2012
To: undisclosed recipients

Hello:
Sales of electronic products facing the world. Absolute orig-
inality, value for money. On this month the product feature
is Seed. Seed.fon Seed.tab Seed.nb Seed.foto. Availability,
astonishing prices.
CLICK NOW FOR EXCITING GIVEAWAYS!!!!!!!
Bring ideas to life
It all starts with Seed
Beautiful day
l k j v

From: penderghastd@gmail.com
Date: Sat 28 July 2012
To: lkjv@ouvert.net

Dear lkjv,

Well, the shit really hit the fan last night. Rach came around. She wanted to pick up the card table she left at my house. Another rare Rach oversight, like the Society of Consumers Against Fraud newsletter. Or maybe it's not an oversight. Maybe her failure to unsubscribe from that newsletter was deliberate, and maybe leaving behind the card table was deliberate too. It's hard to tell with Rach.

At first it was okay. We chatted as I cleared the stuff off the table, folded it up, and loaded it into her car. We had a glass of wine each. I told you Rach was well-oiled like a PR officer and the break-up was no exception; our break-up would have won awards. She was on my couch, nursing a glass of wine, and there was no tension between us—just two friends catching up. And then I made the mistake. 'Hey,' I said. 'Remember those Society of Consumers Against Fraud newsletters we used for the cat litter?'

'The what?' she said. Don't you just love the almost scripted quality of her confusion? 'The what? Oh those! Do you still get them? I'm so sorry! I never read them. I'll unsubscribe. Do you have the latest newsletter?'

I tried to look for it, but then I remembered. I told her I must have left it at work. More scripted confusion from Rach: 'At work? Whatever for?'

And here's what I actually said, as if my life wasn't enough of a bumbling sitcom already: 'Well I needed the mailing address of the Society of Consumers Against Freud. I mean Fraud. See I've started a newsletter from the Society of Consumers Against Freud and I wanted to send it to the Society of Consumers Against Freud. I mean Fraud.'

She stared at me for a second. Like she was waiting for the canned laughter to finish. She said she wasn't sure what I was talking about—'You've started a newsletter, Dave? Why?' So I fetched the extra newsletter that I'd printed at work. It was all glossy and quite pretty really. I handed it to her and she inspected it at arm's length like she was doing a reading test at the optometrist. 'You printed this at work?'

There was no turning back now. 'Yes,' I said. 'I did.'

And it's only because I know Rach so well that I saw her face become cloudy for a second. Then it cleared, just like a fresh-ly flushed toilet with one of those scented things clipped to the bowl. That floral froth really masks everything that came before. Rach smiled, put her glass and the newsletter down on the table, said that I was 'very peculiar'—like she's a com-mentator on Antiques Roadshow now—and thanked me for the wine.

And then she left. Now, I know that doesn't really look like a shit-hitting-the-fan scenario, but honestly, from everything you know of Rach, what did you think it was going to look like? I know what that look was all about. It's the same look she gave me when I ruined her line about my job, the same look she gave me when we went to karaoke for her birthday and all I wanted to sing was 'The Rockafeller Skank'. What kind of grown man spends five hours on a Wednesday night making a fake newsletter? A goof, a time-waster. A little boy desperate for attention. If Rach has any doubts about snipping me out of her life, tonight was a confirmation that she did the right thing.

I drank the rest of the wine after Rach left so I've felt screwy all morning. I don't even have the heart to engage with your latest email (which is your first email). Why didn't you write to me on Thursday? It was so boring at work and by the time I got your Friday email I was clocking off. What's up with that?

D

From: lkjv@ouvert.net
Date: Sun 29 July 2012
To: undisclosed recipients

Hello:
It is the duty of good business to tell you about these deals. Seed.fon Seed.tab Seed.nb Seed.foto. Professionals and beginners choose Seed. Absolute originality, value for money. The trusted brand that takes good ideas to life.
Act now for you may have already won (Online shops)
Your memories are safe with Seed
Beautiful day
l k j v

From: penderghastd@gmail.com
Date: Sun 29 July 2012
To: lkjv@ouvert.net

Dear lkjv,

This weekend's just too damn slow. It's like being in high school again. Okay I know that sounds ridiculous, but stay with me here, lkjv. It's like when you're in high school and there's someone you're just waiting to see, someone you've got your eye on, and there's something nice about just being in the same place, to have the potential for, I don't know, some encounter or conversation. And when you're a teenager that feeling's like ten times larger. Or maybe it's the same as it is now, except when you're an adult you're meant to have your shit together. I don't know what I'm waiting for though. There's nothing to wait for. All the stuff that was on the card table is still stacked on the carpet. The newsletter is exactly where Rach left it. There's no more wine (I've checked).

You make me feel so philosophical, lkjv. At what point does an idea come to life? At what point is it conscious? These are important questions. You ask all the important questions, lkjv.

Maybe I should go outside.

D

From: penderghastd@gmail.com
Date: Tue 30 July 2012
To: lkjv@ouvert.net

Look, lkjv. I sense that you're trying to cool off our relationship here. You're certainly not as regular as you used to be. And that's okay. You were just trying to sell electronics. I understand. I will always remember you fondly, though. We have some good memories.

Check out this waiting room: just a father and his son, playing with the bricks. Every single time his son assembles something that might look like a completed work, the father congratulates the kid like he's won gold and snaps a picture. Imagine being the Facebook friend of that guy. All the obnoxious status updates you'd be subjected to right at this moment. *Just spending some Q-time with my little dude! — At Taylor & Sondergaard.* Johnny Daddykins added 5238 new photos to the album You Totally Must Give A Shit About My Kid's Every Playtime. 'Nice job, Kieran,' he says. 'It's very colorful. Hmm. I wonder why there aren't any blue bricks?'

Oh, but I was saying goodbye to you. Don't worry lkjv, I'm not really that bitter. In fact, I'm jumping back on the hamster wheel, and I'm saving up for a new laptop. I never told you this, but the Asus is still running on XP. Yep, it's time. A new laptop, a fresh start, a clean Spider Solitaire scoreboard. I'm not sure if I'm sold on the Seed.nb yet, but we'll see. We'll see.

With a fistbump that echoes through the ages,
D

From: penderghastd@gmail.com
Date: Sun 19 August 2012
To: lkjv@ouvert.net

Hello:
Beautiful day,
d a v e

SCAFNewsletter2.pdf
1.1MB   View   Download

U (or, That Extra Little Something)

I once had a sister who taught me to share and to forgive. It is unclear if you could call her existence 'living'. She did not have a heart, so the precise hour of her death, too, is unclear. Like a good sister, I hosted her for eleven months, and perhaps she is still, even now, my guest.

He says I've got that extra little something. He says I look like a girl who is not like other girls. A girl who thinks for herself, who is comfortable and sassy, but isn't, like, a total bitch about it. He says I am So Real. The perfect match for the Ampersand brand identity. I'm amused by this idea, as if my body grew into a pre-existing personality, which also happens to be a national brand. But then, I suppose I'm used to my body not quite belonging entirely to me.

He asks me what I know about Ampersand. I say that it is a clothing store that specializes in unisex fashion. I do not use the words: faux-vintage. Twee. Accessories for milky-skinned pseudo-alternative youngsters who drink herbal tea and write poems in pocket notebooks with cream-colored pages.

He flips the Seed.tab and I take up the stylus, too sleek for the serrated digital ink it brings forth. An annual contract:

after which time, I'd guess, another young body who exemplifies the Ampersand brand identity will sign her name in the white cell.

We shake hands.

My sister, lacking a heart, also lacked a name. I think of her as Rsu, a corrupted form of my own name. Inarticulable. A syllable of me.

At the moment you can find me in the brochure for the Ampersand Spring/Summer collection. In each photo, which is printed on matte paper with an Instagram wash, I am posing next to this year's male Ampersand ambassador, who is wearing the same outfit as me with minor modifications. We manage to finesse vague, casual expressions, as if it's only natural that we would be wearing identical outfits while socialising in a sun-lit sharehouse full of sensible bookshelves and creamy stationery. *Ursula and Graeme wear Penny-Farthing shirt ($59.95), Eagle Eye necktie ($29.95) and Greyhound pinstripe shorts ($69.95).*

A ubiquitous feature of every Ampersand shoot is a Scrabble board—not the newest release of the game, but some dustier version with wooden racks, faded squares, letter tiles yellowed like old teeth. They spell high-value words like SUTURES and ECHELON and CITADEL. Ursula and Graeme are obviously intelligent and very fashionable, very expensively educated people.

It's not often that I think deeply about Rsu. This culture is awash with enough stories of malevolent twins and vengeful doppelgangers. But maybe, even secretly, I've always been waiting for some trace of my sister to erupt; an extra tooth, perhaps, or a severed nerve sparking. It doesn't have to be malevolent. Like the way people look for final messages from deceased loved ones. Signs of persistence.

Did Rsu ever have a consciousness?

I've recently become addicted to playing Scrabble against myself. Whenever this blank document stumps me I walk over to my bed, where I've laid out the board, and shuffle the tiles on the active player's stand. I have memorized the entirety of the two- and three-letter words accepted under both the British and US rules. It's actually not difficult to play Scrabble against yourself. Most of the time you'll find that one player gets all the expensive letters, like the Q and the Z and the X, and the other player gets tedious all-vowel combinations, and will never thrive. All the potential, stolen by chance, not unlike Rsu. But that's what happens when you look back over a particular span of time, and decide to *think* of it as a span of time, of the events belonging together: everything becomes a metaphor for your biggest hang-up.

Last time Penny was in my car she switched out my mix CD for an audiobook of Grimm fairytales. The reason she listens to these audiobooks isn't because of the stories, but because she really likes the guy who's reading them. His name is Tim Spiegel and it's not that his voice is sexy exactly, or textured with age, but it possesses a kind of melodic orderliness. Like—if it's possible—a voice that is buoyant and sad at the same time; a balloon drifting off in the sky.

When I tell people I'm an artist they get concerned. Suddenly they are fully conscious of their role as taxpayers. Suddenly I'm a parasite. I should tell them that I know a thing or two about parasites.

Sometimes if I can be bothered I show them the Ampersand catalogue. This can go in two directions—one, it can be impressive and glamorous. My worth as a human is verified in print. People respect things that make cash. Two: it simply increases their disdain. Like I'm delusional, high on my own youth. Like a kind adult never whispered gently in my ear that I won't be young forever.

Here's the extent of my commitment to modelling: a few chance jobs scattered throughout my adolescence. Perhaps you once perused a brochure for a new housing estate, and there I was, riding a bicycle on a path around an artificial lake. Or maybe you once read a names-changed-to-protect-privacy magazine article about health disorders and teen suicide, and the stock image accompanying the column featured the back of my head, staring into a grimy school toilet mirror blurred by pain and Photoshop. Or perhaps you received an orientation day information pack for a university in your state, and there I was, sitting on a costly green lawn in front of a clock tower with four or five other would-be school leavers, my inclusion in the photo, with my non-threatening brownness, signifying the campus's commitment to diversity and multiculturalism. There are many girls in binders, like me, who aren't intent on becoming the next Gemma Miranda whatever. It is simply that there are countless billboards, catalogues, magazine spreads, empty photo frames—a whole advertising universe that needs to be populated by sweet young saleable faces. Scratch that: sweet young saleable *diverse* faces.

Oh Tim Spiegel, the way your voice curls is sometimes just the most endearing thing. I wonder if you get shit from people about reading audiobooks for a living. I wonder whether you still live with your parents, or if people ask you when you're going to get a real job, or if they lecture you about how your voice won't stay the same forever.

Some plucky arts worker has scraped up enough funding to put on a sizeable exhibition in Perth, called *30/30*, which features thirty Australian artists under the age of 30. Penny got in it, and so did I. Penny, with her mobiles; me, with my ink drawings. I've decided to go all-out for this exhibition. I'm going to create the largest and wankiest installation that I can conceive.

That's the other thing about me. I don't know if I really believe that I'm wanky. Sometimes I get so absorbed in making art, and I know exactly what the art explores and I can explain it without resorting to all that *my practice engages in a dialectical interrogation of the discursive limits of* lofty tertiary education crap. But sometimes—and I wonder if my friends would admit to this too—you just sort of pull back a bit, like there's a camera inside your head that pans outwards and outwards, and you think... what is this? What am I doing? Am I really exploring this concept or that concept, or am I really just making whatever the fuck I want?

Penny and I are op-shop-hopping; she's on the lookout for mobile fodder, I'm on the lookout for blankets and old chairs for the *30/30* installation. Tim Spiegel is telling the story of *Little Red Riding Hood*. '"*What big teeth you have,*"' Tim Spiegel says for Little Red Riding Hood. '"*All the better to eat you with, my dear!*"' Tim Spiegel says for the Wolf. '*And with that,*' Tim Spiegel concludes, '*the wolf leapt from the bed and devoured Little Red Riding Hood in one vicious mouthful.*'

Penny says that she'd love Tim Spiegel to devour *her* in one vicious mouthful. I tell her not to defile my car with her intimate fantasies. 'AG,' I could say: an expression of annoyance, remorse, or surprise, but also a colloquial shortening of 'agriculture', as in 'ag college'. Several of the two-letter words accepted in Scrabble are interjections of dismay, astonishment, hesitation, distress. So many nuanced emotions in the simple arrangement of two letters. 'AH,' said Little Red Riding Hood as she was swallowed alive. 'UR,' said the Wolf as he awoke with a belly full of stones. 'OH,' said my mother when the ultrasound revealed, in its oracular chalk, Rsu quietly growing on my neck.

Someone recognizes me at Cellar Door. A rosy-cheeked waitress with a straight brown fringe. She's wearing the *Ginger Schnapps chequered shirt ($42.95)* from the AdShell poster in Forest Chase and the *Cherry Sundae Unicorn pin badge ($30)* from page three of the Ampersand Spring/Summer brochure.

'Aren't you the girl from the Ampersand ads?' she asks.

'I've done some work for Ampersand, yeah.'

'Oh wow! It's like my favorite store.'

'Thanks,' I say. As if I could really take credit for the work of bloodless Ampersand designers, extracting the season's threads from blueprints of wartime clothing; the factory workers gunning away at their sewing machines, relentless as punchclocks. The salesgirl making small talk as she flattens the base of a thick brown carry bag, her lanyard swinging, as if she too is price-tagged. Perhaps I, as well, help to produce Ampersand clothing, by wearing it on my person, by submitting to the camera flash.

'It's so weird to see you in real life,' the waitress says. And with that she whisks away our table number, the Three of Hearts, and retreats behind the counter.

Real life, I think to myself, as Penny goes back to explaining her latest techno-woe. 'Here, I'll show you what I mean,' she says, taking out her Seed.fon. 'See?' She swipes across the menu and back again. The applications whip onscreen and away like unwanted clothes on a sales rack.

'See?' Penny says. 'There's a lag.'

'Oh,' I say, twisting my voice. She keeps demonstrating the lag, but I'm not seeing it.

'It used to be *instant*.'

'Yeah.'

Penny locks the phone and slides it back into her handbag. 'Ugh. It's still under warranty. I'll have to call up about it.'

'Good luck.'

Penny extracts a long packet of sugar from the ceramic holder in the center of the table. The paper of the packet is made from an atypically glossy stock, like the packaging of an Apple device; it is almost a shame when Penny crookedly beheads it and tips the sugar into her coffee.

The phrase keeps on returning, *see you in real life*, like a persistently misdelivered parcel. Penny emerges from her coffee. 'Hey so, tonight after Richard's, Jess is having a thing at hers. Want to go to that?'

Richard: a guy two grad classes below ours, whose body of work consists entirely of slogans typeset in Helvetica. He has a show opening tonight. Jess: a jewelry designer who specializes in video game–themed earrings and lives in a tattered house on the outskirts of Northbridge with perpetually absent housemates. 'Of course,' I say to Penny.

Perhaps when I look back on these days—whatever I will retrospectively define as 'these days', my youth or my twenties or just this vanishing year—my brain will reorganize the moments into a series of violent segues. How exactly did I get from Cellar Door, to Richard's show, to right now, driving through Northbridge humming with too much cider, while Penny continually skips the CD backwards so that Tim Spiegel is saying *one vicious mouth—one vicious mouth—one vicious mouthful* all the way down William Street, while the two girls in the back, friends of Richard's tipsy on the table wine served at the exhibition, toss through the blankets I scoured from seven different op-shops and shriek with laughter, as the traffic lights seem to tilt at every corner, lurching like sights in a theme park ride... day to afternoon to night, fading between each other like some timed gradation, a screensaver, until I'm squeezing my car into a parking space, staggering through Jess's flamingoed front yard, to Jess herself, opening the flywire, two hoop earrings dangling from each lobe. One orange, one blue.

Jess's laptop is jacked into a speaker in the lounge room, and although the songs sound as if iTunes is on shuffle, I know that she has actually spent all afternoon curating this playlist. An uneven circle of people sit on the carpet, including one guy who I'm glad not to know, dropping trivial facts about every song. There are more people outside smoking, flicking their butts into a giant flower pot half filled with blackened rain water. Abandoned bottles cluster in every corner and windowsill. Penny and I hover in the lounge room, impressed at the party-likeness of this party. It's like the work of a really conscientious set dresser.

'Actually that instrument right there is a glockenspiel,' the music trivia guy says.

The other people in the circle are aggressively opening up side conversations to get away from him. 'The thing is it's only called *tandem* cycling when the riders are seated one behind the other,' a girl in a Janelle Monáe T-shirt says. 'When the riders are side-by-side it's called a *sociable*.'

'*What?* I've never seen a tandem bike where the riders are next to each other.'

'Like I said, it's not *called* a tandem bike, it's called a *sociable*.'

'That's the most ridiculous thing I've ever heard.'

'I'm *serious*. Look, just LOOK AT THIS.' She summons Wikipedia on her Seed.fon. 'Shit, my phone's getting so fucking slow.'

'*Mine too!*' cries Penny, injecting us both into the circle.

Jump cut. Two hours later. I drift between two different conversations that are happening simultaneously in the adjoining kitchen and in the lounge room. In the kitchen Jess is delivering an impromptu tutorial on how to open beer bottles using the edge of a table. In the lounge room Penny and the girl in the Janelle Monáe T-shirt are debating the ending of *Inception*. 'OF COURSE IT WAS ALL A DREAM,' yells Penny, her bottle of Rogers perilously inclined.

The music trivia guy's facts are getting sloppy. He keeps confusing Regina Spektor with Fiona Apple. There is a successful *ping!* from the kitchen and a round of applause. I am fixated on a mobile that Penny made last year for her solo show—which Jess must have purchased—which hangs from the light fixture, a bird's nest of cutlery. It's like we have our own private economy; everyone buys everyone else's work.

'The totems aren't for finding out if you're in a dream,' the girl in the Janelle Monáe T-shirt says. 'They're just good for finding out if you're in *someone else's* dream.' She whips out her phone. 'Here, I'll prove it. Oh look, hey you, YOU, stop talking—here's that picture of the sociable I was trying to show you earlier.'

'What?'

'The *sociable*, dammit! It's real! *See here?*'

The group in the kitchen move on to other bottle-opening strategies. Above the little folding table where Jess and her invisible housemates eat breakfast, I spot a piece from Jess's short-lived watercolor phase. It's a painting of duelling Kirbies in *Super Smash Bros. Brawl*—pink, round, fat with threatening cuteness. One of the Kirbies has his mouth open, a black hole, about to suck the other Kirby in. Scrawled underneath are the words: WHAT HAPPENS WHEN KIRBY SWALLOWS KIRBY?

I think that I am turning pink like Kirby. There are three ciders billowing inside me, inflating like a hot-air balloon inside my stomach. The girl in the Janelle Monáe T-shirt passes around her phone to anyone who cares—I see the pictures of sociables, in which a man and a woman—always, a man and a woman—ride what looks like some kind of bicycle hydra, clutching their separate handlebars, pedalling on their separate pedals, smiling like fools.

Jump cut. Two hours. The music trivia guy is mercifully passed out. A group has taken off for a teetering walk to the twenty-four-hour McDonald's but the room still feels full. Something about having a headache makes everything seem far too close. Jess is asking everybody if they have seen her orange portal. 'Where is it? Where is my orange portal?' she says, clutching her left ear lobe as if the hole might close over very soon, using her free hand to overturn cushions. I begin to suspect the playlist is repeating itself. I hear a glockenspiel, cheeky as déjà vu.

The girl in the Janelle Monáe T-shirt is curled up next to me, cycling through random Wikipedia articles on her phone and whispering their titles. 'List of the United States Senators from Maine,' she says. 'European Society of Paediatric and Neonatal Intensive Care. Max Müller (cross-country skier). H.R. Kwai (author). Dendritic filopodia. *Miami Psychic.*'

Penny is also deep in telephonic communion, in the corner, her Seed.fon pressed to her ear. She is sobbing. Every fifteen seconds she peels the phone off her face and dabs the touchscreen. I want to go over there and ask what's wrong but that Kirby-feeling has infected my whole body. I feel like my limbs are small and inadequate, lacking the proper digits. There's no way I'm driving home. Penny keeps on sobbing. I have never known a drunk crier like her.

'List of *Pikkoro and the Multipurpose Octopus* episodes,' the girl in the Janelle Monáe T-shirt whispers. 'Donald Bradman's batting technique.'

I float over to Penny's corner, watch her dab the touchscreen. She seems to be pressing the number five. 'Penny,' I say, trying to hold her slippery face. 'What are you doing?'

She sniffs, wipes her knuckles across her nose. 'Listen,' she says, brandishing her phone at my ear. 'Listen.'

I take the phone, which is spotted with fingerprints and feverishly warm. I press it to my ear—

Thank you for calling technical support for your Seed device. Please keep your model number at hand so that we may best help you with your enquiry.

—and I listen to Tim Spiegel, like a gentle firelight, leading me through the telephonic darkness. Penny continues to sob, and even I am overcome with something, like the sun is rising at my back. His guiding voice: melodious, benevolent.

If you are experiencing technical problems with your Seed.fon, please press one.

If you are experiencing technical problems with your Seed.nb or Seed.tab, please press two.

For problems relating to other Seed devices, please press three.

To speak to an operator, press four.

To hear these options again, press five.

AUF, a useful and peculiar three-letter word, is an obsolete synonym for 'changeling'. Sometimes, the term 'changeling' refers to a human child who is taken away by magical creatures, but it may also refer to the false child left in the real one's place. Stories of children swapped for other children recur across the centuries, to explain away sick children, or children born with deformities and disorders. The idea is that there is some *real* child, sequestered elsewhere, and the newborn is some kind of imposter. There is something miserable about that notion. Newborns, who are exactly who they are, too feeble to protest to their dismayed parents—*no, I am real. I am your real child.*

Perhaps when my mother first saw me and Rsu, a slippery chimera that emerged from the incision on her stomach, we registered as some swap gone wrong, a faulty transaction. Who was the real child?

There is only one photograph of us, the one which was printed in all the newspapers. I was never allowed to see it, and I've never attempted to find it myself. What I *have* seen, instead, is a yellowed clipping of the 'after' picture—Ursula, in singular form. The real child. The one who will pass as the real child.

Perhaps the reason the word 'changeling' is not employed consistently to describe either the real child or the false child is because you can never really be certain which is which. For surely Rsu could have been the real child, and I the false child who supplanted her. At some crucial, secret stage of our becoming, I could have been the parasite, and Rsu the autosite.

Or perhaps the reason I have never been allowed to see the newspaper photograph of Rsu and me together is because I would definitely recognize—in our posture, or our clenched toes, or our tender pink mouths—the single clear protest of *we are real we are real we are real.*

On Monday, when the mental haze from Jess's party has almost lifted, I buy an all-day ticket and travel on all the train lines. I pretend I am some sort of queen, surveying my loyal subjects as they parade before me, presenting their various body parts for my critical gaze—chins, ears, fingernails, Adam's apples, teeth, cleavage. I take their offerings and repurpose them, ink them into an alternative existence. I fasten a woman's sneer to the spotted face of a teenage boy. With my queenly powers, I tell my subjects: the two of you once boarded a train, at separate times, on separate journeys, and now you are the same being.

This train line runs alongside the freeway, hemmed either side by the backs of warehouses and factories. Their gray surfaces are adorned with giant telephone numbers and slogans. At this particular moment, there is a tow truck driving alongside the train, carrying the shells of damaged cars. One of the cars is missing the driver-side door, so you can see the seatbelt flapping inside like a burnt tongue. This little strip of gray is meant to save our lives.

The man opposite me, whose eyebrows I'm refashioning into the fringe of a hat, is trying to look at me without looking at me. I cap my pen and hold my sketchbook up close to my nose like a diner studying a menu. I watch him through the holes in the ring-binding as he fiddles with his earphones. *This is Stirling*, the pre-recorded voice announces, seeming to stumble over the consecutive s's. I try to imagine Tim Spiegel saying it, *This is Stirling*. This other voice, this not-Tim voice, makes me feel like I am inside an untrustworthy universe. In that *real life* the waitress mentioned.

The man with the earphones disembarks. The pre-recorded voice observes, this time meditatively, that the doors are closing. It echoes like a gong through a temple. I put my sketchbook back on my knees and uncap my pen.

Two women with exquisitely beautiful noses take the man's place opposite me. I flip to a new page. The train slides away from the station, and when it reaches peak speed it emits the purest sound, an endless soprano pitch. Beneath it, like a secret melody, the two women are talking in a language that isn't English. When you don't understand something, everything sounds so quick, so assured.

My very first job, back in the day, was an appearance in a French educational video. I was twelve years old and I was wearing a denim pinafore. *S'asseoir*, the voiceover would say, and I would sit. *Manger*, the voiceover would say, and I would eat. *Boire*, the voiceover would say, and I would drink. Between each action, the voiceover would wait exactly eight seconds, so that a class would have time to say the word with the correct pronunciation, or recite the various conjugations—*je bois, tu bois, il/elle boit, nous buvons, vous buvez, ils/elles boivent*. Sometimes, when I am feeling lost, I imagine English words emanating from the ceiling, reducing my movements to a single verb. I make it so that the voice-over is myself, speaking in the same authoritative manner as the voiceover in the French video. *Observe*, I speak over myself, and I observe the two ladies, one of them plucking a loose hair from her blouse, the other lacing her fingers over her knee. *Draw*, and I press my pen to the page, forming a woman standing with her neck crooked, while her long tangled hair culminates in a dress worn by the fourteen-fingered woman beside her.

And now—in the other now, as I try to figure out what to type next; the now in which I consider the Scrabble tile drawn from the green bag, the letter *I*, one point, the most difficult of vowels—the voiceover of myself says, *Write*, and I write. Because the next part is about to become difficult.

I am waiting for a coffee in Cellar Door. I am served by the same waitress as last time, the one who recognized me from the Ampersand ads. My table number is the Queen of Spades. A little card next to the sugar holder informs me that the wireless password is Ce11arDoor, but I don't have a laptop or a smartphone. If I did, I would probably Google *Tim Spiegel*. Who knows what else he's done, where else I've been unwittingly absorbing his voice. He could be the newsreader on the radio, or the television voice that says *the following program is rated M for Mature Audiences*, or the voice at the ANZ bank that goes *ticket number A351—please proceed to teller three*. He could be running this entire city.

Penny texts me a sorry-I'm-running-late. The barista's taking a while with the espresso. I open my sketchbook and review the previous day's work. Penny says she becomes nauseated if she looks at my drawings for too long, as if she can sense the movement of the train. For somebody whose art practice is entirely concerned with mobiles, Penny has a low tolerance for motion.

I turn the page and examine my diagram for the *30/30* installation. A kind of tunnel, or womb, constructed from the op shop blankets, leading to a projector screen of my drawings. I tick off the things I have yet to gather. Pillows. Wire. Scans of my work.

'Espresso?' The waitress sets the cup and saucer down.

'Thank you,' I say, trying not to meet her eye.

The waitress's hand lingers on the Queen of Spades. 'Can I ask you something?'

No. Please leave. 'Sure.'

She slips into the opposite seat. Today she is wearing the *Yodelicious flannel shirt ($44.95)* and the *Kitchen Whisk pendant ($30)*. A few stray hairs have escaped her bun and frame her pale face, or perhaps she left them out of her bun on purpose.

She smoothes her apron over her skirt. 'How can you be sure,' she says, 'that you're the autosite?'

She looks different to when I last saw her, as if she's been injected with something that makes her eyes glossier, of a higher resolution. 'I beg your pardon?' I ask.

'When's your birthday?'

'What—'

'November 30,' she says. '1989.'

I drop my gaze. She doesn't have a name badge. I have never been a waitress, but I am very certain that this is not part of the waitress protocol.

'That's my birthday too, even the year,' she adds.

The long black steams silently. It's the only thing that's moving.

'Your name is Ursula Rodriguez, right?'

She waits for me to respond. I wonder if it would be rude to take out my phone at this moment and text Penny—*waitress is being rly spooky thx for being late!!!!!!*

'Yes.'

She nods. Her eyes become distant. It's as if she's a plane switched to autopilot while the captains swap places. I slip my fingers through the handle of the coffee cup, but I am not able to lift it.

'It's not a coincidence that we've met,' the waitress says.

'You mean, because you've been stalking me?'

'No.'

'Then what?'

She's still got that autopilot look in her eyes. 'I have something you want.'

'What's that?'

She reaches into her apron pocket and pulls out a slip of paper. She places it face-down on the table and slides it across to me.

My phone starts ringing, like a warning, as if some tender wire has been tripped within my borders.

I untangle my fingers from the coffee cup. I turn over the paper.

A color photocopy of a newspaper article.

Two pairs of eyes, tightly shut. Sticky like the wings of a butterfly crawling free of a chrysalis.

A knot of pink newborn limbs.

An unbroken fusion of skin. So whole as to not even register as a connection between two beings. Like the webbing between forefinger and thumb. Continuous.

Swollen with life.

Such ripe, new skin.

I flip the paper over and slam it down on the table. 'What the *fuck*?' The couple at the next table stare at me. The phone still rings and rings. All of a sudden the waitress looks blank, as if consciousness has abandoned her. I can almost perceive her turning gray, receding from the foreground.

The phone's ring becomes elongated, more shrill than reality. All the world's surfaces are ringing, hard and bright—my hands on the table's edge, the chair screeching across the hardwood floor, the fall of my footsteps, the bell on the café door.

The outside world, exploding with sunlight.

Penny hands me a mug of Earl Grey. 'We can call up and make a complaint,' she says, wielding her new Seed.fon, as if to demonstrate that she is adept at confronting businesses about their faults.

My hands are shaking. The journey home was excruciating. Suddenly everyone I saw was a spy, with their angled hats and oversized newspapers; every gesture was a signal, every glance was knowing. It is only now, in my own house, that I can tell Penny what went down in Cellar Door.

'Inappropriate!' Penny proclaims. 'It was inappropriate from the moment she sat down with you! Ugh. I'm so sorry I was late.'

She hasn't addressed the part about the newspaper clipping. Not one word about it. I curl my hands around the mug and wait. It's like when you're a child and you're crying about something and the adult comforting you is trying to guess what you're upset about, and frustration rises in your blood because they're not getting at what you actually want to talk about.

'What are you going to do, Ursula? Ugh. I never want to set foot in Cellar Door again. I can't *believe* that waitress, freaking you out like that.'

Close enough. 'How did she have it?' I ask, loud and wooden, like I'm performing in a play. 'Why would she want me to know that she knows about my past?'

'Do you want me to go back for you? Or we can go back together, when you're feeling up to it? She said she had the same birthday as you, as if that's meant to explain something, but it still doesn't make sense. Just makes it more creepy, like she's been obsessed with you her entire life. That's if she even *has* the same birthday as you. She could've made it up.'

'I don't want to go back there.' I know what will happen. We'll get to Cellar Door, all ready for a confrontation, only to discover that the waitress has moved on. Skipped town. She didn't even have a name badge.

Or we'll get there and Cellar Door won't even exist—instead there will be, in its place, an abandoned hardware store, dusty gray windows, crushed light bulbs. The scowling passers-by will say that the place has been empty for years, whaddya talking about, Cellar Door?

If only I hadn't fled. But then I remember those fat pink limbs, those raw eyelids. Inflating violently across my inner gaze like a billboard for the United Colors of Benetton.

Rsu, I remind myself, *you call her Rsu*. Not just a tumor of flesh.

But isn't that a kind of arrogance, I wonder. To call her Rsu. To not give her a name separate from my own.

I take a trembling sip of the Earl Grey.

'Well then, what are we going to do?' Penny asks. 'We can't just—I don't know—let this *go*...'

I imagine myself reaching out and twisting a knob on Penny's abdomen until she powers off, like an old television, a slow fade and then click—off. Do those things even exist anymore? Things with dials instead of buttons? Instead of smooth glass interfaces?

Later, when the sky has darkened, I drive Penny to her house. When I arrive home I sit in the car with the lights turned off and the stereo on. I let Tim Spiegel's voice surround me, warm as liquor amnii, and I wonder if this is what being born is like—sitting in a car in your own driveway, a home waiting, prepared just for you. Summoning the courage to slide the key from the ignition, to open the door. To lift yourself up. To break the seal between yourself and the world.

I slip my phone out and dial the number for Seed tech support. I stay on the line, pressing five—Tim Spiegel in the car stereo, Tim Spiegel in my ear, echoing and echoing, until my credit runs out.

The installation is almost complete. I sit inside my tunnel of blankets, the fabric expanding and contracting in the air-conditioning. Far off, the projector clicks through my ink drawings. A warm yellow light at the end of the tunnel.

The fabric heaves gently. I crawl out of the tunnel and stand at the entrance as a spectator would. I stare at the ambiguous clicking light. I feel all at once the uncertainty of a thousand adolescent fairytale protagonists. A child carrying a basket for her grandmother. An orphan searching for a vanished trail of breadcrumbs. They all must enter the forest. It is always what stands between them and some crucial understanding. A metamorphosis.

Somewhere behind me, I know that Penny's half-complete mobile is swaying soundlessly. Hovering rods and beams. Like scaffolds for magical creatures—aids in their child-swapping operations, their changeling economy. On another floor of the gallery, an artist is assembling a series of glass vessels; another artist, a sound installation. I am the only one in this space right now. Opening night is in two weeks.

I crawl back through the tunnel and switch off the projector. In the darkness I wait for some feeling to come, but the enchantment is over. There is no magic.

Later, outside the gallery, the giant television screen in the Cultural Centre casts a pale fluorescent light. People tip their faces towards it, glowing like mushrooms. The sound from the television is large, unreal: the reverberating voice of your conscience. I zip up my hoodie. There is a couple walking diagonally across the amphitheater space, in perfect synchrony, like they are riding a sociable. The boy part of the sociable is looking at me. As I pass them, he says, 'Ursula.'

At first he appears to be a stranger—I wonder if he's a spy for the waitress—but then the light from the television changes and it's Graeme, my fellow Ampersand ambassador. Graeme in real life.

'Oh hey.' We do the shuffle two passing acquaintances who aren't sure whether to stop and chat or keep walking do. We decide to stop. 'How are you, Graeme?' I ask.

'Good thanks, and yourself? This is Natalie, by the way.' Indicating his partner. 'Natalie, this is—'

'—your comrade!' Natalie exclaims. She has very red lips. 'Sorry, Ursula, it's a joke we have. Some of the shots from the last catalogue—you two look like you're soldiers in some kind of hipster army. The way they match up your outfits and all that, like a uniform. Kind of creepy.'

'Yeah, I guess it's a bit like that. I'm glad we're not matching tonight, Graeme.' In fact it is Graeme and Natalie who are matching tonight, with their just-showered neatness, their clean denim and cotton T-shirts.

'Where are you heading?' Graeme asks.

'Just home. I was at the gallery. Installing.'

'Ursula's an artist,' Graeme says to Natalie. He turns back to me. 'We're off to see a play.'

'Oh! I hope it's good.'

There seems to be little more to say after that. The sociable continues its journey to the theater and I continue mine through the Cultural Centre. The television says, *there are many undocumented creatures that dwell in the deepest depths of the sea.* It isn't Tim Spiegel's voice, but shouldn't it be? The Grimm audiobook, the Seed tech support hotline—there are always three things. The fairytales promise it.

The word BO, like many two-letter words, has multiple significations. It is a weapon which takes the form of a long staff, and it is also a fig tree. As a proper noun, Bo is the name of a minority population in Southern China, remembered by Wikipedia for only two things: one, being massacred by the Ming army; and two, their funeral tradition of making hanging coffins. Upon learning this last fact, I had imagined something like Penny's mobiles, coffins supported by strings and hooks, but in actuality the coffins are placed against cliff faces, resting horizontally on two rods protruding from the rock wall. Scattered along this uneven surface, the coffins are like irregular watchpeople, posted on invisible footholds, facing the sky. It is suggested that the hanging coffins prevent animals from stealing the bodies.

Despite seeing the pictures, I still think of those words, *hanging coffin*, like they signify some presence just outside perception, in the air behind my head, the dead watching the living.

It is the same night that I encounter Graeme in the Cultural Centre. In my silent bedroom, I open Chrome and type *Tim Spiegel* into the search bar, enclosed in quotation marks. Google delivers 16,000 results in 0.18 seconds. A Tim Spiegel on LinkedIn. A Tim Spiegel, MD. A Tim Spiegel on MySpace, Twitter, Facebook. Thousands of Tim Spiegels, jostling for individuality. But like a new mother on some TV drama, walking past a row of hospital cots each containing furrowed babies only a few days old, each a discrete uncomplicated unit, I know which one is mine: Tim Spiegel Voice Recordist, www.spiegelvoice.com.

It is a sparse website with a clean white background. The sans-serif type is a few shades short of black. There is a concise list of past work, but no audio samples, as if everyone who visits this website, like me, is already steeped in Tim Spiegel's voice. There are no external links, and the contact email, presented so as to avoid being picked up by spam crawlers, is tim AT spiegelvoice DOT com.

If fairytale things always arrive in threes, then I suppose it would be better to make the third thing come to me, instead of simply waiting for it to drop in my path.

I switch tabs and compose a new email:

Hello Tim Spiegel,

My name is Ursula Rodriguez. I am an artist who resides in Perth. In about two weeks, I will be exhibiting some of my work as part of a show called *30/30*. I have attached samples of my ink drawings, but my installation for *30/30* incorporates many other media. My art practice investigates fairytale literature and bodily integrity. This may sound very strange, but I seem to be encountering your voice very often recently—first on an audiobook of Grimm fairytales, and another time when my friend called tech support for her Seed.fon. I would really like to incorporate some sort of aural component into my installation, and I thought of you instantly. Perhaps a short reading of some kind, which could play while visitors interact with the space I have created. I understand this is incredibly vague (and also incredibly short notice), and I am not sure what your fees would be like for such a collaboration, but please let me know if this is something you would be interested in doing. Hope to hear from you soon, U

I attach five of my best drawings, enter tim@spiegelvoice.com in the address field and press send.

My phone rings. Penny. 'How'd install go? Sorry for not sticking around,' she says.

'That's okay. It's all going alright. There's something missing though. Still trying to figure out what it is. I'll probably be installing right up until the opening.'

'Oh don't worry, I've still got miles to go as well. How are you doing, anyway?' She doesn't mention the Cellar Door waitress, but we both know that's what she's referring to.

'I'm... okay.' I switch tabs to Tim Spiegel's website, that comforting sparseness. 'I don't really know what to say about it.'

'Are you sure you don't want to *do* something?'

'I'm not really sure about anything.'

Penny pauses. I wonder if she's going to try, again, to convince me to go back to Cellar Door to demand answers. I hold my breath. I press F5 on Tim's website, as if something would really change. I wonder whether I should tell Penny about my email to Tim. I almost feel guilty for withholding the truth from her. Some things are just hard to explain to Penny. I am always merely approximating something important. Like, right now, I wish I could explain to her how smugly the waitress had presented the newspaper picture to me. As if to say, *look what I own. Look what I know.* I want to tell Penny that some bodies are presumed to be more available for scrutiny than others. Half bodies. Brown bodies. I want to ask Penny what exactly one can *do* about that.

'Well,' Penny says eventually, 'I know I've said this before, but I'm really sorry it happened. It's really messed up. Just let me know if you ever want to do something about it.'

'Okay.' Somehow those two syllables, O and K, seem to carry so much resignation, an unfair weight. 'Okay. Thanks Penny.'

Like an animal shifting in the bushes, the tab for Gmail reports (1) new email. I switch over.

me, Tim Spiegel (2)

Suddenly it is very cold.

'Take care, hon.' Penny hangs up.

I squeeze my eyes shut and open them again. Tim Spiegel. Only a few minutes after I sent my message to him.

An automated reply?

I hover the cursor over the email and depress the mouse button. Release it suddenly.

Hi Ursula,

I am also located in Perth. I have looked at your art. Please send me a manuscript of what you would like me to record, and I will see what I can do.

Best regards,
Tim Spiegel

> *I am also located in Perth.*
> *I have looked at your art.*
> *I will see what I can do.*

My skin prickles with that warm-cold sensation that is almost like love. A concise message, but not an unkind one. I clasp my hands in my lap. I read the message again, which is short enough to take in all at once, like a painting or a haiku. He doesn't say how much he'd charge, or whether he's definitely on board. Or even if he liked my drawings. But he signed off with *Best regards*—not just *Regards* —and this little fact is enough to make me hopeful.

I'm about to start assembling a manuscript for Tim when Gmail refreshes itself. A new email appears above Tim's. 30111989@ouvert.net, no subject line.

I tick the checkbox and move the cursor to the trash can button. But then I look at the address again: 30111989@ouvert. net.

30111989.

30 November 1989?

I open the email.

Hello: Ursula
We are real
Watch out for Seed
Beautiful day
30111989

I am writing to you from the future, but from my particular position I understand that there is no 'future' as such. It's just a way of organizing time, like dropping buoys into the ocean. Now I am plunging my hand into the green bag of tiles; now I am running away from Cellar Door. Now I am being born; now I am born again. Now I am the embodiment of Ampersand's core values; now my body is unsponsored, unincorporated. Now I am inking a woman's eyes; now I am within the camera's eye. Lift your chin a little. Hint at a smile. *S'asseoir. Manger. Boire.* Now I discover the meanings of two- and three-letter words, many classed as *obsolete*, unuttered out of existence. Now I add and multiply; now I carry the one; now I pencil in the final scores. Now the zygote divides. Now something peculiar occurs. A secret arithmetic. A glitch in the matrix.

I haven't been entirely rigorous. I'm sorry about that. Sometimes, even when the event is over, it doesn't feel like any time has passed, and nothing loses its puzzling glow.

I am sitting in my bedroom. I am cutting excerpts from fairytale books and stringing the sentences together. This will be the manuscript that I will send to Tim Spiegel. I've also taken the Grimm fairytale audiobook from the car and I'm playing it on my computer. Right now Tim Spiegel is telling the story of *The Elves and the Shoemaker.*

As I sit here assembling my fairytale clippings, I know: I look fucking crazy. The waitress at Cellar Door confronted me with a newspaper article and my date of birth, but how is it any less creepy that I'm listening to Tim Spiegel narrating the elves' song about making the shoemaker rich as I hack sentences from fairytale books, or that I burned through $15 of credit listening to Tim Spiegel talk about tech support options for products I don't even own, or that all the time my ears are waiting—in queues and elevators and department stores—for that melodic voice? As if it has anything to do with anything. As if Tim has any relation to Rsu, to the Cellar Door waitress, to any of the current weirdness.

The Elves and the Shoemaker is the last story on the audiobook. Whenever we are listening to this in the car, Penny or I will skip the CD back to the beginning. I nudge the mouse so that the desktop jumps out of screensaver. The needle in Windows Media Player is at 5:34, but the total length of this track is 29:32.

A secret track? Does Penny know about this?

I slide the needle along, catching slices of white noise. The hidden track begins at 29:01.

In the current crisis,
our situation
will utterly transform.

Reality is a stand-alone document;
there can be no true maps.
When you weigh up all the benefits,
the document is relatively worthless.
Rethink your monuments,
your map-making instruments.
The sky is a tender vacuum;
the compass turns the traveller.
Accept the unresolvable loss.
There is no better way.
We regret that you no longer exist.
Kindly
surrender.

The track runs out; Windows Media Player falls dormant. I reach for the CD case and flip through the booklet, but it wouldn't be much of a secret track if it was credited in the liner notes. Track thirteen is labelled *The Elves and the Shoemaker* and nothing else.

I pull the needle back and listen to the secret track again.

We regret that you no longer exist.

It certainly doesn't sound like anything the Brothers Grimm would write. I open Chrome and plug phrases from the recording into Google, but nothing useful arrives. None of the Amazon reviews of the audiobook mention the hidden track.

Gmail reports one new email. 30111989@ouvert.net again.

Hello: Ursula
You are the portal
We are real
Get ready for the kick
Beautiful day
30111989

And I just want to scream at the universe, STOP IT, JUST STOP IT, stop piling on the mysteries, stop assaulting me with clues—and Tim Spiegel tells me to *kindly surrender*, and Gmail reports one new email, and Google returns zero search results, and Penny sends me a text, and the banner ad in Gmail says *Save 15% on Ampersand Clothing And Accessories Click Here To Find Out More*, and the green Scrabble bag delivers a lousy hand, seven tiles, 1 1 1 1 1 1 1.

This is the last time that I see the waitress from Cellar Door. She is rollerskating in the Cultural Centre, doing laps around the amphitheater as I exit the gallery, zip up my hoodie, let my eyes adjust to the giant television's light. It's hard to tell, but I believe the waitress is wearing the *Seduce the Auditor button-up shirt ($49.95)*, *Darling Assassin shorts ($33.95)* and *Tricycle Tricycle You Are My Tricycle tights ($29.95)*.

Just a few hours prior, Penny had come over to my installation and observed its growing scope. It's as if the tunnel is actually a wormhole to another realm, expanding into new territory. She watched me crawl through the tunnel setting up the audio equipment, connecting this wire with that wire, but she didn't ask what it was for. Her mobile was as magnificent and frightening as ever, like a creature that my wormhole had brought from the other side. An undocumented creature.

And now, I watch the waitress's hypnotic circles, the buckles on her rollerskates flashing—what is she doing here? Does she know I am watching her? I study the faces of the others in the amphitheater, their faces tipped towards the television, but there is nobody else familiar—no Graeme this time, no Natalie. Just the waitress, circling. Her arc diminishing. Until she coasts to a stop in front of me.

'Hi Ursula,' she says. The rollerskates make her taller than me. Her cheeks are gently flushed, but she is not out of breath.

'I don't know your name,' I say.

'It's not important,' she says.

'It's unfair that you know mine.'

'There's a poignant asymmetry to it, isn't there.'

I pause. 'I suppose you can call it that. Asymmetry.'

She doesn't say anything after that. Now that she is up close, I see she is also wearing the *Ace of Spades pin badge ($22)* on the cuff of her shirt sleeve. A not-so-subtle pun.

'Have you been sending me emails?'

She blinks. 'Emails?'

'Yes.'

Her eyes trawl the Cultural Centre. 'I suppose it's possible that my employer has tried to contact you in other ways, but it's not me who's responsible. My task is complete already.'

'Your task was to show me the newspaper clipping of my sister and me?'

'Yes.'

'Were you really born on the same day as me?'

'Yes.'

The light of the television swirls. There is flute music, the kind that you can only associate with television because it doesn't sound like a real flute, as if the notes have been reconstituted somehow, like boxed juice.

'It's unimportant though,' the waitress says. 'I said it only to supply a plausible reason why I might have had the newspaper article. It's not unusual for parents to keep the newspaper on the day their child was born.'

'I guess.'

'I didn't need the excuse anyway.'

'I see.'

The faces of the spectators turn pink, then blue, then green.

I ask, 'Who is your employer?'

'Guess.'

'Is it Seed?'

'Perhaps.'

'What do you have to gain from keeping it a secret?'

'Who is Seed, really? What is Seed? Is it possible for a corporation to possess consciousness? To possess a will? To *want*?'

'Are you or are you not employed by Seed?'

'I am only pointing out that it is a philosophically difficult question.'

'What do they want with me?'

She studies me, as if she is trying to figure out the brand labels of my clothes. 'They want you for what you do best.'

'And what's that?'

'Creating. Repurposing. You know what they say. You've got that extra little something.'

'But how is intimidating and harassing me meant to convince me to do anything? I don't want anything to do with it, whatever *it* is. I want to be left alone.'

'I see.' Her face is so serene. I imagine that if this conversation was taking place on television—a show like *Lost*, where there is mystery upon mystery, knowing glances, pregnant silences, shadowy cashed-up puppetmaster figures—I would be screaming, *ask more questions!* But I can tell you, in the moment of meeting somebody who knows more than you, the questions don't occur. It's like the totality of your ignorance approaches the sublime. There can be no true maps.

The waitress says, 'We probably won't see each other again.'

'I'd be okay with that.'

She nods. She rolls back a few inches. I wonder if she will disappear, pixel by pixel. Reappear somewhere else in the city with a new face, new directive. I slide my hands into the pockets of my hoodie. A voice in my head says *Walk*, so I walk. As I reach the amphitheater steps I hear the sound of her wheels rolling over the bricks again. Those relentless, infinite loops.

What I like about the word OVA, apart from being an easy way to dispose of a V during endgame, is that it's one of those plural forms that uses fewer letters than the word it pluralizes. In some ways it does an even better job than the singular at conveying what it represents: more compact, almost symmetrical. It's another reminder, however small, that language is arbitrary. It isn't important to know what the words I lay down on the Scrabble board mean, just that they mean *something*, or *meant* something.

Words are all I have right now, though. That's the paradox. They don't bear any actual relation to what they represent, but they're the only tools you have to make sense of existence. And words are okay, for the simple things—when the plainest stimuli pass through me, are turned into code, are understood. But sometimes there is an error in the translation; the stimuli are too overwhelming or ambiguous.

Like Tim Spiegel quietly supplying the recordings I requested, his painfully succinct emails that ask no questions and resist questioning. Like the waitress and her revolving uniform of Ampersand clothing. Like 30111989@ouvert.net, to whom I wrote my first email last night:

Hello. We are real. Do you want to talk to me?

Sometimes when I'm installing, it feels like the gallery is the entire world. If it were possible to exit the gallery, the outside would just be black space, unformed and uncreated. I sit inside my tunnel, making this adjustment and that adjustment. Perhaps I am trying to recreate some prior universe, a home to which I can never return.

'Ursula.'

I apologize again for not being rigorous. For the failures of this record. My map-making instruments will always be deficient. Reality is a stand-alone document.

'Ursula,' Penny says, bending down to look at me through the tunnel, so that the tear along the right knee of her jeans opens like an expectant mouth. 'Is everything okay?' She takes a hunchbacked step inside the tunnel. 'It's looking good in here.'

'Thank you,' I say, falling silent for a little while, pretending I am an ovum, or ova. Full of potential. Singular, plural. Like ill-fitting clothing, language slides around our bodies, and our bodies slide around our selves, and our selves slide over and around and into each other.

Penny still hovers. 'Can I come in?'

'Yes, please come in. I'm about to press play.'

'What's going to play?'

'You'll find out.'

Penny crawls inside the tunnel. There is enough room for us to lie down side by side. I take her hand, which is small and warm, and with my other hand I press play on the stereo concealed between two quilts.

The tunnel fills up with that blank sound of digital air. Far off, the projector clicks through my drawings, like a brain in a dead body, casting a slideshow of memories long after the audience has gone. When Tim's voice begins, Penny's hand tightens, and I too feel as if my heart is rising in my chest, pushing up against my skin, as far as the branches will let it. The cords, the bones—whatever it is that insists on the unity of these parts, the weak circle drawn around the collection of matter christened with the provisional signifier *Ursula*. I accept the unresolvable loss—there is no better way—and the tunnel heaves like the ocean, and the letters slide back into the green bag, and it all keeps on going, and going, and going.

Coca-Cola Birds Sing Sweetest in the Morning

But Audrey is partial to the Panasonic birds, a cheaper but no less handsome variety; they acknowledge the dawn without extravagance, *pip pip pip pip pip*, little notes of fixed widths, such deft even spacing. They are not meant to be here, in the city; Audrey suspects they have migrated from Russet Hill, a network over a hundred kilometers away, renowned for wildflowers. The birds have a talent for evasion, as Audrey has never seen them at the reassignment plant; just as well, perhaps, for to crack open such a tender body, to see the inert parts that produce the sound of her dawn—it would surely be an act of violence. Audrey slips into the morning—or perhaps the morning slips into her, like a suggestion, *pip pip pip pip pip*—opens her eyes to a crisp blue sky, so bleeding-edged in its clarity. It is the kind of sky that reminds her that she was once loved.

The traffic is not so loud that she can't discern the Citrus Man cycling down the street, the clicks of his wheels, the brittle music-box tune that pings from his gramophone. That old song—*oranges and lemons say the bells of St Clement's*. She has never purchased fruit from the Citrus Man, but, as with so many things in this city, she cannot help but have affection for his presence, a belief in his importance—that not one part of this city is dispensable, not him, not the birds, not her, as she slides her legs into her overalls, fills the kettle with water, scoops black tea leaves from a battered tin.

Gently caffeinated, Audrey turns the locks of her apartment, exits briskly to the streets with their striped and creaking awnings, passes the buoyant results of the stock exchange. A man punches a code into an automatic teller machine, removes the bright bills; a publican overturns barstools. Audrey can still hear the Citrus Man's music box, camouflaged now by the eight-fifteen tram, the Coca-Cola birds, the queues shuffling through the bureaus and banks and offices, the shop bells ringing with their first customers of the day.

At the reassignment plant she punches her card and crosses the first floor, where workers disassemble birds and insects and amphibians so that the parts can be reassigned; they clean the cogs, bolts, circuits, screws; they sort them according to grade and size. No part is ever judged unfit to be repurposed. Someday the parts will be reincorporated into new wholes, inserted into new networks, sponsored by a different corporation; maybe the Panasonic birds to whom Audrey listens so keenly in the morning contain parts that once belonged to Coca-Cola birds.

Audrey ascends to the second floor, where mechanics like her collect their day's allotment in closed wooden boxes. Before the animals are sent to the first floor for disassembly they are delivered here, their last chance to be repaired and reintegrated into their network. Mechanics receive a commission for each animal restored, though Audrey believes there is some extra reward in clipping the parts together, resetting the animal; some satisfaction to know that it thrives in some distant network once again conveying pollen, regurgitating nectar, lubricating soil.

But today Audrey opens her wooden box and finds it empty. She checks that it is indeed her box—#9300730/AUDREY KWAI says the label—and opens the lid again. A cold memory revives itself. But then Cornelius the second-floor supervisor leans out of his office, his spectacles already lit with dust: *Ah yes, Audrey—the return machine on Cambridge is out of order. Mind taking a look?*

She did not always work at the reassignment plant: in another life she repaired ticket machines, all kinds, but mostly the ones at train stations, their buttons polished smooth by generations of hurried fingertips. She used to wonder if commuters appreciated the sound of a coin rolling through the slot, the rich clunks as it navigated the machine. A crisp new ticket, an unrepeatable date and time. In this other life, Audrey was a collector of tickets, everything from the theater pass to *Le Sacre du printemps*, hole-punched by an indifferent usher, to the forked slip she pulled at the delicatessen counter, number 25. She liked transport tickets the best: their sharp corners, inkjet smell. Typeface optimized for legibility; understood by tourists, locals, ticket inspectors.

It is because of this past life that Audrey now arrives at Cambridge Street with her toolbox. She has a letter of authorisation from Cornelius, but Audrey thinks she is unlikely to be questioned: a school, a church and silent apartments are all that comprise this corner of the city. Audrey has borrowed a broken Cadbury frog from the reassignment plant to test the machine: when she places the frog in the slot, the machine does not accept it; no numbers click the scales, no coins tumble from the chute.

Audrey pockets the frog. She loosens screws, opens the face of the machine, observes the maintenance sticker that says that the machine was inspected and emptied one month ago. A clutter of animals and animal parts has accumulated like irregular confectionery, not enough to cause a malfunction; nonetheless, Audrey unfolds a basket and empties the shaft.

Return machines are not at all like ticket machines—they are reverse vendors, the recipient of goods in the user–machine transaction, complicating the axis of trust. When Audrey repaired ticket machines, it was not uncommon for her to discover one or two counterfeit coins among the legitimate tender—*slugs*, they're called. Though ticket machines are adept at recognizing slugs, swallowing the counterfeit and refusing to dispense a ticket, over her career Audrey had amassed a sizeable collection of slugs in her toolbox, some nothing more than crude washers, others with an astonishing resemblance to their authentic counterpart, down to the grooves on the circumference. Sometimes, when Audrey is tasked with repairing an actual slug at the reassignment plant, she remembers that other kind of slug, the slippery connotations of both.

There is a sound coming from Audrey's basket, the slightest articulated tremors, *rrrp, rrrp*. Audrey carefully shifts dislocated heads and abdomens to find the source: a bee, legs flailing as if riding an upside-down bicycle, too small for Audrey to determine the sponsor. She supposes it belonged to a park in the city, for bees cannot fly far. She wonders how long it has been inside the machine, kicking and kicking. She extracts a pin from her toolbox, flips her magnifier over her eye. Inserts the pin inside the bee to deactivate it.

Her mechanic's eye is always drawn to the most whole animals, hypothesising causes of malfunction, possible solutions. The sky is still blue, the street is still silent; somewhere in the city the Citrus Man still cycles, and Audrey's most significant days are those that begin like this one, without portent, glowing with the kind of ordinariness on which she leans entirely. But today, as her eyes fall upon the bird in the basket, as she lifts it from the pile, something in the universe pivots quietly, creaks imperceptibly, like the wheels turning in a cassette tape.

She has not seen this bird before. Her first suspicion is that it is, at long last, a Panasonic bird, but as she turns the body in her hands, she knows this is incorrect. She twists her magnifier and searches for the sponsor name—birds, the largest and most recognizable animals, *always* have a major sponsor—but there is no identification.

She turns the bird. No facet of its design suggests a manufacturer. Without opening the body she cannot ascertain what the bird's network purpose was—to disperse seed, pollen; to monitor, to sing. Ten minutes pass before she realizes that the bird has no activation pinhole.

Across the road, the school siren rings. Audrey looks up at the gaping machine, for a moment lost in its very insideness—the belts, pinions, coils. Bolted to the machine's exterior is a sign that reminds citizens that it is a criminal offence to vandalize or steal from a return machine, and in the manner of the train tickets she once collected so attentively, the sign is typeset plainly in capital letters, to be understood by tourists, locals, machine inspectors.

Still, it has to happen, on this empty street, on this unremarkable day—Audrey turns the bird a final time, wraps it in a handkerchief, and pushes it deep within her pocket.

Nobody knows what compels the animals to migrate, but also, nobody knows, *truly* knows, what it was that caused the original crisis. A disaster of first nature. The day that bees were falling out of the sky, as if suddenly turned flightless. Is it a real memory of Audrey's—an infant at the time—this image of bees twitching on the ground in their thousands, their brittle, feeble buzzing, or did Audrey absorb the image much later from a schoolbook? Or is it, perhaps, that this is the memory passed down, made true through its insistent reproduction, a cultural heirloom?

Or could it be that, since the day Audrey threw out her ticket collection—save one, a faded ticket for the river ferry, softened at the edges—something had happened to Audrey's memory itself, a quiet transformation, heaving weakly to accommodate a vast and unimaginable trauma?

At home, after work, Audrey snaps on her desk lamp and unwraps the bird. It is not an ugly bird, but it resists comparison to the birds she fixes at the reassignment plant. As if someone studied a bird and replicated it from memory, with none of the inferiority one associates with replication; as if 'bird' was just a reference point, a figure from a dream.

Audrey angles the lamp, probes the exterior until she detects an interruption. The right tool and the body yields, halves asymmetrically, intimate as a dollhouse; there is something endearing about it, this private arrangement of parts. They all fit together, in an inexact way. Some of the connections are tenuous, and in fact Audrey sees that the bird is inoperable not because of a single fault but a number of parts that have worn away as a result of their imperfect tessellation. She cannot, still, discern the bird's purpose.

There are hobbyists, she knows, who assemble animals, though the Department of Second Nature prohibits their activation in public. While this bird might well be a hobbyist's work, Audrey finds the premise unconvincing: something in the humbleness of the arrangement, the absence of an activation pinhole. Audrey unearths a yellowed pad of graph paper and a pencil, transposes the bird onto these squares, numbering the parts; tenderly, she dismantles the bird and soaks the pieces in white vinegar. Across the night, through her quiet window, it is time for stray frogs to open their throats. Samsung, Toshiba, Cadbury: their creaking dialogue, all the tongues of industry.

Again, the Panasonic birds; again, the Citrus Man; again, the reassignment plant; this time, Audrey's wooden box contains a series of silkworms. All morning she has replaced spools, tested salivary glands; at ten o'clock Cornelius approaches her workbench, asks if she might know why the weight of the animal parts did not match the reading on the return machine from yesterday. *A discrepancy of about sixty grams*, he says; she responds that the scales had malfunctioned, and as Cornelius nods, scribes on his clipboard, she admires the ease of the lie, gliding like a gear with oiled teeth. She returns to her silkworms, sends the inoperables down the chute.

The diagram of the bird is folded in her bib pocket. During break time she studies it in a restroom cubicle, commits the dimensions of the required parts to memory, returns to the plant floor and slips candidates into her pocket. Yesterday's chill of opening her empty wooden box still hovers—somewhere, a ticket machine explodes quietly, not so deep in the past that its reverberations can't disturb the present.

After the silkworms, a wasp. After the wasp, a moth. Through the window, the sky is an imitation of yesterday's, an unsatisfactory facsimile, like a perfume sample in a magazine.

How distant, that blue sky—how faintly persistent—under which Audrey once stood, holding a boy's hand on the river ferry. The world was bright and forgiving then; time was worth marking with tickets. She remembers how the dragonflies floated like helicopters, kissed the reeds at right-angles. That day, she didn't know that those particular reeds are pollinated by the wind, not by insects, so the dragonflies must have migrated from another network; but, whatever their origin, they were witnesses to her short-lived good fortune; she was, to someone's eye, indispensable.

She can still detect it, that facsimiled sky—turning mauve now—as she walks home from the reassignment plant, rotating a stolen cog in her pocket. The diagram of the bird creases against her chest every time she breathes. Cornelius had smiled at her as she clocked out and it pains her, his simple trust, the papercut sting of it.

She is relieved when the sky exhausts its color, and the ferry is small on her memory's horizon.

She notices then, as she rounds the last street corner, the broken window of her apartment, a single decisive puncture; at first she thinks it is a trick of the light, ghostly as an autostereogram, but it refuses to be blinked away. Audrey grips the cog in her pocket, slides it onto her index finger. She climbs the stairs two at a time. Her arrival takes forever.

Turning the locks, bursting over the threshold, to her desk—the toppled beaker of vinegar, rocking in the intruding breeze. Shipwrecked on the liquid surface: two bolts, a screw, a pair of tweezers. Parts have been dragged through the spilled vinegar, spiking the puddle's edges; she can even perceive a trail of pronged footprints, determined as arrows. And the bird, which she had left open on the bench, is gone.

Audrey's hand moves over her heart, to her bib pocket, expecting the diagram, too, to have vanished; she flounders to extract it, confirms: the bird was *here*—then scrunches this tangible memory along the wrong folds, clutches it to her chest like a mourner's handkerchief, while the cold afternoon hurtles through the window's wound.

Before he left, he had the nerve to ask her to exchange some notes for coins, so he could purchase a train ticket to the city where the other woman lived. A thorn which sank deep, piercing some vindictive vein Audrey did not realize she possessed. She performed this favor anyway, and on that last morning handed him a zip-lock bag of coins, buffed to a deceptive shine: slugs, all of them.

It was not meant to have consequences, this feeble revenge; she supposed it would take not more than two attempts before he realized. When the slug rolled through the slot nothing was meant to happen, absolutely nothing, but it was as if the machine was animated by her indignity, summoned to act beyond its regular function; the explosion sent unprinted tickets pummelling through the air, coins flashing—that's what the witnesses remembered the most, coins strewn like dying bees, although Audrey also heard about the young man thrown off his feet, the blast propelling, with malevolent accuracy, a slug into his temple, which remains lodged in his skull to this day.

The investigation labelled the event a freak accident, but she resigned all the same, fearing the inevitable day when she'd be cut loose; it was her but it wasn't *her*, ticket machines are not created to explode. But Audrey wonders if machines are themselves part of Second Nature, if they are categorically the same as the birds and insects that toil away in their networks—all of them lively, willful, migrating out of turn; enacting, in their quiet malfunctions, an unauthorized evolution.

Sometimes, Audrey gets this notion that there is nothing outside the city, no farms, no fields, no vast harmonious networks. In this vision, the animals that the mechanics repair and ship out of the city are all redirected to one factory, where an assembly line opens the animals, roughens the parts, ships them back; some parts will be scattered in parks and thoroughfares for unwitting citizens to pick up, redeem for coins at return machines; and the only real things would be the sponsors, the benefactors of this operation, while the stock exchange results would be algorithmic fabrications of the Department of Second Nature. But then Audrey thinks: where does the honey come from, the fresh flowers, the vegetables and fruit—and the vision disappears, but not wholly, like a prop in a magician's trick hiding beneath the table. It is comforting, the stage of the magic show, the curtain, the dense tablecloth; it reassures the audience that there is some concealed thing making the trick work, something rational; this is, after all, the real world.

Audrey awakens on this new morning, roused not by the Coca-Cola birds nor the Panasonic birds, but by the whistling of the broken window, a disruption to her routine waking. She listens for the Panasonic birds, registers their *pip pip pip pip pip* with the scantest relief; listens evermore keenly now, desiring the city's wholeness—there, the Citrus Man, *oranges and lemons say the bells of St Clement's.* The air is still soured by vinegar; she has not swept the glass, and for all her expertise Audrey cannot discern whether the hole was made by something exiting or entering. She had fallen asleep with the lamp on, and her fingers still grasp two things: one, her river ferry ticket, her last mark of time; two, the pencil diagram, the vanished bird.

Pip pip pip pip pip—Audrey, overwhelmed by the liveliness of objects, holds the ticket to the light, against yet another crisp sky, relentlessly blue. Sometimes it seems that everything in this city conspires to remind her of her impermanence and obsolescence, from the blue sky to this smallest ticket, inkjet fragrant, words still legible despite the intervening years—it's some kind of amazing, the things that outlast us.

This Page Has Been Left Blank Intentionally

Lorem ipsum dolor sit amet, consectetur adipiscing elit. Fuck shit fuck shit etaoin shrdlu. The quick brown fox jumps over the lazy dog, a bright vixen, a vexed nymph blitz. How many wankers does it take to change a light bulb? It doesn't matter, they're only screwing themselves. How many wankers does it take to run a magazine? It doesn't matter, they're all procrastinating. Label one en rule, one em rule, and one hyphen in the following sentence: *'Oh, but I couldn't—' but then she was cut off by Shirley – a most up-to-date girl, sweet hairdo, shocking lips – and the whole thing went sideways*. In order to make tomorrow better, make today shit. A widow is a paragraph ending that is stranded at the top of a column, and an orphan is a paragraph opening that dangles from the bottom of a column. They can create the impression of an excess of white space. Do your best to avoid them. Arch is a chief editor exiting, stranded in a decision-making desert, dangling off the edge of uncertainty. She can create the impression of filler text. Lorem ipsum sit amet, consectetur adipiscing elit. This page has been left blank intentionally.

On this evening they're carpooling, cruising on the Kwinana alongside a near-empty train, panoptically lit, gray plastic handholds swinging like manacles. Swan River odor permeates the passenger-side window even when it's closed. Arch glances up from the wheel to another electronic sign hanging over the freeway, blurting all-caps advice about seatbelts, motorcycles, and lane-changing courtesy.

Chris says, 'What the hell was up with Stace today, anyway? I think she has major trust issues.'

'What? No. She's just shy.'

'It's so hard to do stuff when she's looking over your shoulder, hawk-eyeing for errors.'

'Well, don't hate on her. She's the best we've got. She can tell the difference between a hyphen and an en dash from a zoom of forty percent.'

'It was just a flyer.'

'If there's a single error in anything, she feels like it's on her. And, well, it's kind of on you, too.'

'Yeah, I know. She's just watching my back. Professionalism, whatever. And who's Jules Valentine?'

'What?'

Somehow, without having made a sound, Chris has taken out his Seed.fon. He sweeps his thumb down an email. 'Jules Valentine. Sent an email to us a few hours ago. Says she has some info that might help *Lorem Ipsum* with a story.'

'About what?'

'Doesn't say. There's an attachment.'

'I'll look at it when I get home.'

'Good, because it's taking ages to load right now.' Chris pockets his phone.

They clear the bridge and coast down the slope to the Mitchell. Chris rolls down his window so that the wind beats through the gap, blaring like time travel. Behind them, the tiny lights of the City West dome flash their dated patterns, so sweetly obsolete.

Jules Valentine's attachment is a still frame from the very first Seed.fon ad, that viral marketing campaign that saw fragments of a movie scattered around the city in QR codes, that had all the nerds on the GibsonCalledIt hashtag clamoring in triumph. The sight of the falling girl—by now so relentlessly circulated, reproduced, memed into meaninglessness—injects Arch with a new dosage of apathy. It's not even the best screenshot, having none of the breathlessness of the most popular image of the falling girl, mid-flight, enormous. Arch is already composing a diplomatic let-down in her head. *Dear Jules, thank you for your interest in* Lorem Ipsum. *Unfortunately...*

Bloop.

Chris Riley is messaging you!

Chris Riley
look at that attachment yet?

Archna Desai
Yeah. I don't really know what to make of it.
I'm trying to think of a reply to her now.

Arch pinches the bridge of her nose. She has an essay due next week, a clutter of journal articles to read—but this one routine email, she knows, will somehow take the rest of the night. She gets up to make a cup of tea.

When she returns, her Facebook tab is flashing with something new from Chris.

Chris Riley
i wonder how she got hold of it

Arch frowns.

Archna Desai
What do you mean?

Chris Riley
well its not the same as the movie
like this shot doesnt occur in the actual falling girl movie

She tabs over to the JPEG again. Arch missed out on that whole falling girl collect-a-fragment thing when it happened a while back, actually, because she hadn't owned a smartphone yet. But she did receive one of those prank calls that played 'Little Waltz of the Telephones', the less well-received feature of Seed's campaign. Arch is familiar with the falling girl only through her copies, the endless afterexposure of her hype. But even Arch—who scarcely gave a shit about the whole phenomenon—can discern, now that Chris mentions it, a peculiar inauthenticity in the girl's pose. And yet it is undeniably *her*.

Archna Desai
So what are you thinking then, Chris?
We should meet Jules Valentine?

Those pixels emanating an aura of portent.

Chris Riley
im curious
so yes

Lorem ipsum dolor sit amet, consectetur adipiscing elit. This is what Arch does when she needs to clear up the thoughts in her head. It's easy—you just say to yourself: Lorem ipsum dolor sit amet, consectetur adipiscing elit... and then whatever comes next, until the columns of your mind fill up and you are the illusion of a full page. If you do it just right your eyes can skim over the whole of you and appreciate your form, your typeface, your kerning, without the distraction of having to read into things. You can confirm to yourself that as far as human beings go, you fullfil all the necessary functions. You can say whatever you like in the filler text, even facts that you already know. The most important thing is that you feel like a coherent human being at the end of it.

About *Lorem Ipsum: Lorem Ipsum* is a student magazine named after the nonsense faux-Latin placeholder text that designers often use to demonstrate the layout of a document. The magazine is a collaboration between majors in graphic design, writing, photography, and journalism. About Arch: Archna Desai is twenty-two years old and undertaking her final year of a double degree. She is the current chief editor of *Lorem Ipsum*. This will be Arch's last edition at the helm. A new chief editor is elected each year. Today Arch will be meeting Jules Valentine, a mysterious correspondent with a screenshot of falling girl footage. The tight scheduling and multidisciplinary pressure of *Lorem Ipsum* means that sometimes production occurs in reverse—designers create a layout and the writers match it with content. So with this Valentine interview, it's nice to be proceeding the way a publication actually should proceed. Lorem ipsum dolor sit amet, consectetur adipiscing elit. Everything in its right place.

Arch and Chris wait at a small bar on William Street, watching a four-wheel-drive attempt and re-attempt an ambitious parallel park. A faded notice painted into the pavement reminds pedestrians that there were once wetlands beneath this four-wheel-drive's uncertain pivoting wheel. Arch wonders what the city would be like if everything was labelled like that. This bar that she and Chris sit in, on the former site of an accountant's office, on the former site of a Chinese restaurant, on the former site of Mew's Swamp. Surfaces upon surfaces upon surfaces.

Jules Valentine is five minutes late. Chris is the one who chose this meeting place. The stools they sit on are actually stacks of old books lacquered together. The menu is clipped to one of those Sunshine children's books. It's the kind of menu that doesn't have dollar signs. *espresso 3.5. flat white/latte/macchiato 4. extra shot/decaf/soy .5.* The menu also spells out everything in lowercase, including the café's name and all proper nouns. 'When did this become a thing?' Arch says to Chris, tapping the letters on the menu.

'When did what become a thing?'

'Using all-lowercase. No caps. Especially in company logos. BP, Woodside. Woolworths. Bankwest.'

'Guess they hope to appear more friendly.'

'I mean, I know why they do it. I'm just trying to remember when exactly it became a thing that everyone did.'

Chris snorts. 'And not just e.e. cummings.'

'Yeah. When it became used as a twisted signifier of trust or something.'

Arch spins her dictaphone on the countertop. She considers the menu and wonders if she is prepared to part with 5.7 for a muffin.

The door swings open and a woman with copper hair and Ray-Ban Aviators steps in. She slides her sunglasses onto her head. Takes in the café with one sweep. Zeroes in on Arch and Chris.

'Jules?' Arch says, getting to her feet.

'Yes. Hi.' Extending a hand immediately. 'Archna Desai?'

'Yes—call me Arch. And this is Chris. He works with me on *Lorem Ipsum.*'

Chris says, 'Nice to meet you. I'm getting coffee. Coffee, everyone?' He's already walking backwards to the counter. 'Flat whites?'

A smile interrupts Jules's impassive face. A strangely bitter smile. 'Yes. A flat white would be great.'

Arch sits down, and observes Jules slip into her seat. That copper hair is a dye job. There's something weirdly familiar about Jules. Arch is trying to place it when Jules catches her staring. Arch smiles quickly. 'How did you hear about *Lorem Ipsum*? Do you study?'

Jules says, 'Actually, I graduated ages ago. My friend went to the same uni as you. Worked on *Lorem Ipsum*. She was chief editor for one year, I can't remember which. Before your time, I suspect.'

'Perhaps I know her. What's her name?'

'Elena. Elena Rubik.'

'Ah, okay. I've heard the name, but I don't think I know her.'

'She's dead.'

Shit. That's right. Arch isn't sure how to react with Jules watching her so closely for a reaction. 'I'm sorry for your loss,' Arch says.

Jules shrugs and drops her eyes. Then Chris returns, carrying their table number, a playing card mounted on a silver holder. Queen of Spades.

Arch regroups. She slides her dictaphone to the middle of the table. 'You don't mind, Jules?'

'No, of course not.'

'We're just going to have a casual conversation, but this'll help me jog my memory later. We won't publish anything without your approval.'

'That's fine.'

Chris flips back the cover of his Seed.tab. From the glossy darkness of the touchscreen, he retrieves the JPEG from Jules's email. Fuzzy with motion, inexpertly cropped. This particular unused incarnation of the falling girl.

Jules isn't touching her coffee. Her gaze is still stuck on the table. 'It's weird what becomes famous,' Arch says, to fill the silence. 'What sticks. How you can't remember where you first saw something, some iconic image, and it's as if you've always known it.' She glances at the JPEG. 'When something just appears in your memory, totally without origin, you believe whatever history Wikipedia invents for the thing. It's not like you can verify it yourself. I mean, what year was it when I saw the falling girl for the first time? I have to trust the historical narrative that it was late 2011, that I couldn't have known about the falling girl before 2011, and yet it's like I've got all these implanted memories of people using Seed gadgets, or of people Photoshopping the falling girl into whatever humorous circumstances they can imagine, way before 2011. Before it was even possible.'

Arch looks at Jules, who says, 'I know what you mean,' and nothing else. She's not being sarcastic or polite. It's as if it's just too much effort for her to be insincere. Arch replays the moment when Jules said her friend died, and wonders if she responded right.

'Anyway,' Arch says, gesturing to the JPEG, 'it was Chris who noticed, not me, that this screenshot you've given us doesn't occur in the falling girl movie from all the Seed ads.'

'That's right.'

'And I'm sure you're aware that Adrian Lorca, the maker of the falling girl film, has been missing since last year.'

'Yes.'

'And the starring actress of the film, Karen Hendricks, went missing way before that.'

'Yes.'

'And you rock up,' Chris finishes, 'with a screenshot from Adrian Lorca's unused footage of Karen Hendricks. To us. A low-circulation, low-budget amateur student magazine.'

'Right. Except for one thing.' Jules pokes Chris's Seed.tab. 'That's not Karen Hendricks.'

'Who is it?'

Jules slips a hand into her pocket. She places a metallic blue flash drive on the table. Arch feels like she's in some kind of David Lynch homage. All they need is an amnesiac and a handbag stuffed with cash.

Arch asks, 'What's on there?'

'A video file.' Jules slides it across to Chris. 'Watch it now, if you want.'

Chris flicks off the lid and slots the flash drive into the Seed.tab. He swishes his fingers across the touchscreen. The file springs open.

Daylight. A clapperboard says: 15/05/2011. AN EX-CHANGE OF SIGNALS ACROSS TIME AND SPACE. ADRI-AN LORCA. SCENE 30. TAKE 1.

And they watch that famous falling girl take her first jump.

Even at normal speed, there is something beautiful about watching her fall. This short moment of weightlessness. The human body out of context.

Take two. Back to the beginning. She jumps, falls, runs.

Blinking back. Like the most difficult video game of your life. Like time travel. Like the final scene in *Eternal Sunshine of the Spotless Mind*, Joel and Clementine playing endlessly in the snow. Like the universe looping back, going through the motions into infinity. Everything slightly rearranged, but always the same. The take number increases. Each new number inscribed with more agitation than the last. The girl, jumping, in hypnotic repetition.

About eleven takes in, Arch realizes. She looks up from the endless iterations of falling girls, to Jules Valentine. 'It's you.'

Lorem ipsum dolor sit amet, consectetur adipiscing elit. Arch can trace her interest in typography and design to the Galaxy

Drive-In theater near her home, reputedly the last Drive-In in Perth. During the Drive-In's heyday in Arch's childhood—the Desai family freshly immigrated, developing a surer hold on Western English—there was a huge signboard facing the road that would announce the two featured movies, using those sliding tiles of capital letters. NOW SHOWING it would always say on the first line. Then it might say THE OUT-OF-TOWNERS on the second line, AND on the third line, ERIN BROCKOVICH on the last line. Arch's favorite was when HOW TO MAKE AN AMERICAN QUILT was showing in the 90s, the longest movie title Arch had ever seen, so long that they had to squeeze the AND onto the previous line with the first movie. She wondered what would happen if the cinema needed to show two movies with really long titles. Well, young Arch reasoned, they'd just always make sure the second movie showing would have a really short title. The Drive-In's popularity faded by the time Arch was a teenager—they ceased to spell out the movies on the signboard and the permanent message became MOVIE STARTS 7.30. Teenage Arch reflected that her childhood logic was silly—as if the cinema would alter their schedule of features for the sake of the signboard. But now that Arch is even older she knows that people prioritize form over content all the time—that countless editors all over the world make minute alterations to writers' text because there isn't enough room, or a widow or an orphan needs a snip. Lorem ipsum dolor sit amet, consectetur adipiscing elit. Content dictates form; form dictates content.

It's Friday, a day without classes, a Get Shit Done Day. Arch sits at her desk, chair angled for contemplation. She holds the metallic blue flash drive between her index finger and thumb, probing the edges, its weight, as if she is considering a totem. Is this someone else's dream?

Her diary is open beside her DELL Vostro, radiant with blue-inked deadlines. Jules Valentine's business card is caught in the fold. On one side is written, in Helvetica Bold, STFU. On the other side, Jules had scribbled her mobile phone number. At this moment, by coincidence, Arch's dictaphone recording arrives at the part where Chris asks why Jules's business cards say 'Shut The Fuck Up' on them. *Private joke*, Jules replies, and Arch sees again the impassive face of Jules Valentine, a collection of empty signifiers. Eyes on standby.

I'm not sure if we can meet again. I'm kinda getting out of here, Jules says on the dictaphone. *But give me a call if you want to. I might be able to arrange something.*

Arch stops the recording. She slides the cap off the flash drive. Her laptop is static except for a blinking cursor, but Arch can sense all the activity twitching in the other windows and tabs—her News Feed updating ceaselessly, the banner ads flashing in Outlook, the artist and album title scrolling in her dormant iTunes like a blimp flying over an empty landscape. Everything is just an Alt-Tab away. She can almost perceive the CPU usage in Task Manager jumping from eleven to five to thirty-two percent all in this blinking cursor.

She switches to her inbox. A crisp email from Stace.

Dear Arch,

Please find attached my copy-edited version of your piece. You will find that most of the changes are minimal, though I have a few queries marked in the document. In particular I am wondering what you think *Lorem Ipsum* house style should stipulate in regards to interrupted dialogue (e.g. 'Oh, but I couldn't—' on page 1). I myself prefer using an unspaced em rule for all interrupted forms of speech, though I have noticed we have been using en rules which are followed but not preceded by a space in other cases, as in instances where the interruptions do not terminate in a quotation mark (e.g. in last semester's issue, the Rodriguez piece: *'one vicious mouth– one vicious mouth– one vicious mouthful'*). I am wondering whether it would be simpler, in these particular circumstances, to replace the en rules with unspaced em rules, but otherwise retain spaced en rules as our default dash style. Do you have any thoughts on this?

In any case, if you could please get back to me with your approval of my edits or any queries of your own by Monday 5pm, I would very much appreciate it.

Also, regarding your other query about the travelling coin piece: I would be inclined to reject it, but only because I find that particular literary technique offensively elementary—I am sure my mother gives that very same writing exercise to her Year Three students—but, as Chief Editor, the decision is, as always, entirely yours. But thank you for asking my opinion on it.

Kind regards,
Stace

Arch begins an email to Stace about the Jules Valentine story. She gets as far as typing, *Hey Stace, Chris and I are working on a piece that might raise some problems.* But she can't just write to Stace without addressing all that em rule business. Arch saves the draft for later.

Arch flips over to VLC Media Player, where her dicta-phone recording is loaded. She slides the needle back to half-way. —*had some sort of history, Jules says. The movie had been re-cut and repurposed over many years. It was their ongoing project, an experiment in continuity. Even after their falling-out, you know, they still seemed to like each other. Like, they just got each other. I can understand why they've disappeared. You know, now that their movie is pretty much everywhere.*

Chris asks, *So after that day when you shot your scene for Lorca and you had your run-in with Hendricks, you never saw them again.*

There's a pause here, a pause Arch has experienced in in-terviews before. It's not that the interviewee doesn't know the answer. They're just letting themselves sink through the mem-ory, to appreciate the loss of something.

No, Jules says, *I didn't.*

Arch changes windows, shuffles tabs, and plugs *Elena Rubik* into the Facebook search bar. She finds an Elena located in Perth and approximately the same age as Jules. Arch doesn't know whether a relative has changed her profile, or if Face-book has found some way to account for people who have died, but the information in Elena's profile has been switched to past tense. Worked at. Lived in.

Still, Arch could send a friend request to Elena Rubik, if she wanted. She scrolls down. Her eyes alight on Facebook's question, that chipper faux-innocent helpfulness:

Do you know Elena?

A question that seems to shimmer with loss. Arch replies out loud, 'No, I don't.'

In the library lounge, Arch watches Stace watch the falling girls. Stace Calbourne's face is impassive in a different way to Jules Valentine's. She's the only person Arch knows who probably thinks in complete sentences.

They're coming up to take number twelve. The next falling girl—Arch knows, having scrutinized the footage several times—was the chosen one. Arch watches Stace as the girl takes her jump, and wonders if Stace will catch it. Perhaps...? And there it is. A faint flicker in her discerning editor's eyes.

'Intriguing,' Stace says when the file ends.

Chris yawns. 'I need a coffee.'

'But what would an article about this footage entail exactly?' Stace continues. 'An interview with Jules Valentine? Screenshots from the footage?'

'Just gonna hop over to the ATM machine,' Chris says, invoking one of Stace's most loathed pleonasms, probably on purpose. Arch gives Stace a moment to bristle silently.

'I guess that's what I'm unsure about,' Arch says. 'This seems important, significant, but I don't know why. I don't know how to use this information the way Jules seems to want us to.'

'What *does* Jules want?'

Arch idly drags the needle back and forth. Makes Jules fall and jump in stop motion. 'That's what I don't get. There just seems to be a lot of stuff mixed up in this. It's like she just wanted to get the whole story off her chest for some reason.'

'Well, Adrian Lorca and Karen Hendricks were students here, after all.'

'Yeah, we never heard the end of that. Our most famous bright minds. So I guess that sort of explains why Jules came to *Lorem Ipsum* specifically. And it's like she wants the information out there, but not right away. But there's also this thing about her dead friend. It's like this is all part of her grieving process somehow.'

Stace nods. Her gaze falls back on the uncut footage, and lower, to Chris's Seed.fon, face-down on the table. 'I suppose

I'm concerned about some sort of fallout if we publish this,' she says. 'But I just don't know what it would be.'

Chris arrives with a takeaway coffee emblazoned with the guild logo. He drops his change on the table. 'You know what we should do?' he says. 'No text. Just run some hi-res screenshots.'

'We have to provide some sort of context,' Arch says.

'Context! Nobody owes anybody *context*. This way we can protect Jules. No mention of the flash drive, the whole story with Lorca and Hendricks. I mean it's clear when the pictures aren't moving that this isn't Karen Hendricks. And besides,' Chris flashes a gleeful look at Stace. 'If there's only pictures then there's no text to edit.'

Stace shakes her head. 'You need to ask Jules, in no un-certain terms, what she wants out of this. Maybe she just couldn't stay silent about this anymore. Or maybe—' She shrugs. 'Maybe, Jules wants something else to happen.'

Lorem ipsum dolor sit amet, consectetur adipiscing elit. Do we forget that the words in our books are written in ink that was once wet? Do we forget that a typeface is still the cre-ation of somebody's hand? Even a typeface of such vicious ubiquity as Helvetica? For so much is concealed in a type-face like Helvetica. Even its name, Helvetica, is concealment: the typeface's original name was Die Neue Haas Grotesk. Re-christened for the US market, a typeface born out of post-war idealism and hope, a beacon of legibility, rationality, neu-trality. Soon Helvetica was everywhere and on everything, on public signs, tax returns, street posters, logos. A signifier of efficiency and authority. Until it burned with some kind of Orwellian menace, as if there was some dystopian finality in its horizontal terminators. *We've always been at war with Eastasia* is a sentence made to be typeset in Helvetica. Like technology itself, in a way—that startling newness fading into the quotidian. Another promise failing. Is this history of her business card's typeface lost on Jules Valentine, the real falling girl? Seed missed the memo that there is no such thing as newness anymore, no such thing as authenticity, as trueness, though bless-our-hearts we do try. Whole industries dedicated to the elusive business of making new, of defining again and again the real personality of a corporate entity—rebranding, rebadging, updating, upscaling. Lorem ipsum dolor sit amet, consectetur adipiscing elit. #GibsonCalledIt; there's nothing new.

Arch waits until the phone rings out before hanging up. No prompt for voicemail. All her emails to Jules have returned undelivered. She slips Jules Valentine's business card back into her diary. She's made the mistake today of sitting next to a computer that's not working, so every ten minutes someone will come into the packed lab, make a beeline for this apparently vacant computer, and as they repeatedly tap the keys to wake up the monitor she'll have to tell them the bad news. Everyone in here is purse-lipped and brow-furrowed with mid-semester nerves. Arch is grateful that none of her current units have exams.

Arch jams in her earphones and listens to Jules Valentine again. She Alt-Tabs to InDesign. She's experimenting with layouts of a would-be article, a random screenshot from the footage posing as a placeholder image. She toggles between serif and sans-serif body copy. Left-aligned, justified. Two columns, three. The columns are padded with lorem ipsum filler that she copied from a generator on the net. She wonders if she could get away with actually publishing these templates instead of an article. Whether anyone would get the joke.

Someone pulls out the chair next to her workstation and taps the spacebar on the vacant keyboard. 'It's not working,' Arch says, taking out one earphone and looking up. Chris *nobody-owes-anybody-context* Riley looks back at her.

'Chris,' she says, taking out the other earphone.

'Hey Arch. Still hung up on J-Val?'

'She's not returning my calls.'

Chris consults his Seed.fon for the time. 'Had lunch yet?'

'No.'

'Wanna grab something?' He gestures to the students shark-circling the room. 'Come on. Give up your place to one of these needy bastards.'

They take their lunch to the lawn outside the glossy engineering building. 'I'm beginning to think you were kind of on the right track the other day,' Arch says as they drop down on the grass.

Chris pops the cap of his orange juice. 'With what?'

'Publishing screenshots of the footage without context. I don't agree entirely. But I think making the footage the focus, the bulk of the page, is a good way to go. Leaving it open to interpretation, kind of.'

'There's definitely something striking about those images.'

Arch bites into her alleged Homestyle Country Pie. She watches a magpie hop closer and closer to a discarded sandwich wrapper.

'What's our fascination with this story, really?' Chris continues as he struggles to wind fried noodles around his brittle plastic fork. 'I mean, does anyone really care about the true identity of the falling girl? This behind-the-scenes bonus insight into Adrian Lorca's famous film? Is it the fact that Lorca and Hendricks have disappeared—and maybe Jules Valentine will follow? Is it that we're so desensitized to the falling girl that any new image of her reawakens something? Does it throw the party line of Seed into doubt—that they "discovered" this indie film, already made-up and waiting to be shown to the world, and that you too—yes you, an ordinary sucker—can make shit, can be an artist, now that Seed is on your side? Didn't we, at the back of our minds, doubt all that anyway?'

Arch sighs. She scrunches down the plastic wrapping of her pie. 'It's like you're asking me to pinpoint why exactly the falling girl became a thing. It's impossible to say. I think it's kind of like... I feel like I'm always just coming to terms with the horrifying emptiness of that image, that falling girl. Like it's just absolutely meaningless in a way that's actually quite frightening. A chance image, one out of the many takes that Adrian Lorca could have picked. And yet it holds such sway over us. It persuades us somehow.'

'Persuades us to believe what?'

'Nothing. It's persuasive for nothing.'

Arch's eyes lift to the university banners lining the footpath, advertising to the converted about bright minds and innovation and making tomorrow better. Some time ago the university changed its official typeface to Sansa Soft, a queasy mixture of Aller and Calibri and Comic Sans, a type that has always reminded Arch of those curved beige classroom chairs with the slit in the back. Something weird about that font. Its sleazy soft angles.

A hundred students exit the lecture theater across the pathway. Hundreds more are huddled in computer labs, smuggling caffeine into the library, circling the car park, arriving at the bus stop, working part-time shifts, checking their HECS debts. Thousands of minds worried about the future, if they have the right grades or credentials or foot-in-the-doors for the future. If the future will accept them.

Wednesday night. Arch PDFs the pages of the Jules Valentine story and sends it to Chris, CCs Stace. She's making a celebratory cup of chamomile when her phone rings. A private number.

'Hello?'

'Hi Arch. It's Jules.'

In the moment when Arch's stomach twists, she admires the particular quality of telephone silence. The harmonious crackling pitch of it.

'Um,' Arch says. 'Silly question: are you still in Perth?'

'I am.'

'Are you able to meet up? I want to show you what we've decided to publish in *Lorem Ipsum*. I would really like it if we could go to print with your approval.'

'Sure.'

'...I mean, I could email it to you if it's easier, it's just that, well, all my emails to you have bounced.'

'I'm okay to meet up.'

'Okay. Um. Where's good for you?'

'Hyde Park. William Street side. I'll be at the bus stop.'

'Okay. That's a little bit far from me, so I'll be about half an hour.'

'That's fine.'

'Thanks Jules.'

Arch hangs up, closes the Vostro and slides it into her bag. She's about to leave when she gets a thought. She reopens the laptop and inserts the metallic blue flash drive.

Later, Arch drives along the endless stretch of Wanneroo Road with the radio turned off. A somber song plays on loop in her head. She sails through amber lights, indicates to invisible cars. The sound of the road outside reminds her of that telephone silence. She pretends she is a signal sliding across time and space. She is data. She is divisible by eight. 'Lorem ipsum dolor sit amet,' she says.

She parks her car across the road from Hyde Park. Jules Valentine is framed in the gold glow of the bus stop advertisement, a pencil-moustached Leonardo DiCaprio peddling a wristwatch. Arch crosses the street on the diagonal so that she lands exactly in front of Jules. 'Hi,' she says.

'Hi Arch. How's it going?'

'Good.'

Jules shifts aside on the bench, so Arch sits down. She takes out her Vostro. The power button glows blue.

'I've been thinking about what you said,' Jules says. 'About implanted memories. Like when you can't remember when something happened, so it's like you retrospectively edit your memories so that the stuff happened at the right time, and not when you actually remember it happening.'

The Vostro makes audible thinking sounds. Creaking and grinding. Arch watches Jules. The two screens—Leonardo, the laptop—watch them.

Jules continues, 'This is slightly different—but I was thinking about how weird it is when you think in the opposite direction, you know. Like when someone you know dies, and several years pass, and technology advances. It creates a new normal. Until your present day is different from what the present day was to the person who died. Like in *Cast Away* when Tom Hanks arrives back home after being on an island for four years, and he's like: *let me get this straight, we have a pro football team now?* I mean, sometimes I just think about what kind of conversations I'd have with Elena, you know, if she came back from the dead. We have Timeline now? We have Seed? What's the deal with the falling girl? And suddenly there's all this distance between us, even though we lived in the same time. And then your perception sort of breaks up and you don't think of the present as the present anymore. All of a sudden it's the future.'

The laptop stirs, cricket-like. It prompts Arch for her login details. 'Why did you come to us, Jules?' Arch asks. 'Why are you doing this?'

Jules gazes at the delicatessen across the street. Latent plastic fly strips and dark windows. Gutted fresh flower buckets. She says, 'Let's say you go through some kind of event, that, for some reason or another, changes you, in some devastating way, and there is no going back. It can be an event or a series of events, one moment or several moments: you pick. The more inarticulable, the better. Whatever it is, it is enough to create a rupture in your universe. A terrible wound. And then, nothing. Nothing else happens after that; the event or events are over. Whatever is happening to you stops happening. It is just you and your wound now. So, what do you do? You pore over the facts. You pore over your memories. You replay the moment and the moments surrounding the moments. But after a while there's nothing new. The event is over, after all. What do you do when you run out of facts? You pore over them again. You reread and relive and re-analyse. You go mad, eventually. You want to look for clues when there are no more clues. You want to do something. You want to make something happen. So you can get new information, new facts. Even if you have to make a new wound. You need new data.' Jules looks at Arch. 'I am creating new data.'

Arch, numbly, brings herself to nod. She watches Jules slip into her impassive face again, her gaze floating, hesitating, and then leaving reality entirely. Arch offers a small, sad smile that Jules doesn't see. She turns back to the Vostro and enters her login details. The laptop alerts her to three wireless networks in the area but she ignores it, opening the PDF that she sent to Chris and Stace about half an hour ago. 'Here,' she says, passing the laptop to Jules. 'This is what the article's going to look like.'

Jules lets the laptop rest on her thighs. She angles the screen. And looks at herself, repeated across several pages, light as an epiphany, recurring like a memory. In another time Stace might have disapproved of this, padding out the magazine with full-page images, but Arch thinks in this case Stace would think it is entirely appropriate, these alternate-universe falling girls. One page is white except for a perfectly rectangular column of text, a long verbatim quote from Jules—not the story of Adrian Lorca and Karen Hendricks, but Jules's description of the experience of the shoot. Unedited, unindented, sparsely punctuated. *Sometimes I think I'm still stuck in that moment,* it begins. *Jumping over and over without context.*

The reader falls with her. The comforting tedium of it.

The last page of the article is blank except for a QR code positioned, like a Helvetica slogan, in the bottom right-hand corner of the page. Jules asks, 'Where will this go?'

'To the footage. Chris has uploaded a copy of it. Here—this is yours.' Arch slips a hand in her pocket and retrieves the metallic blue flash drive. She looks carefully at Jules. 'Is this what you wanted?'

Jules scrolls up through the pages again. 'It's good, Arch. Thank you.' She accepts the blue flash drive and exchanges it for Arch's laptop.

'I've copied the PDF to the USB as well,' Arch says. 'In case you can't get a copy of the magazine in print. You said you were getting out of here. I took it to mean you were disappearing.'

Jules nods. 'I am.' She gets to her feet, pocketing the flash drive and taking out her car keys. 'It was nice meeting you, Arch.' She extends her right hand.

They have their final handshake over the brim of the Vostro's monitor. 'It was nice to meet you too,' Arch says.

Arch watches Jules cross the street, unlock her car, slam the door. Snap the headlights on. She watches the wheels pivot, the car turning out. Gliding like a cursor down William Street.

The laptop becomes warm on her knees, so Arch closes the lid. She wonders what it is like for Jules, living in the future, living outside the future. Making copies of herself across the universe in a trail of falling girls. Arch lets her body sink deeply into the bench, lets the bench hold her in the light of the wristwatch advertisement. Hugs her laptop. Allows the columns of her mind to explode with words until there is only whiteness.

Jules's car turns the corner. Light fades like a touchscreen drifting into standby.

Everything That Rises

What can we say is the true origin of the Homestyle Country Pie? Where do we begin the story? Perhaps at the scathing assessment of Valued Participant #4 of Focus Group #7, who declared that the Evergreen Pie Company's latest offering was *soulless?* Perhaps at the board meeting when it was ascertained that a certain clumsiness, a certain un-uniformity in the pie filling, the presence of 'chunks', were crucial to the pie's perceived possession of a soul? Ought we begin with the breakthrough that the pie top should not be completely flat, but possess a dome, a broad and only slightly mammary-like parabola? Or the realization that, if we were to get to the bottom of the cloud of meaning surrounding that signifier, *pie*, what we would find is the enduring image of a pie cooling on the windowsill, in a country house that never existed, in some fabulous pastoral or woody landscape—that this is the true character of the pie, our deepest wish; the pie for which we eternally yearn, the pie in our hearts.

Or would it be more correct to chart the beginnings of *this* particular Homestyle Country Pie, from Batch #9300730, the last in the procession? Should we begin with the sheets of dough, youthfully elastic, dulcified with a combination of pastry-relaxing agents and overnight chilling? Perhaps we could say that all pies were once one entity, one dough, which is then machine-perforated into segments, blocked into base and lid. And there it is now—our Homestyle Country Pie, its unfilled body proceeding, with so many others, like the schoolgirls from *Madeline*. Our Homestyle Country Pie is not the smallest one, nor the naughtiest one; it is not the best or most at anything. It lines up to receive its filling, a mixture of diced and minced beef flesh, peas, tiny carrot cubes. The protective gravy is only three-quarters as thick as its regular consistency to account for evaporation during freezing and baking. Then, conveyed onwards, the uneven mound of its contents wobbling, to be lidded and sealed, excess dough trimmed, edges crimped, punctured with breathing holes, sprayed with glaze.

Perhaps you disagree, thinking that the essence of the pie—the *soul*, perhaps—is its filling, and so we ought to properly begin at the moment of slaughter; at the cattle, like this pie, conveyed in single file, the path strategically curved to obscure the sight of what's ahead. Rendered unconscious, then rendered dead; halved, quartered, chilled. (The meat used in Evergreen pies is ground onsite; the better to articulate the 'chunks' required for the Homestyle Country Pie.) Perhaps we ought to begin at the moment when the vegetables are torn from the earth in their hundreds, washed, diced, blanched, and tunnelled through liquid nitrogen. These bright vegetables, their perfect geometry, crisply suspended in youth—sealed in plain bulk packages, ripe for the moment when they will be thawed, will join the gravy and meat, will be deposited into our Homestyle Country Pie.

One thing could be agreed upon: the pie has a troubled and complicated subjectivity; it and its component parts will endure a variety of hostile temperatures, will have time stopped and started, will age and die according to schedule.

Watch—there it goes—our Homestyle Country Pie, bob-
bing optimistically along, sealed in a dotted plastic wrapper
that bears its batch number and two use-by dates—one for
fresh, one for frozen.

The Australian five-cent coin, like many silver coins, is an al-
loy of three parts copper to one part nickel. On the obverse
side is Queen Elizabeth II; on the reverse side is an echidna,
all puffed and jolly. From time to time there will be some talk
of rendering the five-cent coin obsolete, to cease rounding at
intervals of 0.05. But, through all of these attempts on its life,
the echidna will prevail, rolling sunnily on. A bit of Wikipedia trivia, now: for a brief time in 2007, the five-cent coin enjoyed a bullion value that exceeded its face value—due to the
rising price of copper and nickel, a five-cent coin's metal was
worth six-and-a-half cents.

The five-cent piece is the most liminal, the most transgressive, of all the coins. Its sigil, after all, is an egg-laying
mammal.

Of the 44.8 million five-cent coins that were minted in
2011, we are concerned with just one. We can start when
it had no face, a blank, punched out from a thin sheet of
cupro-nickel, a humble mass of 2.83 grams. Just about everything that happens after the blank is punched out is a
procedure intended to cancel out the side-effects of the procedure before it. The force required to flatten the metal has
made it too hard, so now a furnace must make it soft. The
temperature required to soften the metal discolors it, so the
coins must be dropped in a tank of water and then shuffled
in a washing machine. Through its many cycles, the coins
are cleaned and soaked in chemicals, and then dried in a
tube. Then, off to the upsetting mill, which gifts each coin
with a raised, protective rim.

When our five-cent coin arrives at the Royal Australian Mint, it is snug inside a bright blue drum, very nearly the same shade of blue that will appear, like a beacon, at key junctures of its existence. Indeed, the coin presses themselves are painted blue, arrayed like army tanks. The floor of the Mint is presided over by three robots. There is an orange one, a kind of large pivoting claw-arm, who is responsible for moving the drums. The staff members of the Mint call this orange robot Titan, because it can bear extraordinary weights, but the robot doesn't call itself by that name. It just isn't consistent with its self-image. Sometimes, when there are tourists watching, the orange robot will become shy. It will spend long moments contemplating the drum it is about to lift. It will be seized by the eternal problem of subjectivity. It often wonders why it is a robot and the coin presses are machines; it wonders why they, and not it, have been denied personhood. Eventually, the orange robot will bring itself to lift the blue drum of five-cent blanks. With slow resignation, it will tip the blanks into the coin hopper. They will cascade like so many cheap trinkets.

From the hopper, the blanks will be elevated to the ceiling in buckets, and dropped into one of the waiting coin presses. Our five-cent coin will receive its echidna and Elizabeth, struck by anvil and hammer. It will also acquire its characteristic reeded border.

The five-cent coin's notched circumference is not unlike the crimped edges of our Homestyle Country Pie. Like two celestial bodies, they are headed for eclipse, for tragic collision.

The coins regroup in their blue drum and return to the orange robot, who, this time, tips them into a hopper that sucks them into a counting and bagging machine. There is another robot here, this one called Robbie, who, unlike the orange robot, is entirely comfortable with its name. It suctions up the bags of coins and packs them in cardboard boxes.

Every Australian coin in your wallet or pocket or bank account, as the tour guide is fond of saying, was made at the Australian Royal Mint. But it will be some time before our five-cent coin will see the inside of a pocket. For at this moment it is being shipped out to an ANZ branch in Perth, a bank of the same ominous blue as the drum it sat in as a blank, where it will be counted out, mixed with older coins, and sorted into rolls; where it will be picked up and deposited in a cash register in a Gull service station, again, of that same ominous blue.

And there our coin will stay, for a long time, at the top of the unbroken stack. It is older, actually, than our Homestyle Country Pie, who, quite soon after packaging, is sent forth into the world, an emissary for the Evergreen brand. Let's come back to it, nestled in a box in the refrigerated body of the dispatch truck, among an assortment of Evergreen favorites. The Creamy Chicken & Mushroom Pie, the Nanna's Shepherd's Pie, the Classic Beef Pie—all jostling in their wrappers.

When the pies are slotted into their heated display case at the Gull service station, they have already been browned in an oven at the back of the store. Under the yellow lights they will come into their element. They will each radiate like the tanned, golden cheeks of a veteran TV celebrity. The Homestyle Country Pie will be in the center of the display, its plastic wrapper bearing the cartoon image of a pie cooling on a windowsill, the curls of steam unravelling wistfully upwards. Like game show contestants, each of the pies are positioned in front of a label with their name printed neatly, and their price. The Homestyle Country Pie is $4.90, only slightly costlier than its fellows, on account of its chunks.

The Homestyle Country Pie will be one of the last selected. It will remain unpurchased throughout the lunchtime hours. It will sit patiently and eagerly; it will never allow its face to fall. As the evening deepens, its golden aura will deepen too. The heat-lamped food display will glow like an incubator of something marvelous, some small daily miracle.

It is nearly eleven o'clock, close to the last hour of the day, when the Homestyle Country Pie is pulled from the display with a pair of tongs and slid into a paper bag. This is the moment when destiny is fulfilled. This is the moment when the Homestyle Country Pie sits on the countertop, the heat of its body warming the laminate through the paper bag. The customer, a young woman, hands the cashier a ten-dollar note. It is beautiful what happens. The cashier conveys the ten-dollar note to the till—presses a button, releases the spring-loaded cash drawer. The cashier first peels off a five-dollar note, then looks for the coins. The smallest denomination available is twenty cents, so the cashier reaches for the side of the tray, where the rolled coins are. This is the moment. There are no more ten-cent pieces. A rare phenomenon. The cashier takes up the roll of five-cent coins. Taps the roll against the counter as if he is breaking an egg. Splits the cardboard open. The coins spill out into the small black compartment. The cashier takes our five-cent piece, the one minted in 2011, and pairs it with another piece, minted ten years earlier in 2001, and drops them into the woman's cupped hand.

For a few seconds, the woman actually holds both at once—the pie, the coin—each now on the brink of circulation. It is only a few seconds, and then she slips her change into her pocket. The veteran 2001 five-cent piece, not prepared for this particular fate, bounces off the hard seam of the woman's pocket and lands soundlessly on the Gull welcome mat, so it is only the 2011 piece that will leave the store. The woman doesn't notice. She tears open the wrapper of the pie.

They share each other's warmth—the pie, the woman. She coaxes the pie out of the packaging, just a little bit, enough for a gentle first bite. The pastry is tender, the filling eager to spill. She is the end-consumer, the site of culmination. She is fulfilling a prophecy, redeeming a longstanding promise, a mission statement, a guarantee.

She is walking out into the street. She is walking past the tall sign, like a blue obelisk, that bears the prices of gasoline. She is surrounded by trajectories, not just those of our coin and our Homestyle Country Pie, but the unleaded petroleum, the sterilized ice, the light globes, the advertisements stuck to the bowsers, the song on the radio.

She has barely taken a second bite of the pie. This is it. This is the moment. One second ago she was walking, firmly affixed to the ground, mobile and autonomous, but now she is in the air. She is in the air and the Homestyle Country Pie has left her hands, leaping halfway out of the paper bag, flaking as it arcs into the sky. She is in the air and a Ford EA Falcon passes beneath her, powerful as a whale. She is in the air and the five-cent coin hits the ceiling of her pocket. She is in the air and the message of pain travels out from the point of impact, bristling her nerves, persisting upwards and upwards until her brain is alight with the news; so efficient is the report, so succinct. She is in the air but she is falling now, and so is the pie, and so is the coin, three vessels of meaning, consummating the final slope of their trajectories, destined for asphalt. She is falling like the fading tail of a warning flare.

The woman and the pie meet the ground. Their borders rupture. They become broken containers, meaning spilling forth, but there is not enough meaning to take the full shape of its new container; two tiny universes have just now exploded and it makes hardly any difference at all. The mass of the Earth remains in balance. The coin, whole and secure in the woman's pocket, still denotes an exchange value of five cents, still announces this tiny message of its worth to an absent audience. The woman, the pie, the coin—each of them glistening, each meeting the standards for typicality, impeccable examples of their kinds. Somebody, at some point in time, wanted the best for them, wanted them to go far.

Later, the Homestyle Country Pie will be washed off the road. The person tasked with this responsibility will remove the largest pieces first before resorting to turning on the hose. He will take them up in his gloved fingers—the bruised crust, the slippery bits of filling—and drop them into the paper bag for disposal. The chunks will make it a lot easier.

Later, the authorities will retrieve the five-cent piece from the woman's pocket. It will join other personal effects collected in a stiff brown envelope that is presented to the woman's next-of-kin. It will never re-enter circulation. It will never participate in another transaction. Like its ancestors in 2007, this five-cent coin has acquired some other secret, richer value.

Later, the woman will be cremated. She is slid into her own container and mounted onto a moveable hopper that conveys her—deftly, to avoid temperature loss—downwards into the furnace. It takes ninety minutes for the incineration to be complete and a further twenty minutes for her bone fragments to be sufficiently pulverized. Soon she will have no borders at all, and nothing that can be held within borders. Her body will be simplified into gas and dust.

Later, the hour hand will rise imperceptibly, like the baton of a conductor, guided by subliminal vibrations, interring the minute before that, and the one before that, and the one before that. Later, a million goods will softly expire—will, in a matter of seconds, become unsaleable. Later, all the dies in all the coin presses will be altered to read 2012, then 2013, then 2014. Later, the price of a Homestyle Country Pie will increase to \$5.00, to \$5.10, to \$5.20—climbing ever higher, for all things must keep pace. Later, the hour hand will complete a revolution, will assume the same position as before—but it will not signify the same hour, will never signify the same hour; nothing ever truly returns, reverses course; nothing is permitted the same trajectory twice. Everything rises, for everything must rise—will flare out in a moment of preciousness, bring itself to fruition. Everything reaches the height of itself, and then disperses, evacuates the orbit of its being. The hour rises. It oversees the exhaustion of everything living, the accumulation of expiries.

Luxury Replicants

You need a totem.

    A unique object.

    Small, solid.

    Something that can fit inside your pocket.

    Something only you can recreate.

    This is how you confirm that you're not in someone else's dream.

    This is how you confirm that you are in control.

    Do not show your totem to others.

    Keep your totem hidden.

    If you must refer to your totem, do so discreetly.

    Guard it with your life.

Aeris dies and someone makes a thread commemorating his death. It's all official—the mods have confirmed it's not a hoax—and TheGreatDekuTree tentatively sets up a drive to collect monetary donations for Aeris's family, and because TheGreatDekuTree is a respected long-time member of Luxury Replicants he does manage to collect quite a bit. At first Renzo stays away from the entire thread because it's triggered something for him, he doesn't know what. He's been thinking about Rubik3 again. Not that they were ever friends. Well. They were, sort of.

Renzo-as-Michael Lim is on the train to work, and because he's sitting on the wrong side of the train, the side with the sun blaring through the window, he is feeling very conscious about the weight of his head, its specific and painful submission to gravity. He's wanted to change seats for seven stops now. He scrolls down Aeris's commemorative thread and each time he lifts his thumb he notices the minute streak of warmth—the elliptical print of his finger pad—disappearing on the touchscreen, absorbed after a half-second lag, as if his soul is vanishing. He's listening to Miko and the Exploding Heads and he totally relates to the exploding-heads bit. This sun. He scrolls and he scrolls.

Michael watches an old man slowly rise out of his priority seat and disembark at Glendalough. Michael needs out of this sun, even for just one stop. He swipes up his bag and crosses to the opposite side of the train. He sits down in the old man's place and hopes nobody judges him for it. Leans his head back against an advertisement that features a giant baby holding a stop sign.

He looks at his Seed again but in the seat-shuffle he's accidentally closed the thread. It's probably time to stop thinking about Aeris and Rubik3 anyway. Michael slips his phone into his pocket. He turns his head to one side. It still hurts.

Shuts his eyes. Opens them.

There's a perfectly round hole next to the giant baby in the white resin wall of the train. A subtle aperture, circumscribed by a barely perceptible green ring. Michael looks around the train, but nobody else is seeing what he is seeing. He runs a finger over the recess. There's something else. A mark above the hole. He leans closer. An image? The omega symbol?

No. Headphones.

It's an audio port.

Michael looks around the train again. He unjacks his earphones. Cuts off Miko and the Exploding Heads mid-refrain. But that's as far as he gets, because now he's at Leederville, and he has to go to work.

Today's new arrival is the Message-in-a-Bottle Kit. It consists of a box that is about the size of a spectacles case that contains a small glass bottle, a cork, a shiny slip of paper, a candle, and a packet of red wax pellets. The slip of paper contains helpful prompts for the message you should put in your bottle. 'This bottle was released at [place] on [date] by [name].' Then you're meant to seal the bottle with wax. The candle is for melting the wax. The Message-in-a-Bottle Kit is $24.95.

'Aeris died,' Michael tells Bette during a lull at Ampersand.

'The nineties called, Michael. They want their spoiler back.'

'No, I mean, *Aeris*. From LR. Cancer.'

'Who's she?'

'No, he's—oh, right. No, I mean Ares, like the Greek god. After you left, he changed his name to Aeris, like the *Final Fantasy* character.'

'Why?'

'It's a reference to—' Michael starts, but he's lost her, and she's noisily sorting through a bucket of coathangers. 'Sorry. Should I not talk about this?'

She shrugs. She takes the bucket of coathangers to the storeroom. Bette was SparkleCat on Luxury Replicants. Was.

She quit Luxury Replicants back when they were in high school, years ago, after the whole WhiteKnight debacle. She hasn't so much as lurked there since.

A young man with a tastefully scruffy beard enters the store. 'Hey, how's it going?' Michael says, but the young man just nods, once. He surveys the table of giftware and inspects, in this order: the knitted cactus, the garden secateurs with the enamelled floral handles, the stack of thin notebooks with brown cardboard covers, and then, the Message-in-a-Bottle Kit. Michael thinks of this guy purchasing the Message-in-a-Bottle Kit, for his partner, or his friend, or maybe himself. Filling in the [place] and [name] and [date]. Scrawling his favorite Murakami quote. Rolling up the paper and sealing the bottle and tossing it into the ocean.

Some time later all these identical glass bottles with identical red wax will wash up on some distant beach, like an exhumed primary school time capsule, [place] and [name] and [date] diligently filled. No urgent messages, no dying words. Just doing a thing for the sake of doing a thing.

The young man puts down the Message-in-a-Bottle Kit and exits.

Bette returns. She's got the new posters for the autumn collection, bundled under her arm like giant drinking straws.

'Hey,' Michael says. 'Hey, Bette. Today, on the train, there was this audio port in the wall.'

'A what?'

'An audio port.'

'Whereabouts?'

'Above one of the priority seats.'

Bette's eyes drift and Michael wonders if he's lost her again. She's wearing those guillotine earrings she acquired last season. 'Coralee said we have to put these up,' Bette says, raising the bunch of rolled-up posters. 'Right away. They arrived late, she said.'

'Okay. Here, let me.'

Bette's been working at Ampersand for two years and Michael for one-and-a-half. It is pre-winter, and today, a little behind schedule, is the changing of the guard. New Ampersand ambassadors, a fresh catalogue. Michael unclips the old poster from the lightbox. 'Goodbye, Graeme and Ursula,' he says. Bette says nothing. Michael thought she'd have some quip ready. She's probably pleased to see the old posters go. When Graeme and Ursula were first unveiled Bette said she'd never felt more aggressively marketed-to in her life. She said this because last year was the first time that the girl-side of the Ampersand ambassadorship hadn't been unambiguously white. Ursula still had the vague, unfixed gaze and cinematically knotted tresses of Ampersand ambassadors past, but she was decidedly (and as Bette argued, calculatedly) less translucent, less waif-like. She was even a bit curvy, maybe a size ten or even twelve, not androgynously straight-edged like most ambassadors. Bette wasn't sure how to feel about the appointment of Ursula, Bette herself not white, herself tending towards softness, lumpishness, the likeness of a pear. Should she feel grateful for this attempt at diverse representation, or wary? Was this even to be read as a genuine attempt at diversity? For Ursula's particular brand of beauty was different enough to register as Other without being alienating; she was safely transgressive. They'd never have someone darker than Ursula, someone with a thicker waist, someone shorter. It's all about passing, Bette would say. You can be outside the norm, a little bit, but not too much. You still need to pass. Passing is the most important skill one can ever learn.

But Bette still bought the Penny-Farthing shirt. She still bought the Cherry Sundae Unicorn pin badge.

Today she is, after all, wearing the Executive Decision Guillotine earrings.

All last year Bette and Michael labored under the vague gaze of each iteration of Ursula and her evolving repertoire of outfits, twinned dutifully by Graeme, autumn, winter, spring and summer, this last of which Michael now slides from the frame. 'Hello, new ambassadors.' Michael unfurls the fresh poster.

He's immediately distracted by the T-shirts slung over the pair of lithe bodies. Plain white T-shirts, slightly oversized. Printed on each T-shirt is the falling cat. That black cat from the internet with the red collar whose airborne body is contorted in very much the same style as the falling girl from the old Seed ads. A meme of a meme, now on a T-shirt, available from Ampersand.

'Did you stick in your earphones?' Bette asks.

'Huh?'

'Into the audio port. Did you try sticking in your earphones? What was it playing?'

'I don't know. I had to get off at my stop.'

'Couldn't it have been, you know, something for people with disabilities? Announcing the stations, maybe?'

'I've never seen one before. There weren't any signs or anything.'

Bette shrugs. Two ladies enter the store, approaching the jewelry display case. They chorus *good thanks and you* to Michael's 'Hey, how are you?' Bette's disappeared into the back again. Michael looks back at the new Ampersand ambassadors. Platinum blondes. The guy's wearing glasses, a first. It's that *safely transgressive* thing again. Michael scans the fine print for names. Asher and Kimberly. He nods to his new ambassadors, and the twin falling cats.

There's another customer looking through the rack of coats that Michael didn't see come in. She rubs the lining of the Private Eye trench between her thumb and forefinger to appraise the thickness. Michael considers saying hello but he has no idea how long the customer has been here, and saying hello might be weird if she's been here for a while. The customer moves on to a different coat. Now that Aeris has died, reviving his memory of the Rubik3 mystery, Michael is tempted to return to that old, futile game. Futile, because there's no real way of knowing, no actual clues. But he plays anyway. He retreats to his post at the counter, keeping the customer in his peripheral vision, and thinks: *Are you Rubik3?*

It kind of stuns Michael, actually, when he counts backwards and finds that the WhiteKnight debacle happened almost five years ago. Has he really been a member of Luxury Replicants for that long? Longer, even? Because surely they weren't yet in high school when Bette discovered the forum by way of *Pikkoro and the Multipurpose Octopus* fan fiction, the way Bette was always discovering the cool things before Michael, and they both signed up one after the other, as SparkleCat and Renzo respectively, names that would later mortify them.

Rubik3 was the only other user on Luxury Replicants, to Michael's knowledge, who lived in the same city as him and Bette. He'd gathered that she was quite a bit older than them, from her references to living with housemates or studying at university, so, for the longest time, they never really talked beyond leaving comments on each other's threads. It was only a few years ago that they exchanged PMs, trying to recruit the other to their favorite fandom—which was for Michael, *Pikkoro*, and for Rubik3, *Seeds of Time*. Rubik3's incomplete *Inception* fic, *End of the Gun*, hasn't been updated since 2011. It was around that time when Michael sent Rubik3 a PM to wish her a happy birthday, and received no reply.

Michael revisits Aeris's commemorative thread. It's possible that, at the back of their minds, the members of Luxury Replicants are thinking about the WhiteKnight incident, comparing one 'death' with another, but he is somehow sure that nobody is thinking about Rubik3, whose disappearance was so quiet, the smallest of subtractions, like a pebble sinking through water.

Bette hadn't been all that interested in Rubik3, since they moved in different fandoms. Michael thinks it really sucks that he can't share stuff about LR with Bette that much these days, even though he knows there are good reasons why. Maybe Bette has been mad at Michael, all these years, for sticking around Luxury Replicants while she moved on. But it's something Michael's always noticed about Bette: a kind of withdrawal from him every time he shows interest in something that she's not interested in, or if he fails to show interest in something *she's* interested in.

To be fair, though, sometimes Michael feels a similar kind of betrayal. The other day when they caught the bus together, Michael noticed Bette browsing Seek. She wasn't looking at other retail jobs, but full-time positions and internships, office-type jobs. And Michael *did* feel something, a small piping voice of panic. Bette hadn't mentioned that she'd been job-hunting. He can't imagine continuing working at Ampersand by himself. He feels left behind already.

There's a fic in the Miscellaneous subforum titled *Rubik*, by a new user called lkjv, which has zero comments, which isn't surprising because the convention in the Miscellaneous subforum is to clearly title your thread with the film or series or book you're basing your fic on, otherwise nobody will click on your thread, because the Miscellaneous subforum is for fandoms that aren't large enough to have their own subforum. It first appeared yesterday but it was quickly buried by newer threads; indeed, Michael wouldn't even have found it if he weren't searching for Rubik3's posts. Judging from the scant introduction about choosing a totem, Michael had supposed it was an *Inception* fic, but this most recent update makes reference to Tako, the octopus of *Pikkoro and the Multi-purpose Octopus,* so maybe it's some kind of *Inception–Pikkoro* crossover.

I will do this. I will do this right. I have made up a totem, and this is the secret I will share with you. My totem is larger than recommended, a Rubik's cube, but get this, it's a Rubik's cube with seven colors, seven colors, get it? Seven colors for six faces. An unsolvable Rubik's cube. Kind of like you, Tako. You know. You have more moving parts than an octopus should have. You are endlessly formful and formless. You have everything necessary to begin.

It is autumn and Michael and Bette are turning twenty-one. Soon it will be two months since they graduated, and then three, and then four. This year, Easter and Anzac Day fall on consecutive weekends, and everyone in this city is filled with inertia, only slackly conscious. Michael and Bette ought to be marching towards their future, holding their bachelor degrees aloft bravely; the time for decision-making is swiftly waning. Michael and Bette have committed to shifts almost every day at Ampersand, and while it's nice money to have, it is undoubtedly interim money, temporary money. But whenever Michael gets home all he wants to do is pull his Mac into bed and open one million tabs and read until 2am.

A text from Bette Cho: *my mum says your mum was gonna transfer $$$ for pineapple tarts do you know if she's done that yet let me know ok also come over tomorrow night my parents are going out we can watch TV.*

Michael texts back, *Sure, okay,* but it's late and Mum's already asleep, so he sets the alarm on his Seed and turns it on silent. He scrolls further down the *Rubik* thread.

This is how you will find me, Tako. You have to go to the school. You have to go to the auditorium. You have to crawl underneath the stage. This is where I hid that time, from the HarvestTime™ play. I have recreated the space from my memory, which is also against the rules, but I think it will be okay. There will be a hole in the wall, just a little hole, with a picture of headphones above it. Make a pair of headphones and connect yourself. You can do that, right? Make a pair of headphones and listen. You will hear more instructions.

Today's new arrival is the Crumple Cup, set of four. They are made in the style of Rob Brandt's iconic 1975 design. They have the likeness of a slightly scrunched-up disposable plastic party cup but they are actually made from porcelain. While each original handmade Crumple Cup was uniquely crumpled, these homages are uniformly crumpled to enable easy stacking. They are dishwasher and microwave safe and may contain hot or cold beverages. Crumple Cup, set of four, $45.00.

'All I'm saying is, Rubik3 could be dead, and we wouldn't know. How can you not find that even a little scary?'

'Remember those two kids from school?' Bette says, folding a returned Falling Cat T-shirt. She's having trouble lining up the edges because the hemline is slightly asymmetrical. Michael wonders if he's stepped into an entirely different conversation. 'Remember?' Bette insists. 'The ones who broke into that house? Everyone thought they were crazy. They kept saying that some piano teacher had disappeared. A really quiet Year Three boy and his friend with a broken arm.'

'When was this? I don't remember this at all.'

'Really late. Year Eleven or Twelve. It was news, for like, one day. Anyway. You know what the worst part is? The teacher didn't disappear. She had a nervous breakdown. She was in hospital.'

'What? How do you remember this?'

'It happened, I promise. Anyway. It was like they had this whole mythology mapped out. They were bright kids. They thought they'd solved some big mystery. They believed every word they were saying. And who's to say, really—maybe they *were* telling the truth. Maybe *both* stories were true.'

'Huh.'

'Rubik3's dead. Rubik3 got sick of fan fiction. Rubik3 left LR. Rubik3's in a coma. Pick one. Pick any. Pick all of them.'

A customer brings the Mounted Forces Cowboy Hat to the counter and Michael rings it through. 'Hey, how are you,' he says, and can't bring himself to say anything else. Coralee wanted to know yesterday if they'd been cross-selling anything. Earlier today, Michael had attempted it. 'We have belts too,' he said to a customer trying on the Quick Brown Fox jeans. 'Okay,' said the customer. And then the scene wouldn't advance, like a video game freezing mid-dialogue.

'Hey, are you back on LR?' Michael says to Bette when the customer's gone.

'No.'

'Really? Because last night I was reading this *Inception* fic and it mentioned an audio port in a wall—'

'*Inception*, huh? Yeah, let's watch that tonight. My mum wants us to use these pizza coupons before they expire, by the way, so I hope Domino's is okay. Did you ask about the pineapple tart money?'

'Not yet. Sorry.'

'S'okay,' Bette says. She is wearing her Uppity Giraffe earrings today. She turns out the swing tag on the Falling Cat T-shirt and ferries it to the display shelf, and Michael realizes that she has, with the elegance of Falling Cat, deftly twisted her way out of a Luxury Replicants conversation again.

Did you know that this hat goes with the Honey Ranch neck-scarf?, he could have said to that customer. *Did you know there is twenty percent off all colored pencils and pencil sharpeners today?*

A customer asks Bette if the Pantone socks come in any other shades of blue. Whenever a customer asks Bette a question instead of him, Michael always feels relieved, and guilty for feeling relieved. It's like swinging clear over an alligator-infested gorge while your fellow adventurer plummets to her death.

On 16 May 2009, a user named Sweetpea, who had joined Luxury Replicants about two months earlier, created a thread announcing that her dear friend WhiteKnight—a member of Luxury Replicants since June 2006, real name supposedly Clint Baron—had died the night before, hit by a car while assisting a motorcyclist who had fallen off his bike. He was generally active in the *Harry Potter*, *Fullmetal Alchemist* and *Final Fantasy* subforums, and so his path crossed with Bette's more often than Michael's. Sometimes he left comments on Bette's fics. They may have exchanged a few PMs. And, judging by the accumulation of comments on Sweetpea's thread on that first day, WhiteKnight was more than an acquaintance to many others at Luxury Replicants. Only two users, however, had known Clint Baron in real life: Sweetpea, and a newbie, cedricD.

It is always at this point in the story that the self-appointed shrewdest members of Luxury Replicants insist that they knew *exactly* what was going on.

Still the RIPs flowed—even Michael himself had left a feeble 'I didn't know WhiteKnight very well but sorry for your loss' message in the thread—and Sweetpea and cedricD regaled the others with stories about Clint Baron's heroism, his all-round-good-guy-ness, his humor and sense of fun.

This is how Sweetpea met Clint Baron: she was at a petrol station filling up her car when she was accosted by her violent (only-just-that-night-turned ex-)boyfriend, whom she'd finally worked up the courage to leave. Now there he was, having apparently followed her. It was night-time. She was scrunched up against her car while he hassled her. The gas station wasn't empty—there were at least three other cars there, but nobody came to her rescue. Nobody, that is, except Clint, a white knight from the first time she saw him, striding over from his second-hand Honda, his casual but brave, effective words: 'Is this guy bothering you?'

The funeral for Clint Baron was held on 18 May 2009. They played his favorite song, 'Learn to Fly' by Foo Fighters, as the casket was lowered; his best friend Seth made a speech. Seth made an ID on Luxury Replicants, Seth_g, to thank members for their support, which would be his only post on the forum. The mods, meanwhile, were hanging back from the thread and quietly investigating. They could not find any record of the death of one Clint Baron from Denver. TheGreatDekuTree was the first user to gently ask Sweetpea and cedricD if either of them could post a newspaper obituary for Clint Baron in the thread, but his request was ignored.

Peach was the first mod to make a comment on the thread. She said that it was clear that WhiteKnight was a friend to many in the Luxury Replicants community. She did also, however, reiterate TheGreatDekuTree's request for a newspaper obituary. She noted some confusing points in Sweetpea and cedricD's stories and asked for clarification. And how was it, Peach asked, that Clint Baron's funeral was held so soon after his death?

Peach, the mildest of all the mods. Sweetpea and cedricD were swiftly upset. What was Peach implying? How dare she accuse them of lying, in a time of such grief? Peach's post emboldened some of the more skeptical members of the forum, and one or two mods, to publicly express their doubt, while others, Bette among them, testified that they knew WhiteKnight. They'd had conversations with him. This is a delicate situation, they said, shouldn't the mods tread lightly?

How was it, Michael thinks now, safe in 2014, that it all spun out of control? When did it become such a dogpile?

We thought we were savvier than this. We were meant to be savvier than this.

On 20 May 2009, WhiteKnight's memorial thread was locked. WhiteKnight, Sweetpea, cedricD and Seth_g were all banned. Peach created one post explaining what had happened—something to do with IP addresses, like WhiteKnight was posting from various devices and work computers as each of his sockpuppets, but slipped up somehow along the way—and requested that this be the end of the discussion.

But it wasn't, of course, the end of the discussion. Small fires started all over Luxury Replicants. This is the hardest bit to talk about, because there is hardly anything nameable. Users sneaked references to the WhiteKnight incident in comments. He became a joke, a meme. To 'WhiteKnight' was to pull a tasteless, poorly executed online prank, or to concoct a self-aggrandising story, particularly one that represents you as a Nice Guy Who Saves Women. To be 'WhiteKnighted' was to be duped, led astray by an obvious plot. Threads would spiral into contemplation on WhiteKnight's motives, or a step-by-step breakdown of why the incident was obviously a hoax and anyone who didn't see it coming was an idiot. Then there were others who argued that anyone still discussing the incident was an idiot. Then others argued that anyone criticising anyone else for discussing the incident was an idiot.

But a strange thing happened to Bette. She just didn't want to post anymore. It's something that Michael gets and doesn't get. It's not like Bette was one of the most vocal

WhiteKnight supporters. It's not like she, specifically, was being targeted by all the commentary afterwards. But something about that incident was just too much for Bette to recover from. For a little while Michael would notice Sparkle-Cat lurking on Luxury Replicants, but then, after a time, she stopped signing in altogether. She began to follow fan fiction on journals and blogs rather than messageboards; she would email links to Michael of fics that she liked but only vaguely engaged with anything Michael might have said about things that were happening on Luxury Replicants. The WhiteKnight incident, although its spectre would fade a little over time, remained a steadfast item of Luxury Replicants' lore. But the truth is that despite his distance from it, even Michael felt poisoned by the WhiteKnight incident, as if it was some kind of test that he didn't quite pass.

There is scarcely anything more difficult than humiliation survived alone, Tako says to Pikkoro, offering her a tissue. She has just arrived home from a tough day at school, during which a substitute teacher had criticized her assignment in front of the whole class. Is this an episode of the anime, or fan fiction? Michael can see the scene vividly—Pikkoro, swabbing her tears with a stretched sleeve, Tako's offered tissue, white, the simplest of lines; an atypically thick tissue, handkerchief-like, anime tissue for anime tears. Did Michael *watch* this, or *read* this? Like those two kids who broke into that house—an anecdote, Michael knows, that Bette very well could have made up—sometimes, when you get caught up in stories, when it's a *really* good story, one that explains everything, you can be forgiven for forgetting the base reality. Forgetting what's canon.

Bette has inadvertently downloaded a copy of *Inception* that is equipped with an English Audio Descriptive Service. Neither Bette nor Michael can be bothered to find another torrent, so they just settle in and keep going. It is surprisingly not distracting to watch a movie at the same time as this voice describes what you are seeing. The voice is a confirmation that you are seeing the same visual cues and interpreting them in an approximately identical manner. The voice supplies words for you to describe things more accurately, things you didn't realize had a name, like *balustrade* and *portico*. The voice describes meaningful glances between characters that you might have failed to detect. The voice even describes the Warner Bros logo animation that plays at the start of the movie. The voice is rapt and attentive, both affectionate and matter-of-fact. It could be British or Australian; it's hard to tell which.

The climactic moment—when the inception takes hold, when the sleepers ride the kicks up the collapsing dream levels—is a tour de force of rapid, crisp delivery.

In the hospital, Fischer continues to hold his father's hand. The hospital collapses. The floor cracks open and Fischer falls. In the elevator, Fischer opens his eyes. Eames opens his eyes. But in the hospital, Ariadne is still asleep. In Limbo, Cobb attends to Mal. Ariadne succumbs to the gale. She falls off the edge of the balcony and into the void. She wakes up in the hospital. Cobb sleeps on. The floor cracks and falls away entirely. Ariadne wakes up in the elevator. The elevator slams into the roof in a crash of sparks. Ariadne wakes up in the falling van. Water bursts through the windows.

Bette's fallen asleep. She leans on Michael's shoulder, one hand curled in a fist to her chest, the other open on her lap, the tips of her fingers still shiny with Domino's grease. She's wearing a purple hoodie from Owls in the Navy that is adorned with the text *It's HarvestTime™* and a screenprint of the HarvestTime™ logo, a tree made of love hearts. She hasn't worn this hoodie in a while. Michael wonders if this is Bette's sly way of admitting to writing *Rubik*. Or if it simply means that Bette has recently revived her interest in *Pikkoro* and may demand a re-watch soon. Not that she was ever *un*interested in *Pikkoro*. Just that, from time to time, a particular text will come to rule Bette's life in a persistent, all-encompassing way—like that time in high school when she was obsessed with *Battle Royale*, and would rank her classmates on how long she'd estimate they'd survive in a Battle Royale, and brainstorm unorthodox weapons that they might be assigned. 'Syringes,' she'd say randomly to Michael. 'Bear traps.'

There's this trope from *Pikkoro* where a solid object like a wall turns transparent so you can see what's on the other side, accompanied by a little piccolo trill. Michael has that moment now—*trill!*—as he looks to the living room wall, sees *through* the wall to Bette's bedroom, where he knows that above Bette's bed hangs a poster for *Pikkoro and the Multipurpose Octopus*. It's Tako, in the form of a hot air balloon. His passengers are Pikkoro and the friends she acquires during the show's thirty-six-episode run. The HarvestTime™ headquarters are just visible, a dark bruise on the horizon. It's the most widely available poster for *Pikkoro* but one that Bette, actually, doesn't like very much. She liked *Pikkoro and the Multipurpose Octopus* the best when it was just Pikkoro and Tako—no Yuki the friendly transfer student, no Haruka from the After School Learning To Be Better Club. As far as Bette is concerned, Pikkoro and Tako are all that Pikkoro and Tako require. All of Bette's *Pikkoro* fan fiction, when she still wrote it, proceeded stubbornly from the first season—Pikkoro, forever the loner; Tako, Pikkoro's only friend.

Michael watches Leonardo DiCaprio collect his luggage from the carousel and stride through the airport, nodding to his fellow business-class passengers. The score is triumphantly slow, warm, and if you watch the scene in just the right way, you could pretend that it is actually an advertisement for American Airlines. In spite of it, Michael lets the orchestral waves carry him along. He looks across at Bette, still asleep, and he feels overwhelmed with protectiveness. He wants Bette to be okay. He wants more than anything for them both to be okay.

Bette opens her eyes just in time to witness the spinning top, wobbling, before the screen cuts to black.

That smug bass line of the Hans Zimmer score.

The Audio Descriptive Service voice even reads out the credits. Michael likes the relish with which the voice pronounces *Pete Postlethwaite*.

'What time is it, Michael?' Bette asks.

'About nine.'

'Will you go with me somewhere?'

At the public library near Bette's house, just to the left of the after-hours return slot, she shows him.

'Why didn't you tell me?'

Bette shrugs. She fingers her pink earphones like rosary beads.

'What's it playing?'

'I don't know.'

'How long have you known about this?'

Bette shrugs again. She winds the earphone cord around her index finger.

Michael wonders whether to ask, decides against it, but then asks anyway. 'Are you *sure* that wasn't you, writing *Rubik* on LR?'

Bette snorts. 'What kind of question is that? "Are you *sure* that wasn't you, doing a thing that you already said you didn't do?" Don't be a dick, Michael.'

'Well, I can't think of any other explanation for it.'

'Will you forget about the fic for a sec?' She waves at the audio port. 'We're here now.'

'What are you waiting for? Why didn't you just listen to it when you found it?'

'Why didn't *you*? With the one you found on the train?'

'I was at my *stop*—'

'You were scared,' Bette says. 'You were embarrassed.' She crouches down and pushes the jack into the port. She untangles one earbud for herself and extends the other to Michael. 'Now, come on. No one's here.'

No one's here. For a moment Michael registers her words like a sly joke—*no one's here*—as if Bette is a Tyler Durden–esque imaginary projection. He really is standing alone at a deserted library at night and the earphones are actually hanging limply from the port. Michael crouches down beside Bette and accepts her offered earbud. The cord's short length forces them to lean their heads together as if they are praying.

Michael and Bette each push in their earbud.

—borrow an item from the library, you must first obtain a membership card. To obtain a membership card, you will need to go to the enquiries desk. The enquiries desk is often distinguishable from the loans desk because it is lower to the ground with two chairs facing the counter, whereas the loans desk is typically chest-height with a standing queue. Approach the enquiries desk. State that you would like a membership card. A possible script is: 'Hello, I am a first-time borrower. Could I please apply for a membership card?' The person at the enquiries desk will ask you for details such as your name, address, and telephone number. He or she will issue you your card. This card may entitle you to borrow items from other associated libraries—check with the person at the enquiries desk. A possible script is: 'Does this membership card allow me to borrow books at any other libraries?'

'What *is* this?' Bette whispers. The voice carries on.

There are two ways to take out a loan at the library. The first way is to approach the loans desk. Present your books to the person behind the counter and he or she will scan them and deactivate any security devices on the loan item. These loans will be recorded in a database. The person who processes your loan will also print out a receipt which specifies the due date of your loan items. You must return the loan items by sliding them into the return slot located inside the library, or, the after-hours return slot located outside the library, on or before the specified date. The second way to take out a loan is to use one of the self-service machines located near the library exit. Each machine is equipped with a series of instructional graphics on how to operate it. Like the person at the loans desk, the machine will also produce a receipt with the due date of your items. There are no particular advantages to using either the self-service machines or the loans desk. They are equally valid methods of processing your loan.

Michael glances at Bette and is surprised by what he sees in her face. Not incredulity, not a mocking sneer, but a look of vast, plain, tender understanding. She is moved, and Michael, if he were honest, would admit that he is moved too. He finds himself meditating on this last insight. It is somehow both reassuring and scary. Neither method is better than the other. They are equally valid.

Today's new arrival is the Oh, Buoy! tea infuser. It is a hollow silicone ball shaped like a buoy with holes punctured into the detachable lower half. It comes in four vibrant colors—red, blue, yellow, and orange. Best of all, the halves of the Oh, Buoy! tea infuser can be turned inside out, so you can clean out stubborn wet tea leaves with ease. And it is, of course, dishwasher safe. The Oh, Buoy! tea infuser is $14.95.

The ports become easier to find now that Michael knows they exist. Just that morning Bette had Snapchatted him a port she found at the Coles deli counter. There is even a port right here underneath the cash register at Ampersand. Michael is pretty sure it wasn't there before. The voice conveys advice such as *Do not comment too extensively on a customer's purchase as anything more than the most perfunctory flattery may come across as insincere* and *During very busy periods it is not so important to greet every customer who comes in to the store, but if the store is very quiet, failure to greet a customer will be especially conspicuous, and every effort should be made to acknowledge each customer in those instances—a simple 'hi' will suffice.*

As Michael listens, he overlays his memory of the sound of the *Inception* Audio Descriptive Service voice saying *Pete Postlethwaite* to figure out whether it's the same voice that's issuing forth from the audio port. During Michael's brief stint in counselling, his psychologist always encouraged him to express his feelings in percentages. So Michael would say that he is about seventy-five percent certain it is the same voice. He looks over at Bette unlocking the jewelry display case for a customer and, he doesn't know why, but he is reluctant to share this thought with her. Perhaps Bette already knows, and it was not an accident that the copy of *Inception* that she had downloaded contained the Audio Descriptive Service voiceover. Or maybe it really was just a coincidence; maybe Bette, too, was scared to listen to the audio port alone. Equal validity. Both stories true.

'Hello,' says a customer, and Michael quickly yanks out his earphones.

'Hi, sorry,' Michael mumbles, as the customer stacks her purchases on the counter. The Falling Cat T-shirt, the Love Of All Things Bolshevik earrings, and the Strawberry Bomb brooch, this last of which, once scanned through, the customer immediately unpins from the cardboard and positions on her green cardigan.

'That's a nice brooch,' Michael ventures. 'It goes with your cardigan.' Mindful of the audio port's counsel, he keeps it succinct.

'Thanks,' the customer smiles. Michael feels flush with success. 'Been busy today?' the customer asks.

'Not really. It's been pretty quiet.'

As the customer unbuttons her wallet and presents her Visa card, Michael gauges her approximate age. Twenty-seven? Twenty-eight? He pulls out the thick ribbon handles of the carry bag and passes it over the counter. He meets her eye. Telepathically projects the question, *Are you Rubik3?*

'Have a good one,' the customer says.

'You too.'

Michael watches the green cardigan disappear out the glass doors, the brown Ampersand carry bag with its firm, smooth base. He looks over at Bette and wonders if she witnessed him having such effective dialogue with a customer for once, but Bette is watching her own customer weighing the merits of two silver pendants. Michael reattaches his earbuds, invoking *Pete Postlethwaite.* It's the same voice, he tells himself. Ninety percent certain.

Rubik was updated six hours ago. Two facts now lead Michael to believe that Bette isn't behind it: one, six hours ago, Bette and Michael were just beginning their shift at Ampersand; two, this latest update makes reference to Audrey, a character who appears in one of the early chapters of *Seeds of Time*, and Michael is certain that Bette has never read anything by H.R. Kwai.

> Audrey is good at fixing things. I wish you could meet her. She is kind like you, and really clever. Machines just listen to her. When I watch her fix something, it's like the time we found that injured bird, and it would not stay still for me or even you, but it stayed still for the vet. Machines stay still for Audrey; they will let her help them. I asked Audrey if she could help me modify my PASIV Device but she says that what I am asking is impossible. I wonder if *you* could turn into a PASIV Device, Tako. A PASIV Device is a kind of transportation vehicle, if you think about it creatively. I can imagine your arms stretching and thinning into neat spools of IV infusion lines, your round suckers expanding to pistons, your ocellus forming the central Injection Activation Trigger. For the meantime, Audrey says, she can help me install a lock on my PASIV Device so that no one can tamper with it. She showed me the most basic premise of a lock, which is creating a series of obstacles, impediments, and it is only through a specific alignment of the parts—the creation of a shear line—

that the lock will yield. Tako, some people who I meet, they are so attached to reality. They value it more than anything else. They're always clutching their totems. They get cross with themselves if they get affected by something that happens to them in a dream, if they wake up crying or with their hearts racing. Then there are others who are attached to dreaming. They abandon their totems. They go down one level and then another and another. They design dreams from memories and memories from dreams. Audrey says that reality and dreams are in the end both stories that we tell ourselves. They are two keys that turn the same lock.

A *third* fact, perhaps, is that this update shows Pikkoro relying on another character besides Tako, and, given Bette's penchant for friendships with a maximum population of two, in fiction and in life, Michael can't see Bette writing this fic, even as a joke. It would go too much against the grain of Bette, the well-worn grooves of her neural pathways.

Michael is scrolling down the *Rubik* thread on his Seed and, at the same time, he's jacked into the audio port located just under the window of this carriage of the train. Right now, the voice says:

If you are an able-bodied person who is capable of standing, it is courteous to offer your seat to others in the event that the carriage is full. Some people are hesitant to do this for risk of causing offence; however, there is a variety of reasons why one might require a seat more than you, and an offer of a seat is by no means a speculation or a judgement. Even if you are unsure, it is recommended that you nonetheless make the offer, once, and do not persist if the other person declines. A possible script is: 'Excuse me, would you like a seat?' Vacating your seat and extending your open hand towards the seat is also effective. Alternatively, if you anticipate that the train will become crowded, you can pre-emptively leave your seat. Take care not to stand in a position that will obstruct the flow of passengers. Sometimes it is preferable to take a seat rather than cause an obstruction.

The reflections in each window are almost as clear as mirrors, glossed black by the night, interrupted by the lonely speeding lights of cars on the freeway. The train shudders over the rails. Nobody else seems to be taking any notice of what Michael is doing. Even when Michael brings himself to look directly at another passenger, the other person's gaze seems to slide around Michael, as if being jacked in to the port renders him invisible. Michael has never seen anybody else listening to one of these audio ports except for Bette. He wonders if he should find this odd.

The Aeris memorial thread is starting to lose steam. There are only two new comments since the last time Michael checked the thread. MikiruBeeeeeam has reposted a photograph of Aeris in which he is actually dressed up as Aeris from *Final Fantasy VII*—this impressively bearded white guy in his mid-thirties, pink dress, basket of flowers, *fuck you* smile. What Michael couldn't tell Bette that day, because she didn't want to hear it, was that Ares changing his name to Aeris is a reference to an incident about three years ago, when a user named Rhesus incited a flame war against another user for posting a picture of himself in the Cosplay thread wearing a dress, an attack which only earned Rhesus a tempban and led the other user—though there's no way of really knowing for sure—to gradually disappear from Luxury Replicants. In some kind of solidarity move against Rhesus, Aeris and a handful of other male-identifying users posted pictures of themselves wearing dresses or skirts. Sometimes the pictures would have captions like: *No shame in skirts. No shame in femininity.*

Michael thought Bette would appreciate this story, given her critical observations of Ampersand. Because Michael is now processing some facts using Bette's lens. The matching outfits adorning the Ampersand models would always be unisex, as is Ampersand's brand mission—to design and manufacture clothes that can be worn by both men and women—but these outfits would never include a dress. They'd never make the boy-side of the Ampersand ambassadorship wear a dress. The version of gender neutrality peddled by Ampersand will always veer inexorably towards maleness. It's that *safely transgressive* thing again.

But why would Michael want to tell that Aeris story to Bette, anyway? He can imagine what she'd say already: *What do you want, Michael, a cookie? A Hallmark card that says CONGRATULATIONS?* Michael knows. You don't get extra credit for figuring stuff out. You still cross-sell and up-sell. You still buy the Executive Decision earrings. Users like Rhesus get a temp-ban and reassimilate with barely a ripple; users like—it's so telling that Michael can't even remember the cross-dressing user's name—slowly withdraw from public space; users like Aeris pay the social cost of speaking out but it's a cost they can afford, snug and safe inside their bodies— even Aeris, whose cancer-ridden body would eventually overthrow him, was still in some way kept safe by it; and users like Michael remain silently disapproving of how it all plays out, the injustice of it all, but silent nonetheless.

The train sways, trembles along the rails. It seems to be moving more sluggishly than usual, though Michael, too preoccupied with the voice in the audio port, with Aeris, with the history of Luxury Replicants, does not linger on this thought for too long. Instead Michael notices, for the first

time, a woman sitting opposite him. At first Michael is tempted to play the *are you Rubik3* game, but she looks too young.
She is bent over a book of thick cartridge paper, drawing with
a fine black pen. Her hair is long enough to brush the edge of
the page, dark and carefully loved as the ink strokes she commits to the paper. Focused on some detail near the bottom of
the page, she unconsciously tips the book towards Michael,
so that, upside-down, he can just perceive that the drawing
is of himself—a stretched-out version of Michael, elongated
and thin, skin buckled with age. The earbuds are fashioned
as Venus flytrap–like pods with sinuous stems, cupping his
face tenderly. Then the woman's fingers close around the spiral spine of the book and she tilts the artwork out of view.
She crosses one leg over the other and props the book on her
thigh. Michael realizes he's seen this pose before. In an artful-
ly cluttered house flooded with sunlight, one figure tipping
a book from a well-stocked shelf of creaky paperbacks, the
other figure sitting like this woman now, a paperback pinned
open with one hand.

'Ursula?'

The woman looks up just as the lights go out. The carriage
jackknifes. Arcs backwards. Upwards. The train abandons
the tracks, sleepers snap free of their rails and fling themselves at the sky. The gray plastic handholds lash sideways
until they dangle near-parallel with the ceiling and the distant cars on the freeway hurtle like firelit arrows across the
window. Michael slides across the carriage floor as if dragged
by a tablecloth in a botched magic trick, and Ursula too, her
book escaping her grasp, pages fanning out from the spine,
black veined on white. The fall snatches Michael's rightmost
earbud from his ear, whips across his cheek, and the last thing
Michael will remember is the voice saying in his left ear, *There
are a number of ways to load credit on to your SmartRider card—*
before it cuts out, replaced instead by familiar, earnest violins,

trumpets gently galloping, as if in outer space. *Oh,* Michael will have time to think. *Oh.* And then the vocals kick in, misted, monochrome, from up above, *Non, rien de rien. Non, je ne regrette rien.*

Tako, something horrible has happened. Last night I had a dream. A proper dream—though, as always, you can't really be sure of that, the way things are, here, now. I had arrived home from school but you were not in the living room. You were not in the kitchen. You were not in my bedroom. You were not in the bathtub. I called for you, Tako, Tako, Tako. I wondered if you were in trouble. I knew you had been home recently because your novel was open on the table, and your knitting needles were in the middle of casting on, and the newspaper was folded back where you had circled some jobs that you liked the look of. But then I noticed on the mantelpiece that the photo of us was missing. I was going to leave the apartment and look for you—I'm not sure where I would have looked, but everything seemed closer together in this dream, like I could go anywhere in a few footsteps, as if all the locations of my life were stage settings connected by doors. I ran to my bedroom to gather supplies. But this time when I went into my bedroom I saw you. You were on the floor in the middle of my room. But you weren't yourself. You were deflated, boneless. You were a heap of skin. You didn't look dead so much as empty, like the poncho you knitted me for the play. You didn't look dead so much as never alive. I screamed. I could not look away. I reached for my totem but I woke up before I could even touch it.

I was trembling. I found my totem and I checked it all over. I counted seven colors on one face. But then when I turned the Rubik's cube in my hand I saw that the opposite face had been solved. One side was entirely blue. I didn't make my totem this way. I think someone is trying to trick me, Tako. I am changing all the audio ports to play something else. Please find me quickly, Tako. I am so scared that you are gone.

The first person Michael meets again is Bette. They stand on the edge of something vast, like an oval, or a beach, or the hard blue sky that is so much a part of every universe, regulation issue, a blue screen perfect as death. They don't know what's true, but they'll take it, whatever it is. They are happy to take this moment as true, the baseline of true, and adjust everything else in their memory accordingly.

'Where've you been?' Bette asks Michael, which Michael knows is Bette's approximate way of saying that she missed him.

She is wearing her purple *It's HarvestTime*™ hoodie. She scrunches her hands in the bib pocket. Michael is about to respond to Bette's question, even though he doesn't know the answer, but everything seems to travel slowly, even his thoughts—sliding along straight, silent trajectories, like cars on the freeway as observed from a train. He gets far enough as parting his lips, but Bette says, 'Never mind. You're here now.'

They walk through Bette's tiny house. There are photographs pinned to the walls, each carefully framed, and they feature an orange-haired girl and a brown octopus, selfies all of them, so that none of the photos contains all eight of the octopus's arms and the girl is, more or less, always in a loose kind of embrace. Bette leads Michael by the hand, gently, as if she is a child guiding a wheeled toy across a cracked footpath.

'Are we almost there?' Michael asks.

'Maybe.'

They pick up a little speed. They are walking on the conveyor belt of an airport luggage collection carousel. 'Where are we going, Bette?'

'We're trying to find the beginning.'

'Why?'

Bette steps off the carousel into the arrival hall of the airport. 'That's the thing, isn't it? The easiest way to test that you are dreaming is to try to remember how you arrived.'

They are walking through a factory of workers dressed in mechanics' overalls sorting through broken bits of animals. Then the public library near Bette's house, the brass cover of the after-hours return slot catching the light and flashing like a lost piece of jewelry.

'This way,' Bette says, still gently. 'This way.'

And then they are walking through the Leederville outlet of Ampersand, the repurposed milk crate and wooden pallet shelves, the astroturf, the bunting cut from comic books, the glossy piles of T-shirts and giftware, the backlit posters of Ursula and Graeme. At first Michael is disappointed that Ampersand is here too, wherever *here* is, but like a car on the freeway the feeling just passes on, melts at the edge of perception, disappears.

And then they enter Michael's bedroom, lit only by the screen of his Mac, perched lopsided on his unmade bed, open to the dark *Blade Runner* skyline that forms the header image of Luxury Replicants, the nested subforums bristling with alternative endings, alternative timelines, alternative theories. At this moment, the random quote generator underneath the

Luxury Replicants header says: *You have everything necessary to begin.*

'Are we almost there?' Michael finds himself asking.

'Maybe.' They are in the street now, outside Michael's bedroom. The Cho family car is parked on the street, a blue Ford EA Falcon. Bette's green provisional licence plates are affixed to the front and back windscreens with gobs of Blu-Tack. Bette unlocks the car. 'Let's go.'

She climbs into the driver's side and stretches across the gearbox to unlock the passenger's side. She waits for Michael. The whole shimmering universe waits. Michael takes one last moment to look at where he is, seeing his bedroom for the first and last time from the outside. How small and safe it looks, he thinks, studying it as a scientist might study a diorama. How dear, how precious.

Bette does not urge Michael to get in the car, does not hurry him along, but Michael doesn't wish to keep her waiting. He gets in the car and shuts the door.

Bette inserts the key into the ignition. She creates a shear line. She turns the key.

The street outside is marked by poles, lights, blue fluorescent signs—Amcal, Officeworks, Domino's, Gull—all of them flattened, turned sepia, passing through the car as stripes and shadows, and Michael, having no memory of strapping on the seatbelt that crosses his chest, feels more and more like a child. Time experienced as a dim slideshow.

Pepsi, ANZ, Facebook, DELL.

Bank of Queensland, Taylor & Sondergaard, KPMG, Big W.

Simplicity Funerals, IBM, Bupa, IKEA.

Poles and lights, stripes and shadows.

Bette flicks the indicator, glances up at the rear-view mirror, and then across at Michael. The indicator clicks five times. She commits the car to the turn.

ℛuan x 05

April Kuan is not expendable! April Kuan has more than two lines of dialogue! April Kuan is you! You have seven different outfits. Today you are wearing Outfit Two: gray jeans, green sneakers, Owls in the Navy tee that's the same blue as the Blue Screen of Death. These outfit components can be intermixed, so really you have more than seven outfits.

Today's got a Disc One feel, gleaming like a full health bar. There are zero items in your inventory and a round number of dollars in your pocket. There's a camera on your desk that's trying to pop into the foreground, so you pick it up and hang it around your neck. APRIL KUAN HAS RECEIVED THE CANON.

Your default movement is a brisk run but your home is too small for that kind of exertion. You make coffee. It has no effect.

The first thing you have to do is find your Nexus. It's chirruping in the bedroom somewhere. When you find it, the caller ID says: ARCH.

'Yo!'

'April, where are you?'

'What?'

'Stace and I are at the gallery. Thought we agreed to get here at ten.'

'$#*@!'

'Listen, don't worry about it. There's been a delay and they're starting at eleven instead. Will you be able to get here by then?'

'Yeah! I'm sorry!'

'It's okay. See you soon.'

Cripes. Scull the last of your coffee, tumble out the door and down the stairs, zig-zag all the way to Bull Creek. Swipe your SmartRider and sprint down the escalator and swerve onto the platform.

You can't know about the woman in the Ray-Ban Aviators watching you dodge the closing doors. You can't know that this lady's gaze follows the train as it takes off towards the city, sliding down the center of the Kwinana, the morning sky still glib and blue.

April Kuan! Nineteen years old! An only child, erratic and a little bit lonely; you eat your greens but don't iron your shirts. You might have a dark past? Some secret trauma buried beneath that crazy exterior? Who knows!

There you are, a few minutes past ten o'clock, dashing up the stairs to Peric Chambers, a former law firm turned small gallery, all gray concrete and white walls; sparse, desperate artworks pinned at precise intervals. But what you can't miss is the sprawling contraption in the center of the gallery, a what's-it, a Rube Goldberg machine, resting on a long knee-high plinth. Two artists are bent over a section of the machine, carefully aligning dominoes. Arch and Stace are already there. Arch is asking questions whenever there seems to be a pause in the artists' work; and Stace, bent over her iPad, well—you suppose she's drawing up yet another indecipherable spreadsheet of something or other: so opaque is the nature of her work to you.

'The Rube Goldberg machine has became a metaphor for my entire life,' one of the artists is saying. 'Sometimes I feel like I'm surrounded by plots. Everywhere, plots.'

'I see,' Arch says. Archna 'Arch' Desai, chief editor of student-run magazine *Lorem Ipsum*, the only student to be elected chief editor for three consecutive semesters. It's all because of that falling girl business in the last issue, what we in the biz might call an exposé, but what Arch has always called plain stupid luck.

Stacey 'Stace' Calbourne, lead copyeditor, so solemnly dedicated to the cause of grammar that even her text messages are properly capitalized. She has no God except the Macquarie, a staunch banner-woman of House Style.

Arch looks up. 'Hey April,' she says, while Stace issues a grim smile.

'Hello! Sorry I'm late! Tell me what to shoot, Chief!'

Arch smiles. Addressing the artists: 'This eager one is our photographer, April Kuan.'

Arch is being too kind. Last week, you accompanied Arch and Stace to a flashmob at Bedshed. You took one hundred photos with the lens cap on. Arch was cool about it, but you looked into Stace's eyes and saw APOCALYPSE. BURNING. FLESH-EATING ACID.

You snap back to the present. Arch says, 'April, this is Ursula Rodriguez and Penny Birch.'

'Hello!' you chirp, forgetting their names instantly.

'Shall we start the performance soon, then?' Penny(?) says, lining up the last domino. She says to you: 'Maybe you want to document the installation before we begin?'

Arch smiles at you as if to say, yes, that's a good idea. Stace smiles as if to say, I am adding your lack of punctuality to my List of Grievances.

'Yeah! Sure!' You make sure you flick off the Canon's lens cap and pocket it for safekeeping. 'April Kuan, documentin' the installation.'

'You were saying that you feel like you're surrounded by plots, Ursula.' Stace, shepherding the interview back on track.

'Yes.'

'What do you mean by plots?'

'Well, conspiracies. Other people's plans. There are too many moving parts. You can't trace anyone's motives because you can't see the whole machine.'

This one, the one called Ursula, is kind of familiar. Where's she from? There is something slippery and uncategorisable about her. Something atypical. She has really nice hair.

Tune out, peer through the viewfinder. Through this limited perspective, you attempt to follow the logic of the Rube. It's pretty nice to look at even when nothing is moving, everything conscientiously aligned, like in a kikki.K catalogue, or a miniature scale model in a Wes Anderson film. You can imagine a marble navigating the precise rows of pencils and the grooves of open notebooks, guided by dislocated typewriter keys and pegs. There is even a little origami box on an inclined string cable line. The climactic finish appears to be the dominoes, as the last one's fall will trigger a xylophone mallet to swing like a pendulum and strike a bell. The starting marble will not travel to the very end of the machine; instead it will set off other marbles on meticulously planned journeys.

'So this "conspiracy", like a Rube Goldberg machine, might be a complicated undertaking to achieve a very simple task,' Arch says.

Ursula nods. 'Yes, that's it exactly. There is a kind of aesthetic pleasure to it. The elaborate plot.'

'And you've said before that your individual practice, Ursula, concerns fairytales—do you see them as elaborate plots too?'

'Well, I suppose the antagonists in fairytales can create unnecessarily elaborate plots. When I was younger I often wondered why the wicked witch didn't just transform herself into someone more beautiful than Snow White, for example—I mean she had the power to make herself ugly, why not the power to make herself beautiful? It would've simplified the whole operation.'

'Do you think plots are inherently evil then?'

Ursula laughs. 'I don't know. Perhaps! But with fairytales we have the benefit of omniscience, you see. But in the real world? No.'

Penny says, 'But I'm sure you've had your fair share of plots, Arch.'

Hold the phone! Stace's eyes turn guarded, but Arch remains level. 'What do you mean?'

'You know. You found the falling girl.'

'I didn't find her, actually, she came to me. To *Lorem Ipsum.*'

'Wait,' Ursula says. 'What's this all about?'

Penny sighs. 'Oh Ursula, the way you manage to miss huge pop cultural events, it's amazing. This is like the time I had to explain what lolcats were.' Penny puts her hands on Ursula's shoulders and stares at her like a hypnotist or a really intense parent. '*The falling girl*, Ursula. She was from that short film that Seed used when they became a thing. Everyone went apeshit; the falling girl was everywhere. On everything. That T-shirt that you almost had to hawk for Ampersand, my dear, with the falling cat... anyway. Then the filmmakers disappear, and then Arch publishes unseen footage, Seed freaks out—'

'*Lorem Ipsum.*' Arch looks pained. '*Lorem Ipsum* published the footage.'

'What was she like?' Penny asks, dropping her hands from Ursula's shoulders. 'The falling girl.'

You have never seen Arch look so uncomfortable before. 'She was...'

And here we black out for a bit. Then, a slow fade-in: girl, mid-flight, the gray sky at her back. Fierce and falling, her figure seems to echo, the air vibrates electrically; she is both noun and verb, cleanly separate, scissored. She is here on purpose.

She was evasive, Arch's words float down. *I know she was still mourning. Someone close to her had died. She didn't seem... empty exactly. Just resigned. Resigned about everything.*

'We shouldn't discuss this,' Stace says. Snap back to the present. Stace glances around the gallery as if some Seed spy is about to pounce on the lot of them.

Penny looks disappointed. 'Right, right. Well, in that case... shall we get started?' She checks the time on her phone. It just so happens to be a Seed.fon, the glossy touchscreen embedded in the trademark varnished wooden case, but it's an older model, from a year or two ago.

Ursula hurriedly stands up and shakes Arch's hand. 'It was very nice to speak with you.'

'Likewise. Stace will be in touch with you when the article is ready for your approval.'

Sensing that something is about to begin, the stray gallery-goers begin to congregate around the machine. There aren't many people around—it's a Monday, and the official opening was on Saturday. Ursula and Penny stand beside each other. Ursula says, 'Thank you for coming. Penny and I are delighted to present to you the third performance of *Aller*. We ask that you please refrain from taking videos of this performance, but still photography is permitted.'

There is a bowl of marbles positioned at the start of the machine, each one a different color. Ursula selects the blue marble. You snap a shot of the marble setting off on its journey, rolling down a wooden gutter. *Click.* Then you hang the Canon on your chest and watch. The marble, travelling through places you had just photographed.

Down the wooden gutter. Dropping through holes.

Through the zig-zag pathways made out of pegs and typewriter keys.

Triggering a row of marbles to fall into an origami box, a counterweight that makes its twin box spring up and release another marble.

Hitting a staircase of xylophone keys.

Ping.

    Ping.

        Ping.

            Ping.

After that it all starts going too fast, and you begin to see the machine not as a display of actions and reactions but something possessed by magic. So doubtful are the connections, the tipping points, the pathways. It is almost heartbreaking that it all works. The origami box bouncing along the zip line. The marble dropping, hitting the dominoes. The mallet swinging.

Ding! goes the bell.

The spectators applaud, except for you. You look down at the Canon and stare at the preview image of the blue marble as if it defines your future.

Some of the spectators are crowding around Ursula and Penny to ask questions. Arch catches your eye and the three of you, Arch, Stace, April, slip outside the gallery and meet on the footpath.

Stace shifts timetable boxes around on her iPad. 'Two more stops and we're done for the day. We may have to reschedule the Brad Ruffalo meeting.'

'Alright.' Arch looks to you. 'Thanks for coming out, April. We'll talk more about the article at the next meeting.'

'Hey, no problem!'

You watch the two of them walk off, conferring over Stace's iPad. The Canon seems heavier around your neck, as if data has a physical weight. You let yourself feel it. The marble's inexorable slide.

K X 04

'Do you think plots are inherently evil then?' Arch asks.

Ursula laughs. 'I don't know. Perhaps! But with fairy-tales we have the benefit of omniscience, you see. In the real world? No.'

Penny says, 'But I'm sure you've had your fair share of plots, Arch.'

'What do you do if the machine fails?' you blurt out. Four heads swivel to stare at you. Stace is getting that apocalyptic look again. You can see lava. Sparks. Ash. You grip the Canon.

Ursula asks, 'What do you mean?'

'Well,' you flounder. 'There's a few points in the machine where there's a tiny risk of failure. I mean, I get that you've tested it until the probability of failure is close to zero. But what do you do if it doesn't go as planned, like during a performance? With everyone watching?'

Now Stace stares at you as if you're some kind of exotic file extension. What to do with you? Arch waits for the artists' response. Ursula and Penny exchange looks. 'We had a debate about this, actually,' Penny says. 'We thought we should have some sort of protocol, but I don't think we ever actually decided on one. I thought that if it fails, then that should just be the end of the performance, you know. But Ursula thought it would be appropriate to step in, and correct the problem.'

'It hasn't failed yet,' Ursula adds. 'There's always a chance, of course. But it hasn't failed yet. I guess...' She studies the machine, the milling spectators. 'I'm coming around to Penny's way of thinking, now. Once the machine is in motion, it's not ours anymore. It doesn't have to obey us. It's almost like there's some third thing. A third thing that's not us, and not the machine. Something that wills the objects, that determines how things will behave when they're triggered. It wouldn't be right, to intervene.'

'I see,' you say. The silence itches. You point the camera in a random direction and click.

Arch says, 'So really, nobody has the benefit of omniscience. Not even the person who sets it all up.'

Ursula smiles. 'No, I guess not.'

The five of you stare pensively at the Rube Goldberg machine for a moment, as if it is some kind of light phenomenon in the sky. Flashing with secret signals. Then Penny says, 'Well, should we get started?' Checking her Seed.fon for the time.

Ursula quickly stands up and shakes Arch's hand. 'It was very nice to speak with you.'

'Likewise. Stace will be in touch with you when the article is ready for your approval.'

The gallery-goers coalesce around the machine. You twist through the sparse forest of burgundy jeans and knitted scarves until you have a clear sightline. Arch and Stace are hanging back. 'Thank you for coming,' Ursula says to the assembly. 'Penny and I are delighted to present to you the third performance of *Aller*. We ask that you please refrain from taking videos of this performance, but still photography is permitted.'

You watch Ursula's fingers dip into the bowl of marbles. Each of them is a different color, vibrant as candy.

Ursula selects the red marble.

As the marble rolls down the wooden gutter, you lift the Canon.

Outside Peric Chambers, you shield your eyes against the sun, but it's too late—your perception bursts into glowing circles, like the marbles at the start of the Rube Goldberg machine.

Stace unlocks her iPad. 'Two more stops and we're done for the day. We may have to reschedule the Brad Ruffalo meeting.'

'Alright.' Arch looks around. 'How'd you go, April?'

You blink rapidly. 'Yeah, good! See?' You revive the Canon and flip through the photographs for Arch. They're pretty good. A red marble zig-zagging through pegs and typewriter keys. Dropping into an origami box.

'Wow, April,' Arch says, cradling the camera. 'These are excellent! I didn't even know you were shooting when the performance was underway. Stace, check these out.'

Arch passes the Canon to Stace, who appraises each shot carefully. 'How did you know when to time your shots?' Stace asks. She even sounds impressed, however grudgingly.

You shrug. 'I guess I just figured it out. I don't know.'

Arch says, 'We must have spent about half an hour watching Ursula and Penny set up, but I didn't have the foggiest idea what was meant to happen. I wouldn't have been able to understand the action in time, let alone snap a picture.'

'Nice work,' Stace concedes. She passes the Canon back to you and peeps at her iPad. 'Arch, we'd better keep moving.'

'Oh, yes. What were you saying before? We had to reschedule something?'

'Yes. Brad Ruffalo.'

'Oh, that's a shame. I was looking forward to seeing what was going on there. Unless...' And here Arch considers you. That dishevelled girl over there, still pawing her sun-dazzled eyeballs. The stars align. 'Hey, April. How would you like an extra assignment?'

Stace shoots Arch a look, like *are you serious?*

'Yeah!' you exclaim. 'I mean, absolutely. April Kuan, gettin' extracurricular! What do you want me to do?'

'You're going to meet a gentleman named Brad Ruffalo. He's widely acknowledged to be the best claw machine player in Perth. I can email you the brief, and some questions I was going to ask, but feel free to take the lead on this. You seem to have a pretty good understanding of this kind of stuff. Bring your notes to the next *Lorem Ipsum* meeting and we can talk about expanding the interview into an article then.' Arch looks at you carefully. 'This isn't too much, is it?'

'Yeah! I mean no! I understand!'

'It'll be a collaboration.'

'Yes, ma'am! I mean, yes, Arch!'

YOU HAVE BEEN PROMOTED TO JUNIOR REPORTER!

Stace regains her professional composure and notes this latest reshuffling of responsibilities on her iPad. Arch dips into her satchel. 'Oh, and take this.' She holds out a slim device to you.

'Oh cool! Thanks!' APRIL KUAN HAS RECEIVED THE DICTAPHONE!

You are so excited you almost completely miss Arch's tutorial on how to use it. It's okay—you'll figure it out. You're April Kuan!

For no particular reason, you direct your triumphant gaze across the street, where, overseeing the Horseshoe Bridge, there stands an obelisk of billboards, a different advertisement on each of its four faces. There is a new advertisement, so new it seems to radiate that fresh laserjet smell. The vast background is a blown-up photograph of the sky, high-res, so that the billboard seems to be part of the sky itself, a message from God, and superimposed in white is the logo for Seed, and their new slogan: *You have everything necessary to begin.*

'April Kuan, waiting for a train,' you whisper into Arch's dictaphone. 'April Kuan, whispering into a dictaphone.'

April Kuan! Waiting at McIver! Inventory check: Nexus, Canon, dictaphone. A new train arrives in two minutes. Beyond the train tracks there is one of those giant electronic signs attached to a trailer that says, IF YOU SEE SOMETHING, SAY SOMETHING. It is almost adorably kitsch. Paranoia? Citizen surveillance? So 2001, amirite?

'Field note the first,' you whisper into Arch's dictaphone. 'Camouflage insurgents' hideout with "if you see something say something" sign. Effective? Investigate in own time.'

A group of boys in navy private school blazers approach the platform. They throw their too-big schoolbags on the bench and untuck their white shirts from their gray trousers. Are they wagging? A half-day?

For a moment a memory threatens to bubble to the surface of your brain. A little blister of tension. What's that all about? You shuffle a little bit further down the platform. 'Extension of field note the first,' you whisper into the dictaphone. 'How judgy are those signs? Kind of victim-blamey? Is that the sort of thing that an insurgency organization wants to perpetuate? Or would it be an act of subversiveness? April Kuan, conflicted.'

You tuck away the dictaphone and take out your Nexus. You re-check the brief that Arch emailed you on Brad Ruffalo. You're kind of excited to meet him. An expert claw machine player? It's the kind of very specific skill that you appreciate in a person.

The train arrives and you board a different carriage from the wagging/maybe-not-wagging schoolboys.

The brief directs you to a claw machine arcade in Victoria Park. *HarvestTime,* the sign declares in bulging rainbow letters, and in smaller but no less enthusiastic print, *Fun For All Ages.*

Hey, so, here's an idea: maybe you should make observations of a journalistic flavor, a bit of scene-setting? How impressed would Arch be with that?! You take out the dictaphone. 'Field note the second,' you say, shading your eyes against the sun so you can look through the glass door. 'HarvestTime is Fun For All Ages. During the daytime, on this Monday, it is deserted. I see rows and rows of inert claw machines. Their gently pulsing lights. TOYS they say. ARE YOU THE SKILL MASTER they say. GRAB A DUCK. UNICORN MADNESS. SURPRIZE!!!! I think I can just make out a kind of bowling alley-style canteen, glowing at the back there. That's great because I could use a snack.'

The glass door says PUSH so you PUSH.

And as you wander down the aisle, claw machines lined up either side, there are like one million comparisons popping in your mind. 'Extension of field note the second: being in here is like being inside a laboratory of quarantined plushies,' you tell the dictaphone. 'It's like being in an aquarium supermarket. It's like being in a museum for forgotten franchises—there's Dr Mario, there's Tom and Jerry, there's Huckleberry Hound, there's an entire machine full of minor and obscure Pokémon, there's the eponymous protagonist from *Alpha Cheese* who looks a little too much like Sponge-Bob Squarepants.'

Beyond the aisle of end-to-end claw machines is the canteen, empty and blue-lit. There's a woman there wearing Aviators and a dark red leather jacket the color of dried blood. She's sitting at a table in the canteen, closest to the counter, with an untouched bottle of Coke. There is nobody behind the counter. Is she an employee here? Nursing a hangover? You square your shoulders and Approach With Confidence.

You see yourself mirrored in her stern Aviators. April Kuan, stretched out over a convex surface. The claw machines are mirrored too, pulsing with warped light.

'Hi hi! I'm looking for Brad Ruffalo,' you say.

'He doesn't exist,' the lady says.

'What?'

'Duck,' the lady says.

Is that the sound of... glass cracking? You turn around—

And the Grab-A-Duck machine EXPLODES.

'Holy sh—'

And then the Toy Chest explodes, and the Omegaclaw, and Big Prizes, and the Try Your Luck, and SURPRIZE!!!!, everything exploding, glass and sparks flying everywhere, claws jerked on their chains, light bulbs snapping, and just as quickly bullets puncture your shoulders and the air turns red.

And then, blue.

You hear the distant bells of a descending boomgate.

The whistle of a Transperth train.

K X 03

There's a woman there wearing Aviators and a dark red leather jacket the color of dried blood. She's sitting at a table in the canteen, closest to the counter, with an untouched bottle of Coke. There is nobody behind the counter. Is she an employee here? Nursing a hangover? You square your shoulders and Approach With Confidence.

You see yourself mirrored in her stern Aviators. April Kuan, stretched out over a convex surface. The claw machines are mirrored too, pulsing with warped light.

The woman in the Aviators sees you *SEE*-ing her and waits for you to *SAY SOMETHING*.

'Hi hi,' you say. 'Um. You're not Brad Ruffalo, are you?'

'I'm Jules Valentine.'

'Well, hi! I'm April Kuan from *Lorem Ipsum* and—'

'Duck.'

Oh yeah! You dive underneath the table just as the Grab-A-Duck machine explodes. Jules Valentine pivots, slips a hand behind her jacket, tugs a pistol (?!?!?!) free, fires a line of shots into the arcade. She crouches behind a claw machine containing a chubby assortment of knock-off Kirbies and ejects the pistol cartridge. She removes another one from her jacket. 'Stay there,' Jules says.

'Are you some kind of secret agent?' you whisper.

She twists out from behind the claw machine and blasts away again. Twists back from return fire. You can't see where it's coming from. The floor writhes with sparking cables and acrylic shards. There are rubber ducks everywhere.

'Let's bail,' Jules says.

'Bail where?' you ask but Jules strides out from behind the machine, fires two shots, hauls you up by the scruff of your T-shirt and drags you over the canteen counter. The Canon bangs against your chest but Jules is having none of this *OW MOTHER#$@%* business and pulls you to your feet and rushes you through the sparse kitchen and out the back door. You tumble into an alleyway of abandoned milk crates and painful natural light.

'Sorry about that,' Jules says.

'Where's Brad Ruffalo?' you ask, but Jules is already walking briskly out onto the street, tucking her gun away, throwing glances back at HarvestTime. You keep up the pace. 'I'm on assignment, you see, for *Lorem Ipsum*. I work for Archna Desai, do you know Arch? I'm meant to interview Brad Ruffalo—'

'I know Arch Desai,' Jules says. 'And don't worry. This interview was a cover.'

'Huh?'

'What did you say your name was? April?'

'Yeah.'

You're at a pedestrian crossing now, among a handful of office workers returning from lunch. 'Listen, April.' Jules spins you by the shoulder.

You look into her Aviators. 'I'm listening.'

'I've put you in danger. I'm really sorry about that. But I need your help.'

'Sure!'

'You were just at the exhibition of Ursula Rodriguez and Penny Birch, right?'

'Yeah. The one with the Rube Goldberg machine. I took photos.' You jiggle the Canon.

The red man turns green and you're jostled into crossing the street. Jules glances back at HarvestTime. Then her gaze alights upon the Canon. 'I need you to help me, April.'

'You need me to work with you?' you say, a little too enthusiastically.

She pauses. 'Yes.'

'Awesome! I'll do it!'

YOU HAVE BEEN PROMOTED TO ASSASSIN'S ACCOMPLICE (????)!

Jules thumbs a button on her keychain. 'In here.' She slips into the driver's side of a battered Toyota Corolla. You hop in the other side. 'Can I see the photographs of the exhibition?'

'Sure!' You power up the Canon and pass it to her. Jules studies the preview window. She doesn't take off her Aviators, which is kind of weird. She dedicates at least six seconds to each photograph. 'These are good.'

'Thanks!'

And then Jules studies you. You smile bravely and try to exude confidence and warmth, which is tricky to do while you're wearing a Blue Screen Of Death T-shirt. Jules re-secures her Aviators higher up on the bridge of her nose. 'Let's establish some ground rules.'

'Okay.'

'Rule number one,' Jules says as she retrieves a white card and a blue biro from her jacket and writes down a ten-digit number. 'If we get separated, this is my number.'

'Yep! Hey, why does this card say "STFU" on the back?'

'Private joke. Rule number two,' Jules says. 'If you want out of this, tell me. At any time. I won't ask any questions.'

'Yep!'

'Rule number three,' Jules says. 'You can ask me questions. Any question you want. But you can't ask me questions about why I'm not answering a question.'

'Yep! Don't worry, Jules! That's standard protocol for the writers at *Lorem Ipsum*. Arch is pretty good like that.'

Jules gazes at you with something akin to sadness. Where are you getting these cues from? Sad? Wary? Pensive? There is something uniquely expressive about Aviators, perhaps, some subtle capacity for emoting. Oh. You wish you could write that down or tell the dictaphone. 'Okay,' Jules says. She snaps the lid on the biro and returns the Canon. 'That's all the rules for now.'

Jules starts the car and indicates right. She rolls down her window.

You gaze at the Canon and flip through the pictures, smiling. You watch the red marble work its way backwards through the Rube Goldberg machine.

As Jules pulls out into traffic, your smile falters. You hold the camera close. It's a shot of the marble poised at the beginning of the machine, the very start of the sequence, right after Ursula selected the marble from the bowl—but in this particular shot, the marble isn't red. It's blue.

You stare at it, strafing between photographs, but you can't correct your vision, can't turn the marble red.

April Kuan! Strapped into the passenger seat of Jules Valentine's car, the wind fuzzing your hair. April Kuan, heading off into the afternoon, on a mission to do... what?

'Mind if I take some notes?' You wiggle the dictaphone.

'Sure,' Jules says.

'Field note the third,' you tell the dictaphone. 'Sitting in a car with Jules Valentine.' Jules grimaces slightly, so you try to talk rapidly and softly like you've watched Arch do many times in the past. 'Just escaped a shootout at HarvestTime. What was *that* all about? Jules said that the Brad Ruffalo thing was a cover. A cover for what? And who was shooting at us? Were they there for Jules, or for me? April Kuan, intrigued.'

'They were there for you,' Jules confirms.

'They were there for me,' you whisper to the dictaphone. And to Jules: 'Why?'

'They want the Rube Goldberg machine and they think that you can help them get to it.'

'Who's they?'

'Who are they, ever?'

That makes you think. *'Who are they, ever,'* you whisper to the dictaphone.

Jules is going ten kilometers above the speed limit. You pass another one of those Seed billboards, floating in the sky. The scenery blurs, lags, skips.

'Where're we going, Jules Valentine?' you ask.

'Taylor & Sondergaard.'

'Why?'

'We're busting out Ulysses.'

'Who's Ulysses?'

Jules doesn't reply. She flicks her indicator grimly.

'Right. Rule number three.'

Blurs, lags, skips.

You arrive at the Mt. Lawley branch of Taylor & Sondergaard. Jules fetches a parking ticket and displays it on the dash. You appreciate that kind of law-abiding conscientiousness in an assassin. You hurry to follow Jules across the road. She takes long, even strides, one for every two of yours, even when you're jogging, and it's only now that Jules seems familiar to you, the same way Ursula was familiar to you, as if the both of them were part of some memory implanted in your unconscious that has since been imperfectly erased.

'Where've I seen Jules Valentine before?' you whisper into the dictaphone.

Waiting outside Taylor & Sondergaard, sitting on a bench, is a boy who can't help but look small for his age. He's wearing a fancy private school uniform and his companion is a bulky schoolbag that probably contains his entire life. 'Peter,' Jules says. 'Are you ready?'

The boy nods and slides off the bench. A long-ago graffiti artist has affixed a grubby sticker of the falling girl to the back of the bench where the boy was just sitting. Jules takes up his schoolbag by the handle. The bag's contents rattle. The boy squints at you but doesn't say anything. 'Well, hi!' you chirp. 'I'm April Kuan!'

The boy looks pained for a second. The crest on his school blazer is bigger than his fist. 'Hello. I'm Peter Pushkin.'

'Nice to meet you!'

Jules pulls the glass door and holds it open for Peter. 'April, just follow my lead, okay.'

'Sure!'

The three of you enter the waiting room. There are only four clients waiting, eyes cast down onto their phones or magazines. What does Taylor & Sondergaard do, anyway? A barely audible wall-mounted television murmurs in the corner. Jules and Peter approach the counter as if they have been here before. The receptionist is saying, 'Yes, that will be top-notch. Yes. Goodbye,' into his headset, and then, to your assembled party, 'Hello.'

'Hello,' Jules says. She puts a hand maternally on Peter's shoulder. 'We have an appointment for Peter Pushkin with Dr. Lee.'

'Certainly.' The receptionist makes a few clicks on his mouse. Then he looks at you. His brow furrows in that tactful receptionist way.

'This is April Kuan,' Jules says. 'Peter's mentor at school. Dr. Lee requested that she be present at this meeting.'

'Of course,' the receptionist says. 'Please take a seat.'

'Thank you.'

Jules and Peter choose the seats closest to the children's toys. You trail behind them. In this corner of the waiting room, there is a jumble of loose Duplo bricks on a solid, cube-shaped table, which has a green grooved Duplo play-base fixed into the top surface. That receptionist is kind of ...*looking* at the three of you. Jules folds her arms and Peter clasps his hands on his knees. Jules is still wearing her Aviators, which is super weird. It's probably why the receptionist is still staring at the three of you, right? I mean, it's not *you*, is it? Because you're totally not acting conspicuous. To prove it, you slide a magazine off the top of the nearest stack and begin to read. 'April Kuan, reading about summer thighs,' you murmur.

Then the phone rings and the receptionist is hello-yessing into his headset again. Jules nods at Peter, who kneels next to his bag and unzips it. He removes a handful of blue bricks and places them next to the bricks on the Duplo table. Jules joins Peter on her knees on the floor, and then the two of them start grabbing brick after brick, locking them together into segments, and locking the segments to the playbase. They move deftly, with frightening accuracy—not once do they reposition a brick once it's laid down. They're constructing some kind of city. They start with four walls at the edges of the playbase and then set to work on a broad central watchtower with four turrets.

'We have a nine o'clock, ten o'clock and eleven-thirty on that Friday,' says the receptionist.

They've almost exhausted the pile of bricks. They've been careful to rotate through the colors. You lift the Canon and document their progress. At the Canon's click, Peter interrupts his building to look up at you with that same worried look as before. You glance over your shoulder at the other clients, but none of them is observing this.

'I'm afraid those are the only times we have available,' says the receptionist.

All the bricks are gone. It's not quite a city, you realize, but ...almost like a chunky model of a safe—the central tower is actually the dial of a combination lock. Peter twists a pivoting segment in the middle of the structure, first one way, then the other.

And then the safe utters a click, and the table seems to exhale. Peter flips the playbase up from the table. He reaches into the recess. Jules quickly grabs Peter's schoolbag, splitting both zips to the base, while Peter scoops a black cat out of the safe.

Wait—

Jules widens the mouth of the schoolbag and the cat dives out of Peter's arms and into the bag. Jules connects the zips.

Peter shuts the lid of the Duplo table. He threads his arms through the backpack straps and Jules gets to her feet and grabs you by the sleeve. The magazine falls off your knees and slaps the floor but Jules keeps you moving, elbowing the glass door, while the receptionist says, 'Excellent, eleven-thirty it is, then.' Before the glass door shuts you manage to glimpse one of the waiting clients glancing up idly, belatedly, at your fallen magazine.

The three of you regroup around the corner at the falling girl bench. Peter gently slides the schoolbag off his back and pulls down the zips. The cat climbs out. 'Nice work in there,' Jules says. 'I think we've really got this, this time.'

'Thank you,' Peter says. 'Do you have it?'

'Sure.' Jules reaches inside her jacket. She takes out what looks like a scrunched-up ATM receipt. She massages out the folds. It's a diagram of a bird, rendered in thin, precise pencil. She offers it to Peter, who trades it for a red leather pet collar that he recovers from his blazer pocket. He also gives Jules two glossy tickets, still connected by a perforated line. All the while the cat just sits there, watching the exchange. You're feeling so left out right now.

'Hey,' Jules says. 'Good luck, Peter.'

'Thank you.' Peter slowly pulls on his schoolbag, stowing the bird diagram in his pocket.

'Sure I can't give you a ride?'

'No, it's okay. I can walk back to school. Thanks.'

'Be careful,' Jules says, but Peter's already wandering off, in his slow, ruined way. Jules watches him leave, and then glances down at the pet collar in her hand.

You activate the dictaphone. 'ULYSSES, the tag says. 29 SIGMUND ST. No suburb. No phone number either. Field note the fourth: Jules Valentine has just received a possibly entirely ineffective pet collar.'

Jules looks at you and you quickly shut off the dictaphone and back one step away from her. 'So, uh, Jules, where's Peter going?'

Jules purses her lips. She unbuckles the collar and bends down to fix it to the cat, who sleekly extends his neck to accommodate her.

ULYSSES HAS JOINED YOUR PARTY.

The cat and Jules share a look as if they, too, have seen each other somewhere before. It's like that scene at the end of *Jumanji* when Judy and Peter meet Alan and Sarah and it's really creepy and strange because they *have* met before, and they know it, but all that stuff happened in another timeline so it would be super awkward to discuss it.

'Jules? Where's Peter going?'

'He's also trying to find someone,' Jules says. 'I don't really know.'

'What did you mean before, Jules,' you ask, 'when you said to Peter that you think we've really got this, *this time?*'

Ulysses begins to lick himself. Then—*CLAP!*—he flinches, green eyes darting across the road, to the pedestrian path, where Peter staggers sideways, one strap of his schoolbag falling off his shoulder. Another shot claps out and Peter jolts, teeters on his feet; Ulysses jumps off the bench and races towards him; Jules unholsters her gun—'Get down,' she says—and she shoots at a black Holden Barina parked in front of her Toyota, but the car's already taking off, and the bullet only knocks the side mirror. Peter collapses and the car speeds away, the side mirror dangling like an eye from a socket. Ulysses swerves and chases after the black car, ears flattened, but the car's already too far, small and smug in the distance. Jules runs to Peter. Jules runs to Peter. Jules runs to Peter. Jules runs to Peter.

K X 02

ULYSSES HAS JOINED YOUR PARTY.

The cat and Jules share a look as if they, too, have seen each other somewhere before. It's like that scene at the end of *Jumanji* when Judy and Peter meet Alan and Sarah and it's really creepy and strange because they *have* met before, and they know it, but all that stuff happened in another timeline so it would be super awkward to discuss it.

But, whatever! There's no time to spare. You see the black Holden Barina parked behind Jules's car, the open window, the glint of a pistol. *IF YOU SEE SOMETHING DO SOME-THING!* You spy the handgrip of Jules's gun protruding from her jacket so you yank it free and shoot at the first shape you see in the Holden. The Holden's alarm goes off. Peter turns around, sleepy, horrified. You blitz the trigger again and then Jules pushes your wrist down. 'That's enough,' she says. The driver of the Holden faceplants the steering wheel and adds the *baaaaaaaaaaaaaaa* of the horn to the soundtrack. Peter hitches his schoolbag higher and breaks into a jog. He drops out of sight.

There's something strange about the driver. 'Who's that in the black car?' you ask but Jules untangles the gun from your fingers. The alarm is still screaming. 'Get in my car,' Jules says, nudging you, scanning the street with gun raised. 'Ulysses, go.' And in a tumble of central locking and slamming doors you and Jules and Ulysses are blasting out-ta there.

You wriggle onto your knees and watch the black Hold-en grow smaller in the back windscreen, the driver's horn a perpetual note. 'Who was that in the Holden?' you ask, but then Jules executes a particularly sharp turn, so you slide right-way-around in your seat and belt up. Ulysses is bracing himself in the passenger seat, spreading his claws. How did you lose shotgun to a cat?

'That was a waste,' Jules says.

'What?'

'Going back for Peter.'

'What do you mean?'

'He wasn't necessary anymore.'

'Necessary?'

'To accomplish our task.'

'I know,' you say, even though you're not sure that you know. 'But... it seemed like you cared a little about him, Jules. Even if you were just working with him temporarily. Ulysses seemed to care, at least.'

Jules tightens her jaw and says nothing. Ulysses decides to safeguard against the car's momentum by rearranging himself into the bread loaf position.

Something else occurs to you. 'Hey, what do you mean, *going back* for Peter?'

'You know what I mean.'

'No I don't,' you say, even though you do.

Cars race by you like asteroids. Like exiting souls. Like facts that are avoidable for only so long.

Like the worst segue ever, burning a hole through your periphery.

Jules pulls into a car park off Riverside Drive, leans out the window to press the button for a ticket, and proceeds through the boomgate. It's getting close to three o'clock now; the sky is just beginning to sour. You're outside the Perth Concert Hall, perched atop a mountain of stairs, the oblong windows arrayed like the spines of books. 'Field note the fifth: the Concert Hall is quiet today,' you whisper into the dictaphone.

'The courtyard, vast. It proclaims the following architectural statement: We Have Stairs.'

Jules and Ulysses exit the car. You're pretty exhausted. You turn on the Canon and appraise the blue marble again. 'Let's review,' you tell the dictaphone. 'Arch sent us on an assignment to interview Brad Ruffalo, but Brad Ruffalo doesn't exist and instead we fell into stride with Jules Valentine, who's trying to stop some mysterious trigger-happy forces from getting their hands on Ursula Rodriguez and Penny Birch's Rube Goldberg machine. Now Peter Pushkin's pulled a cat called Ulysses out of a Duplo table and narrowly avoided an ambush from a lone shooter and exchanged a pet collar for a diagram of a bird.' You lean back in your seat and sigh, off-the-record, 'This is going to be one strange-ass article, even for *Lorem Ipsum.*' You slide out of the car.

The foyer of the Concert Hall has that same deserted, distant feel as HarvestTime, set up like a museum, as if everything is separated from reality by a Windexed pane of glass. Jules presents the tickets she received from Peter to a black-clad usher. As the usher examines them, you try to peek at the name of the show, but you're distracted by Ulysses brushing past your leg and slipping into the auditorium with barely a rustle of the bell on his collar. The usher hands back the tickets, and you follow Jules up some cushioned red steps.

The auditorium is lit by a ceiling gridded with square amber lights. It's quiet, muffled as an aquarium. There are a few people sitting in the balconies but the lower area of the hall is completely vacant. Ulysses has already staked out three seats in the middle of a row. You sit like this: Jules, Ulysses, April. You all stare, unspeaking, at the empty stage. At the microphones suspended by wires from the ceiling. At the dormant organ pipes like bones in an upturned ribcage. You raise the Canon.

The row of seats tremors a little. There's a man with floppy hair making his way, crabwise, down this row, on Jules's side. He chooses the seat next to Jules, sinking into it slowly, uncertainly. Before you can ask Jules about what's happening, the house lights dim. The air smells expensive, waxy.

Four musicians file onto the stage. A string quartet. Violin, violin, viola, cello. The scant audience offers applause. Jules tentatively joins in, so you do too. Ulysses reclines in his seat.

The lead violinist nods, and the claps fade. The musicians lift their instruments. They embark on a complex melody. The sound of their labour fills the auditorium.

'Tim Spiegel?' Jules says to the man beside her. The man nods. Jules asks, 'Is this your cat?'

The man turns. He cranes his neck to look past Jules. Ulysses glances away from the string quartet for a moment to meet his eye.

'I need to see the tag,' Tim Spiegel says.

Jules reaches out and overturns the tag hanging from the collar. The engraving, ULYSSES / 29 SIGMUND ST, catches the light.

'Where did you find him?'

'Far from home.'

Tim Spiegel stares at Jules. He has a furry brow, which makes him look perpetually worried. He glances at April, but Jules doesn't introduce you, and Tim doesn't ask. Ulysses yawns, baring tiny white teeth. 'Did Seed send you here?' Tim asks.

'No,' Jules says.

'How can I know for sure?'

'Know what for sure?'

'How do I know if I can trust you?'

'How do I know if *I* can trust *you*?' Jules says. 'You've worked for Seed too.'

'That's different.'

'How?'

Tim Spiegel's frown deepens. He returns his gaze to the string quartet. The cellist draws the bow across her strings. You're feeling pretty left out again. Tim Spiegel pinches his closed eyes. 'I'm sorry, Jules. I shouldn't say those things to you.'

Jules studies him. Her Aviators are emoting again. Finally, she says, 'It's okay. Really. I understand.'

'Thank you for finding Ulysses.'

'It was nothing,' Jules says, even though—as you recall the memory, bleeding in another time, of gunshots, of Peter's collapsing body—it really wasn't nothing.

The musicians fall silent. The second violinist steps forward. The pause is too long to signal the initiation of a new section, but not long enough to signal the beginning of a new work entirely. The violinist rests her chin on her instrument and commences a solo. It starts with a motif that she plucks instead of bows. You've heard it somewhere before. A TV advertisement, perhaps.

'April.'

'Yeah?'

'May I please borrow your dictaphone?'

'Sure.' You surrender the dictaphone.

Jules removes a white piece of paper from her jacket pocket, folded into quarters. She hands both the dictaphone and the piece of paper to Tim Spiegel. 'Read this out, please.'

Tim unfolds the piece of paper. He scans what is written there, his lips moving slightly. Ulysses watches the proceedings. Tim activates the dictaphone. He draws a silent breath: *'In the current crisis, our situation will utterly transform.'*

He's speaking softly enough so that he will not be heard over the music, but you can hear him clearly. Like the violinist's solo, you're sure you've heard Tim's voice before, but in a different context.

'Reality is a stand-alone document; there can be no true maps.'

It was somewhere outdoors. You remember the sky being solid blue, completely lacking in gradient, like the T-shirt you're wearing now.

'When you weigh up the benefits, the document is relatively worthless.'

Why would you hear a voice like this, outdoors?

'Rethink your monuments, your map-making instruments.'

You don't know why you feel sick right now.

'The sky is a tender vacuum; the compass turns the traveller.'

Squash the beginnings of the memory.

'Accept the unresolvable loss.'

Ulysses flicks an ear.

'There is no better way.'

Jules half-turns in her seat.

'We regret that you no longer exist.'

Tim gently folds the page back into quarters.

'Kindly surrender.'

The violinist lets the last note of her solo disappear into nothing.

'They're here,' Jules says.

Jules drags you to the floor. Your head bashes the seat on the way down but it's cushiony so it doesn't hurt. You look around for Ulysses but he has already deftly flattened himself underneath the row of seats. Tim crouches on the floor too.

You hear the inhale of heavy wooden doors opening, admitting a wedge of light into the auditorium, a different shaft of foyer air, and then footfalls on the carpet. The door wafts back on its hinges. 'Move,' Jules whispers, and Tim crawls into the thoroughfare and makes a break for the emergency exit next to the stage. The quartet briskly launches into a new movement. Getaway music. Jules prods you. You squint into the darkness at the back of the auditorium but you can't see anybody. Ulysses has already made his escape. You stay low and run.

You bust through the emergency exit, Jules a second behind you. You're in a concrete parking lot, lit green like the Matrix. 'Come on.' Jules brushes past you, and Ulysses and Tim follow her down the stairs. You take a step in the right direction. Pause. The Canon weighs on your chest.

You slip back into the auditorium, throw a flash of light into the darkness, and duck back out to the car park, tumbling down the stairs until you've caught up with Jules outside in the courtyard. Ulysses and Tim have already disappeared. Jules drags you across the street and packages you into her car. Snaps the boomgate in half on the way out.

'Hold on to this,' Jules says, dropping the dictaphone in your lap.

APRIL KUAN HAS RECEIVED TIM SPIEGEL'S KOOKY VOICE RECORDING.

'Where's Ulysses and Tim?'

'Gone.'

Out over the Swan River, a coral-red hot-air balloon bobs in the sky. The sun is white. But then the weight of the Canon reminds you. You thumb the power button. Waiting for the screen to light up is kind of like waiting for a Polaroid picture to develop. The screen brightens, and offers up your last wild shot into the auditorium.

It's ghostly, barely substantial. But you can see them. A procession of *who are they, ever,* making their way, through the dark hills of the seats, toward you.

They are not typical people. They are dressed in brown suits; some of them wear hats. They are, each of them, tall and armed. Cufflinks and buttons bright with menace. Faces pale, almost to the point of luminescence. Smooth white moonfaces. Not one of them has eyes.

Who are they, ever.

Your Nexus buzzes. Another screen, another message:

ARCH.
Hey April, how did the Brad Ruffalo interview go? Let me know if you want to discuss, otherwise see you at the next meeting. Arch.

Arch.

A thought rolls into your head like a marble.

IF YOU SEE SOMETHING SAY SOMETHING.

'Jules.'

'Yes?'

'I wasn't *meant* to be at HarvestTime.'

Jules stops at a red light. 'That's true.'

'*Arch* was meant to be there. So wouldn't that mean... those people shooting...'

Jules casually flips her indicator. She looks at you.

'Wouldn't that mean they'd have been there for *Arch?*'

'I suppose that's possible.'

'But you said they were there for *me.*'

Jules says nothing. She guides the car around the corner.

'Jules,' you say. 'Are you just telling me whatever will get me to follow you?'

Jules makes another left turn. You could be driving in circles for all you know. You grip the Canon. You wonder if it's heavy enough to knock someone out. Whether you can get enough of a handhold.

'Jules. *Jules.* Why won't you answer my questions?'

'Rule number three.'

'#@$^ rule number three! Answer my #%$^&%@ questions!'

Well, that escalated quickly. Jules changes gear. 'You want to know what I know?'

'Yeah,' you say, even though you don't actually know for sure. Jules's tone has changed. Tinted with something. Not quite wisdom. Not quite glee.

'Your name's not April,' Jules says. 'It's Audrey. You were named for your mother's favorite character Audrey Kwai from a book called *Seeds of Time* by H.R. Kwai, a character who herself was named after H.R. Kwai's deceased daughter. You re-christened yourself April six years ago when your family relocated from Carlisle to Bull Creek, after the incident.'

Sweat on your palms. The Canon slides a little from your grasp, and the movement is enough for the screen to revive the picture of the eyeless suits in the auditorium. You feel like reality is sliding around you, like clothes that no longer fit, like a slackened elastic waist. What? Like reality's pants are falling down? You let out a giggle that actually sounds like a sob. A giggle-sob. Jules keeps on driving and driving. She could be driving you both into the Swan River for all you know. She could be driving to the moon. 'Oh, yeah?' You're trying to be mad, but honestly, you're just scared. 'Oh yeah? So... so what was the incident six years ago, Jules? If you know so #$%@&$* much?'

'You were waiting at the train station,' Jules says, as if she is telling a fairytale. 'You were thirteen and dressed for school. You were a loner, but you were okay with it. You were doing your usual thing. You know. Talking to yourself. There were a few people around, but really, it was kind of like being by yourself, on this particular side of the platform. It was a beautiful day. A lovely voice was saying, *The Next Train To Perth Will Arrive In Two Minutes*.

'Then some boys joined you on the platform. They were about your age, maybe younger. They were also dressed for school. They were sloppy and happy. They were eating chips.

Their shirts were falling out of their trousers. You moved a little further down the platform, whispering to yourself. It was a beautiful day. You had a pie packed for lunch. You had a juicebox. Your homework was finished. Your head was full of ideas and sunshine.

'"Hey," one of the boys said.

'"Hey," you said.

'"What's that all about?" he said.

'"Huh?" you said.

'He pointed at the badge pinned to your school uniform. REPORTER, the badge said. "Oh," you said. You'd forgotten you were wearing it. "I'm a reporter."

'"A reporter for what?"

'"What?"

'"What?"

'"Um," you said. "At the moment I'm writing a newsletter."

'"What's it called?" another boy said. They were all looking at you now.

'"Um. *The Society of Consumers Against Fraud.*"

'"That's not real."

'"Of course it's not real," you said. "It's just pretend. It's just for fun."

'"That's stupid,' a boy said.

'"Um," you said. "I think I'd like to wait for my train now." You shuffled a few steps over.

'"*Um,*" the boy said. "*I think I'd like to wait for my train now.*"

'"What kind of stuff's in your newsletter?" another boy asked.

'"Um," you said. "It's a parody."

'"A what?"

'"Um. It's all made up."

'"That's not what a parody is."

'"OMG I DON'T HAVE TIME TO EXPLAIN EVERYTHING TO YOU OKAY," you said. You shuffled a few steps over.

Your face was red. The whole interaction was getting freaking weird. You felt like they were coming closer and closer.

'On the other side of the platform, a commuter looked at you, and looked away.

'"Why do you have a pencil behind your ear?" one of the boys asked.

'You put your hand up to your ear and felt a sharpened HB pencil tucked there. You'd forgotten you were wearing *that* today, too. "It's just part of my outfit," you said.

'*"It's just part of my outfit,"* a boy said.

'"Oh, I know who you are," another boy said. He stepped closer to you. "You're that girl that runs everywhere."

'"YOU KNOW," you said. "I'VE NEVER SEEN YOU GUYS AROUND HERE BEFORE WHY ARE YOU HERE I MEAN I WAIT HERE EVERY SINGLE MORNING AND I'VE NEVER SEEN YOU GUYS BEFORE STOP HARASSING ME PLEASE."

'*"Stop harassing me please,"* a boy said.

'*"Stop harassing me please,"* another boy said.

'Nobody came to help you. You might as well have been alone. The train was coming. You could hear the klaxons. The boomgate descending. The train's whistle. You were ready to explode.

'And then, something did. There was another whistle. A grinding noise, a long screech, every onomatopoeia in existence going off at once. The train skidded into the station. Literally. It jumped about three meters off the tracks. Cables snapped and sparked. One of the boys actually screamed. He got crushed. They *all* got crushed. All the boys got crushed by this train that flipped off the tracks.'

You are silent. Everything vibrates. The rush of traffic outside Jules's car sounds like a jet engine. Jules nudges her Aviators further up the bridge of her nose. 'And you were the only survivor,' she concludes.

You're all red. The jet engine noise builds and builds. 'And then what happened?' you ask in a small voice.

Jules sighs. 'Well, that's the tricky part, isn't it?'

'What do you mean?'

'Well. You felt guilty about what happened. You didn't feel guilty about what happened. You felt guilty for not feeling more guilty. You barely gave the event a second thought. You went to a counsellor. You didn't go to a counsellor. You told the police everything that happened. You didn't tell the police everything that happened. You requested the CCTV footage. You didn't request the CCTV footage. You couldn't bring yourself to work on your fake newsletter again. You continued to write your fake newsletter as if nothing happened. You went to school. You didn't go to school. You became depressed. You didn't become depressed. You couldn't take that train line again. You continued to take that train line every day. You left a suicide note that said only the word RESPAWN. You didn't leave a suicide note. They found your body. They didn't find your body. You went on to become a successful reporter. You didn't want to become a reporter after that. You changed your name. You didn't change your name. Who can say, April, Audrey, what really happened?'

Jules stops at a red light. You have no idea where she's taking you. You're stuck in a car with this person that you just met who possibly saved your life from you-don't-know-who at HarvestTime and you don't know what she's going to do next and she seems to know everything in existence but she's not explaining things to you, not the things you actually want explained anyway, and is any of what she's saying even true? The Canon has gone cold in your hands. The photograph of the eyeless suits has, for now, gone away. Jules looks at you, and her Aviators are completely opaque. Reflective voids.

You reach out and take her Aviators. It's just one quick movement—there—and you're holding the Aviators in your hand.

Jules Valentine doesn't have eyes. She has two shallow cavities smoothed over with skin. And she looks at you.

And that's it—you're screaming. The traffic light stays red. Jules looks at you. The scene is jammed here just like one of those nightmares. You scream as if it's going to wake you up. The light is stuck on red. You claw at the car door but you can't open it. Jules looks at you. You scream and scream. The Canon and dictaphone fall off your lap. Jules looks at you. Jules looks at you.

Escape.

K X 01

'In the current crisis, our situation will utterly transform.'

And the breath you release is one you feel you've gripped there, in your lungs, for years. As the air exits, you fold your hands around each armrest, like an aeroplane passenger bracing herself for landing. You are landing.

Ground yourself. There's Tim Spiegel, murmuring into the dictaphone. There's Jules Valentine, who is just now becoming alert to the auditorium. The eyeless suits will arrive any second now. The violinist plays her solo. You let your hands slide off the armrests, accidentally touching Ulysses's tail, which darts softly away. You don't know what precisely to do differently. You have only a few more seconds to decide. You turn on the Canon, shielding the screen with your hand.

The shot of the eyeless suits is still there, gleaming bright as one of Ursula's marbles.

'Accept the unresolvable loss. There is no better way. We regret that you no longer exist. Kindly surrender.'

'They're here,' Jules says. Dragging you to the floor again. The inhale of the swinging doors, the muted footsteps of the eyeless suits.

How does Jules know what she knows?

You follow the path left by Tim and Ulysses.

Don't bother to go back to snap the picture.

Run down the Matrix staircase.

Burst into the sunlight.

Don't even blink when Tim and Ulysses hop into a coral-red hot-air balloon and sail off.

Bundle yourself into Jules's car.

Get your dictaphone back.

'Are you alright?' Jules asks as she snaps through the boomgate.

'Yeah.'

Your strategy this time around seems to be Keeping Quiet. It is very effective. You turn off the Canon. You peek at your dormant Nexus. The message from Arch is already there, marked read.

IF YOU SEE SOMETHING CURL UP INTO A BALL OF DENIAL UNTIL YOU ACCEPT THAT THIS NEW REALITY IS IN FACT REALITY.

You risk a question. 'Where are we going now, Jules?'

'We're going to the Rube Goldberg machine.'

'At Peric Chambers?'

'Yes,' Jules says. 'We have everything necessary to begin.'

April Kuan. Nineteen years old. Time mobilising around you, taking up arms, all the potentialities multiplying into infinity. Somewhere a train flips in the air, and keeps on somersaulting, like a fish thrashing out of water; sparks cut the sky to the bone. Survival is only a matter of inches and milliseconds. Of approximate coordinates. Trial and error.

April Kuan. Nineteen years old.

Peric Chambers has closed for the day. Jules picks the lock while you stand guard, reverberating not-so-privately with your own special collection of traumas. April Kuan, equipped with Nexus, Canon, and dictaphone, bright megabytes of data, an excess of surfaces for memory to grow on. Jules rustles the lock; the door yields. You climb the gallery stairs.

The gallery is empty except for the artworks pinned to the walls. Like two-dimensional claw machines, in a way. You don't have the heart to take field notes anymore, but you feel that that should be one. *Field note the sixth: there are things that look like other things. That's the premise of a metaphor. There are things that are entirely different from other things, but they can be alike in one specific and vivid way, and that's how everyone makes sense of the world, comparing unlike things.*

Jules says, 'We don't have much time,' which makes you want to laugh, because it's not like you both have ever spent that much time in one place before you're bolting off to some other place with eyeless suits hot on your heels.

In the center of the gallery rests the Rube Goldberg machine, partially dismantled and raised on a plinth, like a sacrificed body. The remainder of the machine's components are in a cardboard archive box next to the plinth, ready to be set up tomorrow morning. The label reads: *ALLER, U.R. & P.B.*

You load the pictures of the Rube Goldberg machine on the Canon. Together, with Jules, you align pencils and dominoes, balance marbles on precipices, steady rulers and ramps. Your pictures are an excellent reference. You steal glances at Jules, trying to peer behind her Aviators, but the angles of her lenses are just too cunning, and you can never see beyond them. You feel bad about taking Jules's Aviators and screaming at her before. I mean, you were having a profoundly terrible moment and all, but maybe that was kind of rude. You wonder what happened to Jules. Whether you should feel sorry for her or not. Whether you can trust her or not. Whether you should actually feel bad. The jury's out when it comes to Jules Valentine.

And as you work, you find a safe place to nestle inside your head. You make a commitment to see this through. Just keep moving. You fix the xylophone mallet. You position the bell. You place the bowl of marbles at the start of the machine. You verify the set-up on the Canon.

'I think that's ready to go,' you say.

Jules gets to her feet and steps back. 'I think you're right.'

You hang the Canon around your neck. The machine seems different in this afternoon light. Somewhat larger, filled with shadows, less crisp. Jules plucks a marble from the bowl. 'Play Tim's speech, please,' she says. 'On the dictaphone. When I say "go".'

'What's going to happen?' you ask, as you retrieve the last track on the dictaphone.

Jules poises her marble at the starting point. It's a white marble, like an eye without a pupil.

You sigh. 'Rule number three?'

'I don't know,' Jules says. 'I don't know the answer to your question. This is the first time I've reached this place.'

'Oh, okay.'

You turn the volume wheel. The amber screen of the dictaphone waits for your signal, while you wait for Jules's signal. Jules steadies the marble. 'Hey,' she says, a lifetime of weariness in that single syllable, soft and frayed. 'Thanks for your help today, April. You were invaluable.'

JULES VALENTINE HAS DEEMED YOU INVALUABLE.
YOU... WIN?

Jules doubles her focus on the marble. 'Okay. Go.'

She releases the marble, and you press play.

'In the current crisis, our situation will utterly transform.'

Down the wooden gutter. Dropping through holes.

'Reality is a stand-alone document; there can be no true maps.'

Ever so faintly, you can hear the solo violinist, the ghost of her speaking in the background, as if the dictaphone you are holding is actually a living diorama, a moment trapped in a shoebox.

'When you weigh up the benefits, the document is relatively worthless.'

You think of Peter Pushkin, clutching the bird diagram so tenderly.

'Rethink your monuments, your map-making instruments.'

The rolling marble. Descending the xylophone staircase. The notes ring out like epiphanies.

'The sky is a tender vacuum; the compass turns the traveller.'

You think of Ulysses, his watchful green gaze.

'Accept the unresolvable loss.'

One marble's journey ends, another begins.

'There is no better way.'

Marbles hum and drop.

'We regret that you no longer exist.'

The bow of the mallet.

'Kindly surrender.'

Ding! Goes the bell.

The recording clicks out. The mallet swings back. At first everything seems to vibrate with a kind of hyper-stillness. Theatrical, projecting all the way to the cheap seats. Objects performing stillness. Jules looks mournful. But then, the plinth creaks. You hear a clunk like tumblers turning in a lock. The plinth seems to not so much come alive, but come awake.

It hums, and then, at an imperceptible speed, it begins to sink into the floor. Through the floor. The Rube Goldberg machine rattles, but it does not collapse; the marbles tremble in their graves. The plinth continues to descend.

Perhaps you should have expected it. There's a change in the air. You turn around.

They're here. Five, six, seven of them. Smooth white moonfaces. Melted eye sockets. Smart neat suits and smart neat guns. This close, you can see that there is a small purple sigil stitched on each of their lapels. A kind of tree.

Jules, now, turns. Stares down the eyeless suits as if she has already won. She even permits her lips to rise in a smile. The plinth creaks with finality. You can smell the oaky breath of the exposed pit.

And then the air cracks. Jules goes down like a hulled ship, through the space where the Rube Goldberg used to sit, falling into the darkness. Her jacket flares open; white STFU cards flutter outwards like the ghosts of dominoes. They follow her down. Jules Valentine, shot through with tunnels, red and glistening. Jules Valentine disappears and doesn't ever seem to land.

You look back at the moonfaces, their smoking guns. You look them straight in the gleaming barrels.

Bullets soar like the strings of the most moving soundtrack you've heard in your life.

Pummel your Blue Screen of Death.

You let yourself get really close this time. Closer than you've ever dared to be, even closer than you were that day on the train platform. You shut your eyes. The better to trace the trajectories of pain, hurtling through every nerve, searing asteroids of your personal solar system. You wait for flashes, for a lightning storm of memories, but it is just this—asteroids, pain, burning tunnels. Interrupted signals, tripped wires. The immediate moment, stretched thin to a tenuous gum. The long groan of your universe. Everything horrible and beautiful cast in the present tense.

The swooping boomgate. Glass and bells exploding.

Don't bail until the last

possible

second

K X 00

April Kuan is not expendable! April Kuan has more than two lines of dialogue! April Kuan is you! You have seven different outfits. Today you are wearing Outfit Two: gray jeans, green sneakers, Owls in the Navy tee which is the same blue as the Blue Screen of Death. These outfit components can be inter-mixed, so really you have more than seven outfits.

Your Nexus is ringing. Not an incoming call, but an alarm, a gentle clamour, and you open your eyes. And there you are, noun and verb. You are.

Inventory check: Canon, Nexus, dictaphone. Dictaphone? You feel its weight in your hand, the raised buttons, the satisfying clunk of the record switch. You play a random track and encounter your own excited voice: 'Field note the first. Camouflage insurgents' hideout with "if you see something say something" sign. Effective? Investigate in own time.' You fumble for the Canon and shuffle through your photographs. Eyeless suits. A combination safe built from Duplo bricks. Marbles. Marbles in transit.

Blue, red.

It's nine-thirty. You hang the Canon around your neck, pocket the Nexus and dictaphone. You skip coffee and run to Bull Creek station and board the next train to the city. You run to Peric Chambers. Take on the stairs two at a time.

Bursting into the gallery. There's Ursula Rodriguez and Penny Birch, assembling the Rube Goldberg machine. There's Arch Desai, conducting the interview. There's Stace Calbourne, overseeing the accuracy of it all.

There's... someone, documenting the installation. A scruffy-haired dude.

You flinch at the sound of his camera flash.

Ursula Rodriguez is saying, 'It's French because when I was younger I modelled for a French educational video where I'd perform basic verbs—sit, eat, drink. A voice would say the word in French and I would perform the action. Sometimes when I am stuck I hear that voice in my head issuing instructions. Walk. Read. Nod. *Aller* means "to go". "To proceed". Sometimes you just need to do a thing, and you need to just keep on doing. And it's how you survive.'

'Simply keep functioning,' Arch says.

'That's right.'

'Shall we begin?' Penny Birch asks, checking the time on her phone. A Nokia Lumia in a hard, bright case, *Watchmen* yellow.

Arch leans back to catch the photographer's eye. 'How are you going, Brad? Are you finished?'

'Yep,' the photographer replies.

Stace and Arch stand up to shake each of the artists' hands. 'Thank you for your time,' Arch says. 'We'll be in touch.'

Penny Birch slides the Nokia Lumia in her pocket. Why do you notice this? Sensing that something is about to begin, the stray gallery-goers begin to congregate around the Rube Goldberg machine. Ursula and Penny stand beside each other. Ursula says, 'Thank you for coming. Penny and I are delighted to present to you the third performance of *Aller*. We ask that you please refrain from taking videos of this performance, but still photography is permitted.'

The Rube looms like a foreboding airship. Like a bomb. You're seized by an impulse. Take out the dictaphone. Turn up the volume dial. Get the last track ready.

You hide the dictaphone in your pocket and join the crowd.

Ursula's hand dips into the bowl of marbles. A yellow marble. She places it at the starting position.

As Ursula sends the marble off, you press play. Tim Spiegel's voice rings out, bouncing off the gallery's hard white walls: *'In the current crisis, our situation will utterly transform.'*

Ursula and Penny stir. Stace immediately flips open her pamphlet of exhibition notes to figure out whether she's missed something. But everybody else is transfixed by the marble, accepting the voice as part of the installation—including Arch, who smiles at the line, *'Reality is a stand-alone document; there can be no true maps.'* Ursula is urgently scanning the crowd for the source of the voice, but, true to their word, uttered in some other lifetime, Ursula and Penny do not step in, do not interrupt the performance.

The marbles drop. The origami box springs up.

You also scan the crowd, wondering if, like Brad, Jules Valentine has been repositioned somewhere, recast in a different role, but you do not spot her red jacket or Aviators. You grip the dictaphone in your pocket. You can almost perceive wheels creaking, tape spooling, the dictaphone's unfathomable secret clockwork just like this Rube Goldberg machine, even though the dictaphone is digital and not like that at all.

Dominoes tilt, clip.

We regret that you no longer exist.

The mallet swings.

Kindly surrender.

Ding! Goes the bell.

The crowd applauds. You wait for the plinth to click awake, to descend. You wait for the portal to emerge, for eyeless suits, for Jules, for anybody. But the crowd applauds—oblivious, satisified—and then, bit by bit, the crowd begins to disperse. The recording runs to the finish. The Rube Goldberg machine remains stationary; the marbles are inert. Futile orbs. A benign murmur begins.

'Hey, April!'

You turn around. 'Oh, hi, Arch,' you say, numbly.

Arch is clutching a dictaphone which is very much like the one in your pocket. She smiles. 'My apologies, April. If I'd have known you were attending this session of *Aller* I would have asked you to photograph instead of Brad.'

'Oh. Um, that's okay! I don't mind.'

'See you at the next *Lorem Ipsum* meeting?'

'Sure!'

You watch Arch walk away and join Stace at the top of the gallery stairwell. The Canon is heavy like a hand over your heart. It is Monday and you are not sure where you are meant to be. April Kuan, confused.

Slip out of the gallery. Clunk down the stairs. Into the morning light, the busy sidewalk, thick with lives. You wonder what the time is, and you remember Penny Birch consulting a Nokia Lumia, the hard yellow acrylic case.

You tip your gaze—across the road, to the obelisk of billboards. There is a new advertisement, so new it seems to radiate that fresh laserjet smell. An advertisement for Nescafé.

As your fingers dip into your pocket for your Nexus, the rubber case catches on something else. You pull it out: a white business card, creased in the middle. STFU it says, and, in blue biro, a phone number. Jules's rule number one.

Plug the ten-digit number into your Nexus. Push the green telephone.

We wish to advise you that the number you have dialled does not exist.

You keep the Nexus pressed against your ear. It projects only silence. A null space, just like the void below the Rube Goldberg machine.

The door to Peric Chambers swings open and out steps the photographer. The elusive Brad Ruffalo. He lights a cigarette. Flicks ash.

You keep holding the Nexus to your ear even as you turn away from Brad Ruffalo and walk down the street. *Aller.* Go. Proceed. The Nescafé billboard drops out of view. There are people everywhere with cellphones pressed against their ears or cradled in their hands, busily creating data, and not one of them sports the telltale wooden case of a Seed.

You redial Jules's number.

We wish to advise you that the number you have dialled does not exist.

The voice seems to grow lovelier each time you redial.

We wish to advise you that the number you have dialled does not exist.

We regret to advise you that the number you have dialled does not exist.

We regret that the number you have dialled no longer exists.

And, finally, when you are ready, you push the red telephone.

Slide the Nexus away.

You keep walking. April Kuan, on this brand new morning. April Kuan, starting over.

April Kuan: you have everything necessary to begin again.

Acknowledgments

My deepest thanks to Deborah Hunn and Ann McGuire for supervising my PhD at Curtin University, and for continuing to look out for me. To my friends and colleagues who shared their insights on various drafts of *Rubik*, especially Eva Bujalka, Erin Pearce, and Vicky Tan. To Brooke Davis, Rebecca Higgie and Mel Pearce for your generous advice and encouragement. To Janelle Booker at Curtin's counselling service. To Cherish Marrington and Anna Dunnill for inspiring Ursula's drawings and Michael's adventures respectively. To Final Fantasy Online for giving me the best years of my adolescence. To the Pearce family for welcoming me into your home. To the Cullen family and the Katharine Susannah Prichard Writers' Centre for the Bobbie Cullen Memorial Award. To my own dear family for loving me. To Alice Grundy, for being *Rubik*'s champion, and to Rachel Crawford and Olivia Taylor Smith for bringing *Rubik* to the US.

About the Author

Elizabeth Tan completed her PhD in Creative Writing at Curtin University in Perth. Her work has previously appeared in *Westerly, The Lifted Brow, Voiceworks* and *The Sleepers Almanac*. Her webcomic, Mais Pourquoi, can be found at et-maispourquoi.blogspot.com. *Rubik* is her first book. She lives in Australia.